Also a

The Thorn & Thistle Series

New Ink on Life

INKED
WITH A KISS

———

JENNIE DAVIDS

carina
press

carina
press®

Recycling programs
for this product may
not exist in your area.

ISBN-13: 978-1-335-21592-5

Inked with a Kiss

Carina Press
22 Adelaide St. West, 40th Floor
Toronto, Ontario M5H 4E3, Canada
www.CarinaPress.com

Printed in U.S.A.

To my dad and grandpa.
When I told you I wanted to be a romance writer,
I'd been expecting teasing and instead received
nothing but support. I'm sorry you couldn't live to
see this dream come true, but this one is for you.

INKED
WITH A KISS

Chapter One

Jamie

I tried not to stare too long at the bare skin in front of me. Kind of hard since I was tattooing it. The freckles, so many of them, were a distraction. They got me in the mood to do some exploring. Not good. I was a professional. Besides, the freckles belonged to Sierra Clark.

I had no business being intrigued by the freckles or the woman. Twenty-five. That's all I needed to know about her. She was twenty-five.

On the days that Sierra's name was in my appointment calendar, I skipped the coffee.

Sierra, on the other hand, looked like she could use some stat. She sat in my chair, eyes closed, head tipped like she was seconds from falling asleep.

I had that effect on people.

I'd just never had it on her before. Usually I was being regaled with stories of festivals she'd gone to and the newest dance club she'd found, all things that made me feel old and boring. Tonight, zip from her.

Rolling my chair forward, I bent closer to her bicep.

"What made you decide on a giraffe?" Because there was a conversation that would keep her awake.

"I love how sweet they look with their big eyes and

those two things on top of their heads." Her eyes looked into mine, a light brown that was about the tamest thing on her face, what with her bright red hair and her usually blinding smile. "I knew you'd be able to make one super cute."

I had. I'd designed a chibi giraffe with the characteristically large eyes and small body.

"No special meaning at all?" I asked, dropping my gaze back to the arm I was working on. The giraffe's arm, not hers, because I would not focus on that.

"No. I thought my others needed a leggy friend."

This was her fourth tattoo with me. Always chibi animals. So far never a story to tell with them. That was a rarity. Most people who got ink had a very specific reason for getting it.

Yet when I was done, Sierra gave each of them "the look" satisfied clients gave beloved memorials.

I stretched to dip into my ink, purposefully keeping it further away so I had to reach. It helped keep my back from getting too cramped by the end of the day.

"Did you know giraffes can run over thirty miles per hour?" I blurted out.

And that was why I normally let her do the talking. Something happened to me around her. Something that should not.

In the station behind me my boss, and sometimes friend, MJ, snorted.

"I didn't know that. What else do you know about them?"

Well, crap. I racked my brain for more than that random tidbit from a book my daughter and I had read when she'd been on a kick about animals and thought she might want to be a zoologist. Now she was on to cars and combustible engines.

I missed the animal books.

"Um, I think maybe the mother gives birth standing up and the baby just drops. Though that seems like it could hurt them, so I might be wrong on that one."

"Yikes."

"Elephants carry their babies for two years and then tend to live together for most of their lives in a family group."

Unless MJ had developed the ability to snort in surround sound, then my co-workers were getting in on the action. I ignored them and thankfully Sierra did the same.

"Oh, I like that better." Her voice livened, not quite as fast and high and reminiscent of the chipmunk I'd tattooed on her side, but not the monotone she'd come in with.

The results I'd been after, just not the means.

"I think you just gave me my next animal." She slowly and carefully pointed to her right thigh. "It can go right here."

I looked, of course, I did.

I could see an elephant there. See myself spending hours putting it there. Easing my foot off my pedal, I waited for that image to leave my brain before I put needle back to skin.

She adjusted her head on the headrest, facing me more directly. When we were done here today, the scent of lemons would linger. Bright and fresh.

I was pretty sure the only thing I smelled like was my dryer sheets. I wasn't big on scents after being up close and personal to everyone else's all day, but lemons were nice. Refreshing.

"Do you have any animal tattoos?" she asked. "I know there aren't any on your arms."

I automatically looked down at my arm sleeves even though I dang well remembered what was there. Each goddess had been chosen with care for traits I respected or aspired to have. The performers on my left arm were no different. "No, no animals there. I actually have an elephant. On my back. I've always admired their family dynamic." Admired might not be quite the right word, more like was jealous of.

"Oh. I'd love to see it."

My stomach went haywire at the thought of her wanting to see something on my body. My skin was pasty white from spending most of my time in the shop, and even if I had spare time to spend outside, Portland wasn't exactly known for its sunny weather. Even my skin wasn't interesting. Not like hers.

"I'm not sure you'd like it. It's traditional style."

"I'm pretty sure I'd like anything you do."

Whether intentioned or not, my brain took the words as flirty. Which meant that even though I had a dozen years on her, I was back to feeling like the baby giraffe we'd talked about—dropped on my head and left reeling.

"Thanks," I managed. "That's nice to hear." She faced forward again, and not having to look into her eyes made breathing a whole lot easier. Swallowing too.

All right, enough trying to draw her out with some conversation. I obviously was not capable of it around her. Time to get directly to it.

"Everything okay with you today? You seem a little off. If you're not feeling well, I can stop."

She shook her head, her red hair swirling around my chair, and smiled. Not the wide, bright one I associated with her, but it got my heart racing all the same.

"No need to stop. I've been looking forward to this

all week. I'm just stressed about work. My yearly review is coming up."

She'd sat with me all these times, hours together, and I didn't know what she did. I'd never initiated any questions, relieved to let her talk as much as she wanted. Until tonight. Until she came to me, withdrawn and subdued, and I'd wanted to vanquish whatever caused it by drawing her out.

"Where do you work?"

"Haven Bridge." As if knowing I had no idea what that was she added, "It's a crisis center for families. I'm a caseworker there."

Caseworker. Never in a million years would I have pegged the woman who came in here with a wide smile and a wonder-filled gaze in that kind of field.

"What does a crisis center do? I'm not familiar with them."

"Oh, we do so much. It depends on each person and their situation, but it all comes down to supporting them. We help fill out paperwork and protection orders. Help find safe housing. Find services if they're struggling with mental health or addiction issues."

Passion rang in her voice and brought a flush to her skin.

Something swelled in me in response, making me want to get right out there with her and help.

"Wow. It's awesome that places like that exist." I dabbed at her skin with the towel. "Awesome that people like you do that."

"I just wish I could do more. There's so many people that need help."

"You're going to nail that review. If I can feel your dedication from one conversation, I'm sure your boss, who sees you every day, knows it too."

Her smile flashed, wide and true. "Thanks. I hope you're right. It's all I want to do. I've known since I was a kid that I'd be doing it."

Such certainty. It'd taken me a while to gain the courage and enough in savings to know I could support my family before I went after tattooing. My first career had been an insurance agent, not something I could say I was passionate about, though I had liked being the person someone talked to after an accident. It'd been my job to assure them everything was going to get taken care of. In that it'd been a continuation of my calling of sorts—handling situations.

"You'll—"

I stopped as knuckles rapped on the wood partition outside my station. MJ, the owner of the shop, stood just outside. She jerked her chin at me, a greeting and an acknowledgment she was interrupting all in one. She held up a paper that looked like some kind of statement in her hand. "Are you gonna need the credit card next week? I'm looking over everything now."

We'd come a long way, so that MJ was even letting me use the company credit card for anything. It'd taken a long time to earn that trust. A trust that I was damn proud of and would never jeopardize. "No."

"Are you sure?"

That was new. It sounded like she wanted me to use it. I turned, giving her my full attention. "I don't need it."

"I don't want a rebellion on my hands if your choice is crap."

"Did you want to plan it?"

She took a quick step back, shaking her head. "Shit, no."

"Well, then leave me alone. I've got it taken care of."

MJ looked doubtful, but jerked her chin in a nod

and then she turned and headed down the hallway toward her office.

I moved to shading the giraffe.

I wasn't looking at Sierra. I was focusing on the tattoo like I should be, but my skin prickled with awareness as if I was in a dark alley and being watched. Except this time my body was telling me an on-the-go redhead was the danger.

"So what are you planning?" she asked.

"We do a team building outing every few months. This month it's my turn to plan it."

"Oh, nice. So what are you going to do?"

"Probably Powell's. I can always count on them to have a book reading or poetry."

"Oh."

That one word held all the disappointment my coworkers would no doubt feel when I mentioned where we were going.

"Why? You got a better place?"

"I do. I'm sure I do." Her feet started to bounce. I pressed harder around her skin to make sure she didn't end up with a botched giraffe. "Are there any guidelines?"

"No more than twenty bucks per person. Open late because we do it after we close up. No bars or clubs."

Sierra nodded. "I can totally work with that. How long do I have to plan?"

"We're doing it next week."

"Awesome, I got this. You just wait, it'll be lit."

Right, because it being "lit" had really been a concern. No, what concerned me was that I was going to have to be in contact with her over the next week.

And until I did, I'd be both dreading it and anticipating it.

Sierra

I opened my laptop. Three new cases. Three new families needing help. How many of those I'd already been assigned could I check in with before lunch? Did I even need lunch? I'd had a bagel for breakfast. People needed help and I needed to give it to them.

I'd intended to leave close to on time so I could be at Thorn & Thistle and join them on their night out. But I was pretty sure Jamie's invitation had been more out of politeness since I'd planned it, rather than any desire to have me there.

Here, I could get through some of this backlog so that I could get to the new cases.

When I got into social work it'd been all about wanting to show people the programs and options available to them so they wouldn't feel so helpless. When I'd envisioned it, I hadn't known a huge chunk of my day would be sitting at a desk drowning under paperwork, or computer files in this instance. I spent more time in front of this monitor, with its annoying flicker, than I did with actual people.

People like Angel Rodriguez. Hm, they sounded familiar. A quick scan of the notes brought it back. Damn. They needed housing. Again. I clicked onto my list of options.

Before I could start checking, the metal folding chair next to the desk I'd claimed for the day was dragged across the concrete floor. Holy crap that was loud and annoying. Kind of like the girl flopping into the chair.

"Ugh. This day already sucks," Jordan, our seventeen-year-old receptionist, said. She stuck her hands into the pocket of her hoodie. "Those career counselors stayed behind and talked forever. I just wanted them gone so I could put the room back."

My lips twitched. No one did put-out better than Jordan. "How dare they stay after trying to make people's lives better. Didn't they know they were inconveniencing you?"

"I know, right?"

Mm-hmm. Before I worked here, Jordan had been a client of Haven Bridge, and once she'd emancipated from her parents she'd been hired on. There was no one who knew the center better than her, and under the prickly exterior, no one more protective of it.

I nudged her chair with my foot. "Aren't you supposed to be at the front desk? You know, greeting people and spreading your cheer."

She lifted her shoulders, the movement mostly lost in her oversized sweatshirt. "I'm legally allowed to have a break. I had to come back here before I went off on someone."

"Lucky me."

"Yes, lucky you." With a glint in her blue eyes, she leaned forward, her dyed black hair sliding over her shoulder. "I heard something."

Ah. Now we were getting to her reason for being here. Jordan got all the dirt. So many people just viewed her as a teenager who had no part in the adult world— even my colleagues who should know better—and didn't guard what they said around her.

"Spill."

"There's going to be more budget cuts. Like next year's looking bad. Real bad."

The words echoed in the small office. Cuts. Cuutts. Cuuutttssss.

Panic was visible on Jordan's face, the same panic

that was now eating a hole in my stomach. If there were cuts, we'd be the first under consideration. Seniority—we didn't have it. Jordan's position wasn't deemed essential but her hourly wages would be less than anyone salaried.

Like me.

No. I would not lose something I loved again.

And this job, I loved it. This is where I made my mark.

Shake it off. Shock wouldn't help. Once it got a hold of you, it was near impossible to pry it free. Best not to let it get a grip in the first place.

I turned to see how Jordan was faring.

Ah, that face. Not good. Not good at all. I went to pat her shoulder but caught myself in time. No touching. She didn't like to be touched.

"You'll be fine," I said. "They'll find a way to keep you."

Jordan snorted. She flicked me a look like she was the one with the expensive degree and had to protect me from my naivete.

But I had to believe they'd keep her. They could not kick Jordan away from the only stable thing in her life.

As for me, it wasn't like being disposable was new.

Not that I'd let it come to that. I'd prove Haven Bridge needed me as much as I needed it.

Jordan sighed, her body lowering with the action until she rested her chin on her folded arms. "Let me see one."

Yes. Anything to get a fighting expression back where it belonged on her face. We had to rally, especially right now when we were both being confronted with the possibility of getting kicked out of this place that meant so much to us for different reasons.

I pulled off my crocheted sweater, already missing the feel of the yarn against my skin. I lifted the sleeve of my shirt and uncovered Daphne, my little turtle.

Jordan lifted her head. "I love the dimensions on this one."

The flurry of my heartbeat slowed as I stared at it. "I love everything about it." From the way Jamie had drawn it so its body was twisted half to the side, to the way it peeked over the corner of its shell with its big eyes, and best of all, its sweet and bashful expression.

My first tattoo, the word *empowered* in script over my ribs, had come when I'd turned eighteen ready to make my mark on the world. After that I hadn't had a big desire to get another one. Then I'd hit the field study part of my degree, and been confronted with the reality that no matter how hard I worked, a lot of people weren't going to get the happy ending I did. I'd been desperate for something cute and comforting to look at.

It was only once Jamie had given me my first animal and I'd experienced the pick-me-up from looking at it that I'd developed a true addiction.

An addiction that would have to wait. My last one wasn't even fully healed. It'd be a while before I could afford another one.

Jordan pinched the skin of my forearm, manipulating my tattoo so it looked like Daphne was moving. "There's ones that could make it look like the shell was real. All 3-D."

Jordan had had a thing for my tattoos since the moment she'd seen them. At first I'd thought it was the classic "too young to get one so that automatically made them cool." I'd quickly learned for Jordan it was about techniques and other things I didn't really understand because I didn't have the same interests. My interest in art ran more to a certain artist.

Art was not something we prioritized at the center. The only art supplies we had on hand were crayons and coloring sheets we printed off for younger kids. Our limited funds went to the essentials. Medical services, shelter, food, educational opportunities, paying the small salaries we did receive.

Giving up on schooling me on my tattoos, Jordan slouched back in her seat, once more the picture of a sullen teenager. "But yours are cool too."

"Gee, thanks. Now don't you have to go back to the front desk?" And I needed to get back to these files, as many of them as I could.

That's what we had to do. Show them how much they needed us.

She pushed to her feet and then glanced at the computer screen. She tapped the second name. "He's going to need to go to Middle Point." And then she was off.

I made a note beside the name she'd pointed out for possible entry to our alternative school for those with behavioral issues. She'd know. Jordan had a sense for picking up on things like that. And unlike me, she'd actually already seen him. Later today, hopefully, if I could just get to my priority cases first.

Now that I was alone the panic was once again trying to consume me. Feet tapping under the desk, I continued on through my files. My pace was as frantic as always, but as I clicked on the next one and updated the calendar with upcoming court dates, it wasn't because of thoughts of helping our clients. No, it was thoughts of how to make sure Haven Bridge understood all they'd be losing if they got rid of me.

Fifteen minutes after my shift ended, I clicked out of

the computer and pushed my chair back. I was done. No
more tonight. Earlier I might have had thoughts of calling off going with the Thorn & Thistle gals and staying out late, but not now. I needed to have some fun,
be active, be around people. Recharge so I could come
back tomorrow and go at it even harder. Plus there was
the bonus of Jamie. It might only be courtesy that had
made her ask me there, but I'd be glad to be near her.
Being around her made everything seem like it was
going to be all right.

I arrived at Thorn & Thistle as it was closing for the
night. Once I was inside, my gaze immediately sought
out Jamie.

She was at her station, bent over the counter, sketching.

The other artists talked and laughed across the tattoo shop, but she didn't break her concentration. That'd
been the thing that'd attracted me to her from the moment I'd met her. She was so solid, not just physically,
but personality-wise. She seemed so sure of herself, her
place in the world, and her ability to handle it. That appealed to me hard.

Yup, from the moment I'd met her, I'd been attracted
and hadn't been shy about letting her know, hoping to
experience the effect of Jamie in bed. I'd come on pretty
strong and she'd deflected just as strongly.

That'd been the end of that.

Now when I came to get tattooed, I sat in her seat,
talked and then offered to purposefully shut up so she
could keep some of the peace I soaked up from her.
She never took me up on it. It'd been the same now for
the last three tattoos. Well, except for my very last tattoo. Then she'd initiated some conversation and I'd even
caught a blush.

Jamie glanced up and her eyes locked on mine. My pulse kicked into high gear. She straightened, put away her supplies with concise movements, and then headed my way. Even her walk was steady as was the way she held my gaze the entire trip.

No. I would not salivate over the way a woman walked, not even if she'd stopped looking at me like an excitable puppy she wasn't sure was house-trained.

"Hey," she said, stopping in front of me. She shoved her hands into her jeans' pockets, making her black and white plaid shirt billow around her. "I'm glad you could make it."

"Me too. I'm ready to see you when you're not jabbing me with a needle."

She flashed a smile that was gone before I could really even appreciate it. It reminded me of ones people gave when they were trying to hide imperfect teeth, but I'd seen hers and they were fine. She just didn't go all out with her smiles.

"Well, since you haven't told me where we're going, I'm relieved to hear it."

The owner of the shop, MJ Flores, walked by with a client whose forearm was now rocking a snake under a layer of protective wrap. Once the person had exited, MJ locked the door and turned back to face the shop with a grin. It wasn't exactly what I would call a happy grin, more like one that promised trouble.

Oh, yes, I'd made the right decision in coming tonight.

As the other artists started to gather around, Jamie stepped closer to me, her shirt brushing against mine. "Let me introduce you to everyone. This is MJ," Jamie said.

I nodded to the hard-looking woman.

She inclined her head to me, her black pompadour hair so well gelled it didn't even move. "Ah, it's our tagalong for the night."

Jamie turned to indicate a pale petite blonde who had come up next to MJ. "This is Cassie."

"Hi." I smiled and held out my hand to the woman who I'd never really interacted with. She was always quietly working every time I'd been in the shop.

I made it through the row of artists. Maya, a white woman with dyed neon-red hair, and the loudest of the bunch. Vivian, an Asian woman who had a friendly smile and wore kick-ass lace heels, a pair of which would be making an appearance in my wardrobe. Lastly, Gina the piercer, her tan skin paired with short dark hair, who would not be joining us because she had a date with her wife.

Now these were women I could see adding to my repertoire of friends. Best yet, unlike so many of mine, they wouldn't be complaining that they had to get up early for work or study for a dissertation. I could see some late, fun nights in our future.

"So where are we going tonight?" MJ asked, looking at Jamie.

Jamie shrugged. "I don't know. Sierra's got all the details."

I bounced on my toes as I faced the group. "I'd just like you to know I saved you from a poetry reading."

"Boo."

Jamie crossed her arms over her chest, looking unbothered by the collective groans of her co-workers.

"Never fear, I got something better in mind." I blew on my knuckles before brushing them against my shoulder. "Get you some comfy clothes because we're hitting the trampoline park."

"Ohh," Cassie said.

Maya stepped forward and held up her palm for me to high-five. "Good choice. I approve."

"We're heading out in ten minutes," MJ said and then marched off back to her station.

As everyone scattered to their workplaces, I turned to Jamie. "So what do you think? I did good, huh?"

Jamie smiled, her lips lifting just long enough for me to marvel at the way it softened the sharp angle of her chin, before it was gone again. It left me free to look at her surprisingly full cheeks, about the only thing on her that looked soft. Well, that and her eyelashes, but since she didn't seem to wear makeup, I had to be close to see them. Like I was now.

"You did good," she assured me.

"Why thank you." I pulled at the side of my pants and dipped a quick curtsy.

She chuckled and shook her head. I'd expected her to be put off by me, and instead she looked almost indulgent. "Much better than the reading. Those jumping places are fun. Last time I went I landed my back pullovers."

"I don't know what that is, but it sounds very impressive." And her boastful tone was too cute.

"I'll have to show you," she said.

"I'd like that."

A new trick would be a nice distraction and a chance for some one-on-one time with her, so I wasn't complaining.

Jamie's cheeks pinkened, her gaze dropping away from mine.

What was this? Yeah, I'd seen something similar the day I'd been getting tattooed, but I'd shrugged it off as the possibility that she liked the more subdued version of me that had been my mood. But I was back. I was ready to have some fun tonight. So why were her cheeks still getting so adorably pink?

"I—" She broke off, pulling her phone out of her pocket. She frowned as she read whatever was on the screen. Making a face, she typed a reply. Slow going since she pecked with one finger.

When she looked up, the charged energy in my blood fizzled. Her apologetic smile said it all.

"Something's come up. I'm sorry, but I've got to go," she said, confirming what I'd already figured. "Thanks for putting this together. It's going to be great."

I couldn't even get a response out before she was striding back to her station.

Noooo. I didn't believe in relying on any one person for help or comfort, not anymore, but after today, I knew my best chance at feeling better was walking out the door.

Chapter Two

Jamie

I pulled up to my parents' house and relaxed my grip on the steering wheel. At least my brother wasn't here yet. It was so much easier if I could intervene before he got everyone riled up. Ryan went into things with a burn-it-all-down attitude. I preferred to be the wet blanket.

Stepping out of my car, the grass hit my shins. What the hell? It didn't look like it'd been touched since I'd done it two weeks ago when my dad's back was sore. But he said it was feeling better.

My mental list of possible reasons was interrupted by my brother's car pulling up. The low slung, sleek thing sounded like it was growling as it slowed and then stopped. Yet another way we were opposites. When looking for a car, I checked the safety ratings and how it would drive in the few snowstorms Portland got a year. My brother went for flashy and expensive.

Somehow people were more impressed with his methodology.

Ryan turned off the ignition and flung his car door open. He stepped out, lips pressed so tight I could hardly see them. The muscle in his left cheek pulsed.

Well, I'd known it wouldn't be good. He never called

me to just chitchat. I wished he would, wished that we were still close like we'd been when we were kids. But it seemed he lumped me in with our parents. Because I chose to help them, their actions became mine.

"Hey—"

He slammed his door and brushed past me, flattening the grass as he headed to our parents' front door.

Breaking into a jog, I passed him, planting myself in his path. "All right, what—"

"No. I'm not letting you do this. Not this time." Hands balled into fists at his side, his body vibrated with tension.

He was taller than my five foot six by at least four inches, but I stared back unflinchingly. I'd caught him humping his pillow when he was ten. Nothing he did would be intimidating after that.

"I'm not letting you talk me out of this. They need to take some goddamn responsibility."

I held my hands up. "Hey, I just want to know what's going on so we can come up with a plan to approach them."

"No. I'm not making a fucking plan. I don't need a plan to tell them I'm fucking done." He dodged around me and stormed up the steps. Before I even made it to the porch, he was pounding on the front door. He didn't let up until the door opened and our mom's face peeked out.

"Ryan?" Her gaze slid to me, widening even more. "Jamie? What are you two doing here?"

Not answering, my brother shouldered his way in and headed down the hall. In his crisp suit, if not for his five o'clock—well, nine o'clock now—shadow, he looked like he was storming into a boardroom for a takeover.

My mom's eyes locked on me. "What's going on?"

"I'm not sure."

I stepped into the entryway, using the additional light to look her over. Still in work clothes. Eyes the same brown as mine, no signs of red around them. She smelled of nothing more than White Diamonds, the same scent she'd always worn.

She closed the door, sighing. "What's he going to complain about now? I'm the worst mother ever, I get it. I haven't even talked to him in a month."

There was no point in reminding her that Ryan had an arsenal of things to be pissed about. She had blinders and excuses when it came to herself.

As we made our way to the living room where the TV blasted, I cataloged everything. Pile of mail on the counter. Dishes in the sink, not spread all over the counter. Laundry was, if not put away, at least in the bedroom and not in heaps around the house. I worked my mouth from side to side, relaxing the tension. Everything looked all right. We were doing okay.

Avoiding my brother's pacing route, I nodded at my dad as I made my way toward the fireplace and sat. The rough stone should have an imprint in the shape of my butt at this point.

My mom was still lowering herself to the blue cushion on the couch, when my brother rounded on our parents. His face was a mass of angles that mine just didn't have, and all of them looked like they could pierce his skin and cut a bitch.

"Did you think I wouldn't find out?" He thrust his hand in his pocket and pulled out a piece of paper.

I was too far away to read it, even if I'd been wearing my stupid glasses.

"I'm not an idiot," Ryan snarled. "I know your little

'weekend issue' is more like a trojan virus infecting everything. I took precautions."

Dread slithered up my spine, tightening each vertebra in its wake.

My mom stared right back at him with her trademark innocent expression. My dad wasn't concerned enough to look away from the TV.

Everyone knew what was going on here but me, yet any second their heads would turn toward me, expecting me to fix it.

I pushed to my feet and made my way to my brother.

He turned, blocking me as his gaze drilled our parents, an ugly twist on his lips. "This is illegal. You'll go to jail."

Jesus, what had they done? I snatched the paper from his hand.

A credit application in his name. Not exactly something to get mad at our parents for. It… Oh, god. No.

Slowly, I lifted my head. "You didn't."

I hated the edge of pleading in my voice. But damn it, things had been holding steady.

My mom lifted her chin. "What? What is it we're supposed to have done? He hasn't even told us what he's accusing us of."

I stared down at the application and then to my brother. "You're sure?"

"Yup. I have an alert on my credit so it lets me know when anyone tries to access it. You better check yours too. If they did it to me, they'd do it to you."

That penetrated the layer of calm that seemed to have been a gift from the womb and had only thickened over the years. Bile swam in my gut. Fuck. Had they already tapped me out? My bank provided free security, but I didn't pay extra for any bells or whistles.

My score was good. After living with the uncertainty of my parents' erratic bill paying, I'd made sure of it. Never a late bill. Credit card paid off every month. Had they ruined it?

My mom rose and tugged the paper from my hands. One cursory look and then she handed it back to my brother. "That identity theft is becoming a real problem."

Oh her tone was innocent, so very innocent.

The thing was if she were really innocent she'd be begging for us to believe her. The fact that she wasn't was an admission in itself.

Swallowing down the last of my misplaced belief in them, I closed my eyes. It was so much harder to open them than that it should have been.

"You didn't get anything." Ryan thrust the Winston chin in our mom's face, his blue eyes narrowed to slits. "You'll *never* get anything."

My dad tore his gaze from the TV. No innocent face for him. No, his go-to was confusion. "If nobody got anything than why are you going on and making such a big deal?"

Seconds passed as I tried to process how he could think this was less than a very big fucking deal. Precious seconds. I needed to move, get in there and block my brother before he tore into them.

Except Ryan remained perfectly still. Gone was the usual disgust when he looked at our parents and in its place was pity.

"I'm done," he said, his voice calm in a way that I hadn't heard him use with them since he'd hit puberty. "I hope it was worth it. I hope trying to steal some credit was worth losing your son."

He turned and faced me. His mouth was relaxed,

showing what were actually full lips, and his eyes had lost the tension lines framing them.

A chill shot down my back.

"Call if you need *me*." He turned on his heel and strode out of the room. Seconds later the front door clicked shut.

The need to go after him, beg him to give them one more chance raced through me. I locked my knees. It wouldn't be for him, or even them. The desperation was for me.

I was truly on my own.

Huffing, my mom folded her arms over her chest. "He's always so dramatic."

They'd tried to steal from him and he'd calmly walked out. Out of their house, their lives, and he probably wasn't ever coming back.

She had to care. Somewhere inside she had to care. I had to believe that. Otherwise what was I doing all this for?

I sank down onto the edge of the fireplace, my hands hanging between my spread legs. "What's going on? Why would you do that?"

My dad tipped his head back and groaned. "It's no big deal. We've gotten behind on some bills. Last month your mom sideswiped a car so we had to pay the deductible and—"

"Were you drinking? Do you have a DUI?"

Since the day I'd been old enough to get my license, they knew to call me if they needed a ride, no questions asked or lectures coming their way. They'd never taken me up on it before, their drinking done at home. Had that changed too?

"No. It was a Thursday."

I let out my breath. That was one good piece of news

in this shit show. They were still keeping their drinking to the weekends and holidays.

"Why would you risk—?"

I stopped. There was no point in asking why they would risk Ryan's credit like that. They wouldn't care how it affected him. As functioning alcoholics their only concern was making it through the week without anyone learning that their weekends were spent with their BFFs Miller and Smirnoff.

"Why would you risk going to jail?"

"We were going to pay it back." My mom leaned forward, bracing her arms on her thighs. "I didn't think he'd even know. It's not like he'd give us any if we asked. He always says no. And I bet you don't have any money now that you're tattooing."

Accusation vibrated in her tone. Resentment. Not an ounce of apology or regret.

I'd known Ryan and I didn't come first. Hard not to know when they would rather spend their time with the liquid in a bottle than their own children, but never had they intentionally targeted us. We were just the innocent bystanders. Trying to steal from their own child—no, worse, acting like they were the wronged ones—well, that ripped the sheet off the cadaver.

Why would they do this? What had changed?

My dad smiled at me. My mom tapped something into her phone.

Apparently it was only my stomach that was roiling. Only me with this desperation to make everything right.

Their son had just walked out of their lives. I couldn't make that right.

But I could do something about the insurance and the bills. I also needed to check my credit.

God, please don't have let them have fucked me over.

Between my apartment and half the mortgage on the home my ex-wife and our daughter lived in, my money was all spent. What if they'd gotten to it? They had all my info—birthdate, social security number. My mom knew her own maiden name.

"The money is due." My mom's voice dragged my attention back to her and her crisis. "What are we going to do?"

I sighed and rubbed my hand over the back of my head. "I'll talk to your creditors." After that it'd be time to explore treatment programs. Again.

My mom looked away from her phone long enough to smile at me. "Oh good. If you get them off our backs, everything will be fine."

I straightened my shoulders, trying to ditch the exhaustion weighing me down but damn, sometimes it felt like they'd been siphoning my energy since I was a kid. When would they hit empty?

Nope, not gonna happen.

I had this. We were just experiencing a setback.

I settled a steely look on both of them. "Guys, you can't do this. Not ever again. You run into problems, you come to me."

My mom glanced at my dad and they shared a long look before she nodded and scooted to the edge of the couch. "You're right. We were just trying to save you the trouble."

Right, or the more likely scenario, that they were trying to prevent me from learning something that would blow their attempts to convince me they were fine.

"I mean it," I said. "No more pulling this shit."

They both nodded.

"You could have—"

"Well, it's getting late." My mom jumped to her feet.

"We have to get to work in the morning. I'm sure you're tired from all you do."

Knowing I'd reached the end of their willingness to listen, I let her usher me to the door.

My mind triaging what I needed to address first, I walked to my car, crushing more of the grass.

If enough people walked on it, maybe I wouldn't have to mow it. That'd be one less thing on my list that had doubled thanks to tonight.

I collapsed into my car. Ten fifteen. How was that possible? Surely, I'd been in there for hours.

But no. The girls from the shop couldn't have been at the trampoline park long. Less than the hour you paid for which meant they'd still be there. MJ would not let them leave a minute sooner than the time she'd shelled out for.

Wanting nothing more than to rush home to my computer and get into my bank accounts, I instead headed downtown. Bonding nights were important for the crew. Tonight was my responsibility.

Instead I'd left Sierra to take care of it. Sierra with her contagious smile. Sierra, who hummed pop songs while she was getting ink. Sierra, who awakened a desire in me to experience things I might have missed out on.

Tonight I wasn't turning away from that feeling of excitement and longing, but instead heading right toward it. Toward her.

Chapter Three

Sierra

"Come on. You got it."

"Reach with your left."

They made it sound so easy. Keeping a death grip on the little yellow peg protruding from the wall with my right hand, I reached out my left. I stretched and stretched and wiggled my fingers. Nothing but air. To get to the green grip I'd have to swing myself in that direction. Yeah, not gonna happen. I was staying here. Right smack dab in the middle of this rock wall with everyone looking up at me.

Ugh, why couldn't we have stayed with the trampolines? Maya had seen the rock wall and demanded to do it. I'd eagerly joined in thinking it'd be fun. This was not fun. There was no laughter. There was no nice distraction from work. There was just me up here by myself, proving that my occasional walks and dancing weren't cutting it in the fitness department.

"You're gonna have to move some time." Encouragement, MJ style.

She did have a point. My arms and legs were getting tired. Beneath me was a pit of foam I could fall into. But then I wouldn't be going after what I wanted. And

right now I wanted on top of this beast of a wall like
everyone else had.

"Wow, you go."

"You're killing it."

"Damn, go, girl."

Um, why had my tattooed cheerleading section suddenly become so enthusiastic? I hadn't moved.

I angled my head to look below me. On my left side
a climber was approaching and fast.

I had a perfect view of the top of the person's head.
Light brown hair pulled back into a ponytail. Close
enough now that the lights shined off the few grays
mixed in. I knew that head, that hair. I'd stared down
at it for hours as she worked on me.

My muscles hummed with renewed energy. Jamie
was here.

Her fingers curled over the hand grip next to me.
Now those I didn't recognize. While she tattooed me
she wore gloves. Her fingers were long, her nails short
and polish-free. I wasn't even going to look at the state
of my manicure. I was sure I'd left chips of bright pink
all the way up.

Jamie pulled herself up and then she was there, not
even a foot separating us.

"You made it." If a voice could smile, mine was.

"I did."

She'd changed clothes since I'd last seen her. She
had a Lycra black tank top that clung to her and showed
off her biceps. They were flexed and visible in a way
mine were not.

Taking the chance it'd unbalance me, I ducked my
head so I could see more. I swallowed a moan. Gone
were her jeans. She had on leggings that went to her
calves. Her large, beautiful calves. I bet they were the

reason she didn't even look like she was sweating. She'd earned those with some serious physical activity.

Okay, I needed to look away. As beautiful as they were, they were distracting and not going to get me out of my current predicament. Not to mention, except for a few charged looks, she hadn't given any signs that she'd appreciate my thirstiness at her in her workout clothes. Which also meant I needed to stop willing her to go up one peg so she'd get a killer shot of my cleavage.

I focused on her face. Not exactly a hardship.

Lines branched out from the corners of her eyes and mouth, and her jaw was bunched so tight it looked like it would need to be pried apart with a special tool.

"I take it whatever called you away, didn't go so well," I said.

Jamie stilled. Absolute stillness like when we asked for a volunteer to go first in group therapy. "Why do you think that?"

"You're holding your tension in your jaw."

"Huh." She let go of the wall with her right hand and rubbed the lower half of her mouth as if trying to feel the tension for herself.

I gasped and clung tighter. "What are you doing? Put your hand back. You're going to fall."

"Nah. I've got this." She flashed me a grin. Yes, it was cocky, but somehow on her it wasn't annoying. Unlike when MJ had grinned at me earlier on the trampolines after she'd jumped over my head.

Too soon the grin faded away.

Which brought us back to whatever was weighing on her. Here was my chance to show her just what I could do, which I was pretty sure she thought was talk a lot and spend my time partying with friends. Most people made that assumption about people my age. She was going to discover just how multitalented I was. Impromptu therapy on a rock wall—I was digging it.

"You want to talk about it? I'm a good listener."

"Yeah?" Her beautiful biceps showed no signs of strain as she looked at me, like she was trying to decide how to make that new tidbit fit with the others she'd collected about me.

"Very. I'm trained in it and everything."

Jamie's gaze went to the wall in front of her, that jaw tensing right back up. "Everything's all right. Something came up that I wasn't expecting. Something I missed. I need to do better."

Not only admitting there was some kind of problem she'd missed, but dedicated to correcting it. That was some next-level adulting and it gave me very little chance of showing off my skills. But damn did it make me respect her more and reinforce my image of her as capable and so steady.

"It sounds like you already have a plan to fix it, though I'm guessing you're being too hard on yourself."

"Not too hard. Just disappointed." Jamie's gaze moved to study more of the gray slab we were attempting to climb. "Why are you up here by yourself?"

"Oh, well, I'm not quite as good at this as everyone else. So they made it and I'm slowly"—very slowly—"working my way up."

"Someone should have stayed with you."

"Well, you're here now."

A look of determination came over her face and somehow she squared her shoulders even with the way we were hanging. "That I am." She tilted back her head and squinted up at the wall. "So what's the plan?"

"Plan?" Yes, I supposed hanging here until my arms dislocated wasn't an actual plan. "I'm debating between a dive into the foam or trying to grab the hold that you're on like everyone keeps telling me to and ending up in the foam. So my plan involves foam."

"Hm. Well, plans are kind of my specialty, so how about a new one?"

"What'd you have in mind?"

"I'll stay with you and help guide you up."

Ohh. I'd be showing off my cleavage and get the chance to check out her legs some more. Yes, please.

"Lead the way."

I joined her in looking up to our endpoint. Halfway. I'd only made it halfway. Yeah, Jamie's arrival had given me a jolt of adrenaline, but how would my arms and legs hold out for all that?

Jamie's gaze went from sizing up the wall, to sizing up me.

Like her, I'd changed out of my work clothes and into some leggings and a workout top. I wasn't ashamed of my rolls, but I didn't usually draw attention to them which this hunched position was doing. My curves were more of a plus on the dance floor. Pretty sure I had them to thank for snagging many a lay.

Jamie flicked her bottom lip with her tongue. As the seconds ticked by and her gaze didn't move on, we were definitely heading past cruising and into checking out territory.

No way. Was Jamie feeling me right now?

My body started to react to the prolonged stare. Of course it did, it was a complete slut around Jamie.

I'd been wanting this since the day she strolled up to introduce herself in the lobby at Thorn & Thistle, so casual and at ease in her ponytail and jeans and a plaid overshirt. What perfect timing she had if she wanted to make it happen. My roommate was out for the night if we needed my place.

"Okay," she said, her voice huskier than normal. "So I'm thinking your best bet is to go back down and put your right foot there and your left there and—"

"You want me to go back down?" She would not be saying that if she knew how much trouble I'd had getting up here.

Her smile flashed again. It highlighted a small scar right above the middle of her upper lip. A faint line, but I wanted to reach out and trace it.

"Yeah, I think it'll give you the best route. The one you're taking has too much dead space."

It was nice of her to give me credit for taking a route instead of just blindly following the instructions yelled to me from below.

"Okay. I'll try it. Here I go."

I stretched my leg as far as I could, toes pointed and wiggling.

"Almost there. Another inch or so."

An inch. I could do that. My thighs burned. So much burning. Any second now a muscle would snap because this was it, as far as I could go.

"Just a little further."

Clenching my teeth, I elongated everything I could.

Yes! There. My toes touched something firm.

I'd done it. I was back down.

"Good job."

I glanced up to respond and the words tripped up on my tongue. While I'd gone down, Jamie was still in the same place. I was looking directly at her ass.

Sweet Jesus and I'd thought her calves were things of beauty. Like them, her butt was strong and muscular.

"Now come up here." She patted the peg she wanted me to grab.

The going up part was easier, or maybe it was the reward of being beside Jamie again, of being close enough to discover, not only the scar above her lip, but the faint paler strip of skin around her eyes, probably from sunglasses.

Soon she had me two pegs higher than when she'd showed up.

"Doing okay?" she asked as we paused and caught our breath.

The "we" was being generous. While I sounded like this was some high altitude peak we were climbing, she hung there, her chest rising evenly, her breasts—Nope. I needed to look away if I wanted any chance of making it up.

"Let me get back at you with that one," I panted. "I don't even want to know how sore I'm going to be tomorrow."

"Put some muscle rub on tonight and I bet you'll be okay."

"Hm. Yeah, that's probably better than my warm bath idea."

Her head whipped toward me. Her brown eyes were far from chill. They looked like they could spark a flame on kindling. Because she was thinking of me in the bath? My mind was right there with her.

"Right," she said, licking her lips. Was she imagining it now? "That would work. You'll smell better that way too."

My nice visual of the water dripping down my body and her gathering it with her tongue shattered. "What?" I choked out, laughing.

Jamie winced. Her cheeks turned a bright pink almost

instantaneously. "Argh, I need to stop doing that with you.
I just meant the rub can be pretty pungent so if you had
a bath you wouldn't have to deal with that."

"Well, I'm glad you don't think I stink."

"No. Not at all. You're like lemons." She winced.
"And there I go again."

"Hey, don't stop on my account. I'm liking it. Almost
as much as I like those pink cheeks you're sporting."

"I have no control over those when I'm around you."

I swallowed and tightened my grip. Yes, I was pretty
sure I was experiencing Jamie Winston's version of
flirting.

Wow, was it doing it for me.

"You like tart things, huh?" I asked, testing.

"I would go with invigorating."

"And is that how you see lemons?" *Me.*

"Yes."

Her cheeks went impossibly brighter. I sure hoped
we weren't doing permanent damage to her capillaries
as we stared at each other.

I waited for her to blink, to sever this awareness
flowing between us. She did, but it was still there,
warming my body, no eye contact needed.

"You good to go on?" she asked.

Uh, well, no, not really after that. I nodded gamely
anyway and made the move to the hand grip she pointed
at.

We were quiet as we continued on. I figured she
needed to concentrate on how to get us up there and I
needed to decide if I wanted to make another move on
someone who'd been so quick to redirect me last time.
Yeah, it'd been two years since we'd first met, and I
knew a lot could change in a short time—boy did I—
but I didn't like to look back, and normally I would be

all about showing her what she missed out on. Those little grunts when she boosted herself up, though. They were putting images in my head that I'd like to really explore, as were the glimpses of her flexed muscles.

"Here?" I nodded in the direction of a green plastic peg above my head. My arms trembled. It'd be interesting to see which would hold out longer—my arms or my sanity.

"Yeah, go for it."

I grabbed it. My muscles quaked and I had sweat in places I hadn't even known I could sweat, but I got it.

I blinked. Jamie's hand filled my vision. "Grab it. You made it. We're at the top."

"I made it? Oh thank god." I slapped my hand into Jamie's.

Using every bit of my remaining leg strength, I pushed so she wasn't hoisting all of my weight. It was the least I could do since she was the major reason I was up here.

A cheer rose up from below. Someone whistled.

On wobbly legs I made my way to the edge of the wall and bowed. Jamie went for a more subdued wave to her crew.

Turning to face her, I grinned. "We did it."

"We sure did." She held up her palm for a high five, but I was already flinging myself at her for a hug. I caught her hand between us as I smacked into her.

Laughing, Jamie's free arm came around me, steadying us.

I didn't know what was the best out of the situation— her laugh, the feel of her body against mine, or the sense of comfort that had me wanting to lean in even more, rest my head on her shoulder. It was the last part that had me pulling away.

Since her hand was still there, raised, I smacked my palm to it.

My skin tingled where we'd connected. That or it was an aftereffect of my death grip for so long.

Jamie's laugh gradually stopped. Her smile faded until that too went away and the joy was only in her eyes. "That was fun, but I guess we should get moving."

She turned and started toward the edge of the platform where a ladder was attached.

I snatched her hand, pulling her to a stop. "Where do you think you're going?"

"Down."

I pointed behind us. "We're going that way."

Her gaze went from the very safe and sturdy ladder to the drop behind me.

I waggled my eyebrows. "You ready?"

She stared down at my hand. Right, I probably should have let go of that by now. Before I could release her, she squeezed my hand, her gaze meeting mine. The joy was gone, but there was something new—excitement, and it was sexier than any wink that'd ever been thrown my way.

"I am now."

Our hands still clasped, we ran to the edge and then jumped.

Jamie

I pushed myself upright in the pieces of orange and yellow foam. Sierra surfaced next to me laughing. It was so loud and infectious that I joined in.

When I'd arrived tonight it'd been all about obligation. Now it was all about feeling good. Thanks to Sierra.

I was stupidly pleased even after our laughter petered out that her smile lingered, and not only because her smile produced little lines around the corners of her eyes that showed some wear on her body, but I was witnessing the proof that she'd had fun with me.

I tore my gaze away before I gave in to temptation and started counting her freckles.

"Whew. I needed that," I said.

"Me too. If you hadn't shown up who knows how long I would have hung there."

"Not too long. Your arms were shaking pretty bad." Thank god they had been. I hadn't been lying when I said I needed that. I'd needed to help her get up there. I'd needed the reminder that when people were struggling, that's when I excelled. I'd made sure Sierra made it, just like I would with my parents.

Laughing, she reached out and smacked me. Since she hadn't yet stood, her hand landed against my thigh.

This time I didn't join in on her laughter. I was too busy processing the feel of her hand on me. I wasn't thinking about her age, or my age, or how active she was, or how tired I was. My thoughts didn't go past waiting for the heat of her hand to penetrate the stretchy fabric and reach me.

She stood, her black leggings showing off all her curves, clinging to her skin, drawing—

"Jamie. Hello, Jamie. Anyone home?"

I dragged my attention from Sierra to Vivian who stood at the edge of the pit, holding out a phone. Going by the soccer cover it was mine. "You've got a call," she said.

I didn't want to take it, even though the reason I always had it on was so I could be reached anytime. I wanted to stay right here, where my biggest concern was what I could do to keep hearing Sierra's laugh. Yeah, 'cause that was a good use of my time.

I shot Vivian a look when I saw she'd already answered. At least it was my ex-wife and not my mom like I'd been expecting.

"Hey, Nicki, what's up?"

"So I got a veeeerrrry interesting call."

"Oh yeah?"

Nicki growled. "Don't play coy with me, Jamie Winston. I just got off the phone with your mother. She wanted to make sure I was doing okay because she was worried I might be too overwhelmed with the house. You know with how 'big it is and how much work it must be to upkeep' it."

I groaned and shot Sierra an apologetic glance as I exited the pit. This was a phone call best done in private.

Very few people knew my parents were alcoholics and I didn't need to be announcing it to anyone else, but the other reason I wanted privacy, maybe more so, was because I didn't want anyone to know that I'd failed to keep things running smoothly.

Was *still* failing. My mom must've picked up the phone as soon as I'd pulled away from the curb. Oh yeah, she'd really taken heed of my warning. "Sorry about that."

"Jamie, tell me what's going on. Why is she suddenly so *concerned* about me?"

"Because she got busted. I went over there tonight and found out that they filled out a credit application in Ryan's name, trying to get money."

"Oh." None of the shock that had rocked me was in her voice. I didn't even hear any plain old surprise. "And that brought me into it how?"

"They need money and wished I had it to give to them."

"Ah. Yeah, that sounds about right."

I couldn't fault the bitterness in her tone. How many times had she accused me of not helping my parents, but enabling them?

I suppose I had. But the alternatives were equally as bad. I'd tried to get them help. So many times. You couldn't force people who refused to believe they had a problem. They could still hold jobs. With the automatic bill pay I'd set up, they made their payments—well, except for this car insurance deductible I had just learned about. It would take a long time for them to hit rock bottom. At least by going over when they called, I could keep an eye on things.

Yeah, I was doing a bang-up job on that front. They'd attempted credit fraud for fuck's sake.

"How you holding up? You could have stopped over here afterwards," Nicki said. "You can, you know—come over. Anytime. It doesn't have to be about Riley."

"I know."

And I did. The divorce had ended our marriage, not our friendship. I didn't think anything could. Besides the bond of raising our daughter together, we had met at vital times in our lives. We discovered who we were as adults together. Unfortunately that discovery included that she didn't need me anymore. Riley was well on her way to raised. My responsibleness had first appealed to her. Now it smothered her.

Friends or not, I couldn't go there. Not tonight. I didn't want an I-told-you-so.

"Good," she said. "Don't forget it. You're the best thing that ever happened to me. Heck, you're the best thing that ever happened to them, even if they don't realize it."

"Thanks." The heaviness that'd hovered over me as soon as I'd been handed my phone lifted. It was nice to be appreciated by someone.

Though Nicki wasn't the only one.

I stopped reining my gaze in and let it go to Sierra. She'd been appreciative of my help. On the wall while guiding her I'd had purpose without the weight of duty and it'd felt surprisingly good. Almost as good as having her pressed against me when she'd gone in for the hug. As I'd always suspected she was the perfect armful. So soft and warm and somewhere I wanted to stay awhile.

"Just a heads-up," Nicki said. "If your mother calls again I'm going to tell her to mind her own fucking business. At least this time she remembered to ask to speak to Riley, but she was already in bed."

"Sorry she dragged you back in. I know no longer having to deal with them was one of the better parts of us going our separate ways."

"True. That and not having to watch your news shows anymore."

News shows. It's a wonder we'd stayed together ten years with the way she disrespected Rachel Maddow like that.

"Yeah, well, I still have to watch those *One Tree Hill* wannabes. Every time Riley is over she turns them on."

"Oh, I've taught my daughter well," she said. "Which reminds me. She was going to call you tomorrow to see if it'd be okay if she skipped out on Sunday. Some friends are going to one of those escape room things and she wants to go with them."

Riley would rather hang out with friends she saw all week at school than me. A sharp pain stabbed at my temple, radiating all the way down to my jaw, giving plausibility to Sierra's claim that I held tension there.

I'd known it'd be coming. Riley had been pulling away these last few months. I still wasn't ready. I didn't think I'd ever be ready. My time with Riley was the most important thing in my life. But I didn't want it to be forced time.

"Yeah, that's fine," I finally answered.

"Jamie." Nicki sounded like she was holding back a laugh. "She's thirteen. She's not going to want anything to do with us soon."

"Yeah, yeah. I'll talk to you tomorrow."

We got off the phone and I faced the climbing wall. My co-workers were nowhere to be seen, but Sierra remained. She watched another person attempt to climb, but it was obvious from the way she turned as soon as I put my phone away that she'd been waiting for me.

My pulse stuttered. Why did that make me feel so good?

"Everything still okay?" she asked when I was almost to her.

"Yeah, all good."

"Whew. I'm glad." She smiled and hitched her thumb over her shoulder. "We're going to go get something to eat at the bar down the street. You joining?"

"Nah, I'm going to head home." I couldn't quite believe it was disappointment I saw on her face. My own daughter didn't want to hang out with me. What chance was there that a twenty-something-year-old would?

My disappointment made sense. I was leaving her adrenaline-inducing company to go check and make sure my credit hadn't been stolen. "Thanks for putting this together. Everyone loved it, not an easy feat with our group." And she'd managed it without doing something really out there and wild like I'd been expecting.

"Not easy for some." She put her hand on her hip

and cocked her head, a gleam in her eye that had my systems firing up in preparation. "If you're stuck, call me. I'm your girl."

Flutters went off in my stomach. Could she be... No. She wasn't serious. She was flirting. Maybe? After being with Nicki ten of the last twelve years, and in a three-year relationship before that, I was out of practice at reading the signs. Not that I'd been good at it in the first place. But still my stomach wouldn't settle. "I really do need to be going."

"Oh." She blinked and when she opened her eyes the heat of her gaze had been dampened. "Well, then I guess I'll see you when I'm ready to get my elephant."

"You will." This time there wouldn't be dread. There'd be nothing but anticipation at seeing the chibi-animal-loving caseworker who had brought new excitement to our outing with her fresh idea.

A fresh idea.

That's exactly what I needed. My parents were obviously hitting a rough patch, but my usual wasn't going to cut it. There were only so many websites I could show them, so many quizzes I could try and have them take, so many addiction hotline numbers I could place around their house.

I needed something new.

My gaze went directly to Sierra. As I stared at her I didn't see her youth and energy as reasons to stay away, but instead be inspired by. "If not sooner."

Chapter Four

Sierra

I scanned the list of crisis counselors, looking for any with openings. Ha. It was like trying to snatch a marionberry shake before they were out of season. A three week wait? What part of crisis did they not understand?

I jumped when a knock came from outside the office I'd snagged for the day.

Twisting in my chair, I found Wendy, my boss, in the doorway.

My heart, which had been adding a few anxious beats since I woke up, now had validation to go all out. She was starting it right off. No end of day for us. Good. Even I would get sick of Beyoncé if I had to keep repeating her power songs in my head all day.

"Hi," I greeted Wendy. Before I could decide whether to stand or invite her to sit, she slid into the empty chair wedged between the desk and the wall, the placement funky thanks to the teeny, tiny room.

My gaze dropped to the paper in her hand. This was it. I was meant to be here, to do this. Please let her see that, to see what I gave. I searched her face for any clues. It was hard with Wendy. She always had a tired, drawn look that only disappeared when she was in front of the kids.

"What's up?" I asked, not wanting to play "does her frown look deeper than normal?" anymore.

"Well, as you know, it's time for your yearly review. First I'll give a quick overview of how we feel you've been doing. Then we'll go over areas of improvement. You'll sign it and that'll be that."

I nodded, my gaze locked on that paper. The desire to snatch it from her and read it myself was strong. No need to draw it out by saying every word. Unless this was going to be a compliment fest. In that case bring it on.

"So just like last year, we really love how hard you work. You're always ready to tackle a new case. Your energy and enthusiasm are things we really appreciate here."

My chest eased. Whew. Okay. They saw what I was putting out. Acknowledged it.

Wendy glanced down at the paper and made a face. "In the 'need to work on' column, it would be making sure all of your forms and paperwork are filed in time. And to be more thorough on your case notes."

I nodded. That was almost identical to what was said last year. "I'll keep working on that."

"Good." Wendy leaned forward and pointed with her finger where she needed me to sign. "There's one more thing."

"Hey, no add-ons after I signed."

Her lips lifted in a small smile, but it didn't last long. "Yeah. The thing is next year's numbers aren't good. We'll have even less to work with."

And that right there was why even with the good review I couldn't get lax.

Even with the heads-up from Jordan, the confirmation was a blow to the gut.

"I'm sorry," I told her.

She nodded. "We're just letting everyone know so that they can keep it in mind."

Pretty sure it wouldn't be anywhere else. "Okay."

"Well, I'll let you get back to work. Good job, Sierra. We're glad to have you here."

And I was going to keep it that way. I still had time to fight. I'd make the most of it.

Sighing, I looked back at my computer screen and growled when I saw that the appointment for three weeks out had been snatched up.

"Uh, why does your face look like that?"

I growled louder, this time at Jordan.

"Did your review go that bad?" she asked.

"No. For your information it went well. Really well."

"Yeah, you look it. Anyway, there's someone out front for you."

"For me?"

"That's what I said." She held up her hand in a slow your roll move. "I don't know who. I didn't ask."

I nodded and pushed back my chair. I didn't think I'd done anything to piss her off today, so I would trust she wasn't leading me out to someone who had a vendetta against me. She'd spot a disgruntled partner or parent of a client in seconds.

As soon as I saw who was at the receptionist desk, my pace picked up, along with my pulse.

Jamie lifted her hand.

"Wow. This is a surprise."

When she'd told me she might see me sooner—the phrase having haunted me for the last few days—I hadn't expected it to be at work. Actually, I wasn't sure she'd seek me out at all. I'd thought we were going to have to go the ignore-the-mad-chemistry-between-us route.

"Yeah. Hi. After you talked about your work, I looked it up online. It said you needed donations."

Before I could fully take in that Jamie had been interested enough to look up where I worked, she bent down and when she rose she had a large box with a picture of industrial paper towel rolls on it.

"I gathered some things and my daughter contributed some toys she doesn't use anymore and we wanted to donate it."

Oh, she knew what made my knees weak—old, no longer wanted stuff.

"Sweet. We always need donations. Thank you and your daughter."

I didn't know much about Jamie's daughter beyond that she was a healthy-looking girl with blonde hair and blue eyes. In the most recent pictures at Jamie's station she looked to be an early teen. No matter how many times I stared, I couldn't make out much resemblance, except in their stance. They both did this thing where they leaned back and tipped their chin up. Like Jamie was doing now.

"If you want to follow me, I can show you where we keep our donations. It'll give you a chance to look around since you're interested in the center."

"I'd like that." Carrying the box with no signs of strain thanks to those biceps that I now knew were under her yellow and blue striped shirt, she followed after me.

"These are what we call the communal rooms. People can use them to hang out and connect."

As we walked further, I pointed out each room we passed. I glanced over my shoulder, checking her eyes. Nice and glaze-free.

"Let me know if I'm talking too much. When I first started here I gave the tours of the center to potential donors but I was pulled off after a day. They said to show what's important and I think all of it's important so I show everything."

Jamie's mouth twitched. "Keep going. I'm liking it."

"Okay, you asked for it."

Since we used most of the rooms for multiple things, it was a lot. My throat was getting dry by the time we reached the hallway that led toward the back of Haven Bridge where the public wasn't allowed.

"This used to be a conference room but now we use it for storage and donations." I led her to the corner where we had boxes and bags piled that we hadn't sorted yet. "You can put it anywhere. We'll make good use of it."

"I don't doubt it." Jamie bent, putting the box on the floor.

My gaze dropped to her ass then her legs. Her jeans were a loose cut, but her calves and fine ass seemed to take it as a challenge and filled them out.

She stood and now that there wasn't a desk or a box blocking my view, I took all of her in. Her jeans were frayed at the knees and ankles and her undershirt rode up enough to expose the bottom of a belt. I wanted to push her shirt aside and see if there was a surprise flashy buckle under there waiting to be discovered.

I stepped forward, my fingers tingling. Even after her multiple rebuffs, my mind refused to let go.

Yeah, I wanted orgasms with her. But there was more, another layer that I hadn't experienced with anyone else. Not only did I want to collapse with her on a mattress, I also wanted to stare into her face, to trace her laugh lines and kiss all along her jaw. It was something I shouldn't want, but I couldn't help myself.

Years ago I'd gone to a haunted corn maze and been terrified. In certain spots there were places you could check your route and the actors didn't spook you. That's what Jamie felt like to me—the safe reprieve of the no scare zone.

I couldn't imagine how that would carry over to having sex with Jamie, but I would love to find out.

Should I try and find an empty room and then she could do more than look at my lips?

I squeezed my elbows in to give my boobs a boost and stuck my hip out to the side. I hadn't figured out yet what kind of woman she was—breasts, ass, thigh—so I was trying to give her a little bit of everything. "Is there anywhere else you'd like to see? We have some other storage rooms." A little cramped and dark, but hardly anyone ever went in them so they'd be nice and private.

"Uh, I…" Her gaze snapped up from where she'd been looking at my waist, to my face. She brought her hand up and rubbed the back of her head. "I'm actually interested in what you have for alcoholics."

All the thoughts circling in my head—of what she'd taste like, how good it'd feel to squeeze her ass—came to a screeching halt and then others fell into place. There'd been clues. Her insisting that the outing not be at a bar or club. Her not joining us to eat at a bar afterwards.

I straightened and shooed thoughts of sex and back rooms aside.

Purpose tingled in my blood. Oh, she'd come to the right place. She wanted information. I was going to give her so much of it, as much as she could take.

"First I want to assure you your privacy is completely protected. Also this is a judgment-free zone."

Jamie tilted her head, staring at me with the beginnings of a frown.

"Follow me and I'll give you an idea of what's available." I started walking, hoping that movement and my voice would drown out any second-guessing she was having.

Jamie's brows drew even closer together. "Oh-kay."

"So we don't offer treatment here unless you're a client, but we have plenty of recommendations. There are all kinds of options that work with all kinds of lifestyles. All throughout the city. Day and night."

She nodded and didn't look like she was going to make a run for it.

"Over here are some flyers and a calendar with dates and times of meetings." I showed her the bulletin board. Beneath it were pamphlets for domestic violence victims, legal aid, shelters, and dependency programs. "I've heard only great things about the Silver Springs facility. They take a whole life approach." I pulled out another pamphlet. "This is a counselor that does group therapy. Oh and this one is more general and is about identifying if you have a problem and how to seek help. And here's a great outpatient one."

Jamie took them, scanning the first one. "Thank you. This is what I'm looking for."

I put my hand on her arm, right over her tattoo of a woman juggling three weapons while balancing on a ball. "It's not easy, but I'm really proud of you. We will find something that works for you."

Jamie

I thrust the papers away from me. "It's not for me. I don't have a problem." And as I knew firsthand, that's exactly what an addict would say. Deny. Deny. Deny.

Sure enough, Sierra's smile faded, her eyes going knowing.

"I really don't. I don't drink. At all. Or do drugs." I rubbed my hand over the back of my head. "It's my parents."

She blinked, her body losing the feral do-gooder edge to it. "So you're here to get information to give your parents?"

"Yes."

"Oh. That would explain why you were so interested in where I worked."

"Yes. Well, no." I dropped my hand, all the rubbing obviously wasn't helping me communicate. "I was— am—interested in this place. It's incredible. When you first told me about it I wasn't thinking about my parents. It was only after something came up that I remembered all the things you said you guys do."

If I'd learned where Sierra worked when I first met her, a month ago, heck even last week, I would've thought it very admirable and been happy places like this existed, but I wouldn't have associated it with somewhere I might need to make use of. Why would I? Everything had been manageable with my parents.

It was now, when I needed to know of its existence, that I learned where Sierra worked.

I'd seen the exact thing at the shop. A certain client would come in at just the right time. It'd happened with Vivian when she was talking about some new medicines her father had been prescribed. Her client turned out to be a pharmacist and caught that the medicines were dangerous when combined with some supplements. Gina had scored an early viewing of a house more central to both her and her wife's work not even on the market yet when she was piercing a real estate agent.

Sierra tapped the side of her head. "Prediction—your parents were the reason for the tight jaw on the rock wall."

"Yeah. I thought you might be able to offer something different than everything I've already showed them. They think it'll be like they see on TV, locked up for thirty days, wearing uniforms and eating Jell-O cups."

Sierra's hand returned to my arm again. "It doesn't have to be. There are so many options available. We'll find you something."

My Athena tattoo shifted as my muscles twitched under her hand. Freckles dotted her skin to her knuckles and then thinned out, becoming intermittent around her fingertips. I didn't think the touch was something she was aware of. It was more an act of reaching out to offer comfort.

Usually that was my role. To calm and comfort, to take care of things.

It made my insides shift and not all in a good way. It felt wrong to be on the receiving end.

She squeezed my arm. "I'm sorry. I'm sure you already know this, but you can't make someone get help. It has to be up to them. I bet that's one of the most frustrating parts."

"Yes." How did you convince someone that they were ruining their life when they had jobs and looked nothing like alcoholics depicted on TV? But god they had to recognize this time they'd gone too far. "Maybe this time, maybe these"—I held up the pamphlets—"will do the trick." There were some outpatient options they hadn't seen here before.

"What about you? Would you like me to get anything for you?"

"Me?" I jerked back. I wasn't here about me. I thought she understood that.

"Yes. I can get you some info on Al-Anon meetings or private counseling to talk through how it's affecting you. There's also some great books or even blogs written by family members of alcoholics that might help you."

"I'm fine. Good. It's them that I need to work on. It's them I need to get help for."

Oh god, she was giving me the "I can't help you if you're not honest with me" face. I was very familiar with it. I was usually the one wearing it.

"They've been like this for a long time," I said, desperate to get that look off her face. "I've grown up with it. I don't know any different. So this doesn't really affect me. I'm just here trying to get them help and prevent it from escalating."

Hearing all the "I"s in that sentence it felt like instead of making my point that I didn't need help, I'd made hers.

Except I didn't. I didn't need help. I was paying my bills. I made sure my daughter was provided for and that I spent as much time with her as I could. My appointments were booked solid for two months. It wasn't my life that needed help.

"Well, thanks for these," I said, holding up the papers. "And for showing me around."

"Of course. If you need some more recommendations, feel free to call me." She bumped her shoulder against mine. "I'd like that."

I relaxed infinitesimally at that brush from her. At this point her flirting was welcome. Especially that she'd done it after I'd just admitted I hadn't been able to help my parents in the past. She wasn't looking at me like I was some big failure.

I nudged her back. "I'll do that."

There was a hop to her step as we continued walking. "Good."

Had I put that hop there?

I liked seeing it. Liked even more that I might be responsible.

Her constant motion wasn't as draining as I'd thought it'd be. All this time I'd viewed it as a negative. Something to be avoided and certainly a reason that nothing could come of my attraction. I mean, how many times had I been told I was boring. Nicki, my wife and best friend, hadn't been able to stand it anymore and had left to find more excitement in her life.

Being married to a tattooer sounded a lot more exciting than it was. It mostly consisted of long days at work with a weird schedule that made it hard to mesh. When I was home I still needed to work on sketches for clients and update my portfolio.

Hell, my co-workers, most of whom were in their twenties, agreed with Nicki's outlook. They looked to me as the mother of the shop, the person they went to when they had a problem, not for a good time.

Today I didn't feel old and tired. The opposite. It was refreshing to be around someone so passionate about something. It was beautiful the way her eyes sparkled when she spoke of this place. It was inspiring, the bounce in her step.

We walked back to the front of the shelter, it filling with more noise and people than when I'd first come in. As when I'd arrived, there was a girl at the desk.

Sierra stopped and addressed the teenager. "Did you meet Jamie earlier? Because I think you'll find her veeeeerrrrry interesting."

It was damn hard not to do a quick check over my shoulder, but Sierra's brown eyes were locked on me.

The teenager's gaze raked over me and seemed to be questioning Sierra's definition of the word.

Moving behind me, Sierra put her hands on my shoulders, leaning to the side to look at me. Her breath blew across the back of my neck and the tiny hairs there rose as if trying to catch every last vibration from her. "Jamie is a tattoo artist and has lots of her own. Maybe if you're nice, she'll show them to you. Rumor is she has an elephant that's pretty cool." She winked at me before lifting her hands and stepping away.

No. I wanted them back. Might need them so she could balance me. Because, wow, all of her pressed against me, the wink, the smile, it was all…was this how it was to be drunk? Is this what my parents felt all weekend?

"Jamie, this is Jordan. She is our Haven Bridge expert."

The girl wasn't looking disinterested anymore.

Jordan pushed up from her chair. "You're an artist?"

Nodding, I set down the papers and then slipped off my overshirt and placed it in Sierra's waiting hands. I pushed the sleeves of my T-shirt up to my shoulders. "I am. I work at Thorn & Thistle."

She bent closer and I slowly rotated my arms so she could have a good view of each tattoo. Once she'd inspected all of my visible ones, she went back to my left arm, focusing on the Greek mythology section of my sleeve.

"Wow. I've never seen shading so good. I can never get mine like this. My contrast is always screwed up."

Ah. This was more than an interest in tattoos. I was with a fellow artist. "You draw?"

She ducked her head, tucking a long black strand behind her ear. "Yeah, I used to all the time. I can't as much now, but yeah."

I didn't know her circumstances, but she was young—god she didn't even look old enough to have a job—and I imagined it couldn't pay much. I'd also noticed the hardened edge to her face. I'd seen it on a few of the kids we'd passed here. Good supplies cost money and took up a lot of room, two things I'm guessing she didn't have a lot of access to.

"So you're interested in tattoos?"

"Yup. I'm always checking out Sierra's." Her eyes widened. "You do hers?"

"I did."

"I bet your stuff is really sick if it wasn't baby animals."

"Hey," Sierra cried out as I chuckled.

"I can see where you'd think that, but doing chibis on her can be better than the coolest dragon or pirate piece on someone else."

The teen rose a skeptical eyebrow. "How?"

"For one, because she loves them so much. There's nothing like the thrill of putting down ink on someone that they love. Two, and this is the best, she lets me have control of the tattoo. Yeah, she tells me what she wants, but that's it. She lets me do my thing. That's better than someone who gives me the most awesome subject, but won't let me do anything with it."

Thank god my days of doing quick walk-ins and just replicating what someone pulled off of a magazine or online were over.

Jordan nodded, her face thoughtful. "Yeah, like getting the choice to trace the cover of a comic or creating some killer fan art. It's gonna be the fan art."

I held out my fist to her. "Spoken like a true artist."

She smiled, showing off crooked front teeth, and bumped me back.

"See," Sierra said, smiling at me. "I'm a good client. Thrilling even."

That she was. About as thrilling as a roller coaster. She gave me the same flippy feeling in my stomach. Plus she liked to throw me for loops. Like introducing me as interesting, and being worried that I get help, and now flashing a smile that practically invited me to play. I was throwing in my own loops by wanting to.

I turned toward Jordan, literally putting my back to Sierra. It was the only way I had a chance of concentrating on the teenager.

"Is that what you want to do? Be a tattoo artist?"

She shook her head. "I'll definitely be getting some 'cause they're cool as shit. But nah, I'm into illustration. I want to do graphic novels."

"Oh, nice. My daughter's just gotten into those. That's an exploding field. You work on paper or computer?"

Jordan snorted. "I don't have any programs. When I can paper, but I'm out of practice."

Art was like a muscle in that it worked best if used frequently. But thankfully, it wasn't a muscle. It lived in your soul. Your unique perspective never went away whether you were practicing or not.

I bent down, ignoring the way my left knee cracked, and waited until it was me and not the floor Jordan was looking at.

"There's no time limit. I didn't start tattooing until I was twenty-seven. I had to wait 'til I got my family stable and had enough money saved to support us while

I established myself. Was I behind the game of everyone else my age? Yup. Did I catch up? I sure did."

She looked like she was storing my every word in her memory so she could pull them back out when needed.

I reached into my pocket and drew out my business card. MJ gave me crap about still using them, but you never knew when they would come in handy. The deli down the street had plucked it from their free lunch giveaway five times.

"Here's my card. When you're ready for that tattoo come to me. I'll hook you up."

Jordan took the card, the hardened teenager back. "You'll forget me by then."

I stared into her blue eyes, figuring someone who'd obviously been through some tough times had already learned that you could tell a lot more from a person's eyes than what they said. I let her see the truth of my words.

"It doesn't matter how many years go by, Jordan. I'm going to remember you and when you come to me, I'm going to ask how your illustration is coming. I'll be happy for you, even if it's only something you do in your spare time because you love it."

One side of her mouth lifted and she tucked my card into the pocket of her hoodie. "Yeah, okay."

"Okay." I glanced at Sierra over my shoulder. Her soft smile combined with her I'm-picturing-you-naked look nearly set me on my ass.

Yup, she was definitely a roller coaster and I was close to getting motion sickness. Yet, I wasn't ready to get off. The steady ground was waiting for me later.

I pushed to my feet. "Well, I've got to get to work." I leveled Jordan my best motherly "I mean it" look. "Call me when you need a tattoo."

Turning, I reached for my shirt, almost hating to take it because Sierra's fingers were playing with the collar. I stared into her brown eyes. "Both of you."

"Oh, I will." Sierra's gaze traveled down the length of me and back.

I didn't want to wait months until she needed some new ink to see her. I didn't want to have to wait to actually feel this, to feel something.

Did I have to?

I clutched the papers in my hand. Yes, my parents had gotten off course, but I had everything else going smoothly. And as much as I knew it was a bad idea, that there was no possible way it could work, I also knew that not investigating this with Sierra was something I would regret. I'd denied myself a lot of things in my life, but I didn't want to deny her. Not when she stared at me with longing she didn't hide.

It was time to do something for me.

Chapter Five

Sierra

My knees bounced as I sat in the lobby area of Thorn & Thistle.

Around me the tattoo guns buzzed, taunting me because I wasn't getting one this time. My thigh twitched where my next one was going. Occasionally I could spot the top of Jamie's head as she worked on someone. Instead of organizing my ideas into some kind of pitch, I waited for another glimpse of that brown hair. Each time I saw it, I felt less likely to shake the building off its foundation with my fidgeting.

Minutes went by without a glimpse and then Jamie stood, a dark-haired woman following. Talking, they left Jamie's station and headed my way.

I sat up straighter, every cell in my blood perking up, waiting for the moment she would see me.

Jamie glanced up and then did a double take. "Sierra?"

"Hi."

As her client continued to the door, Jamie gave a distracted goodbye. Her attention remained on me.

Without the stupid partitions in the way, I got my first good look at her. Tonight Jamie had jeans and a T-shirt with a logo of a tattoo convention, no plaid overshirt. With or without it she looked good. It wasn't the clothes that made her sexy, it was how comfortable she was in her skin.

"Are you here to see me?"

How I wanted to say yes, especially because she looked so pleased at the idea.

"I wish," I said. "But I'm here to see MJ."

Jamie blinked. "For a tattoo?"

"Not a chance. You're stuck with me. Client for life."

A slow smile lifted her lips and her eyes crinkled at the corners. "I think I can live with that." Lowering herself on the bench next to me, she stretched her legs out in front of her. "If it's not top secret, what brings you to see MJ?"

Right. Not here to stare into her eyes and get the same calming effect as my weighted blanket.

I slid toward the end of the bench and angled toward her. "You remember Jordan?"

"Yeah. Is she okay?"

Not even a second to try and place her. First bringing donations and now keeping her word when she'd said she'd remember Jordan. It was like she'd gained access to a list of all things that made me willing to wear underwear that was mostly strings and uncomfortable as hell.

So often people came in and donated their money, which yeah, was appreciated, but it was obvious they'd come for the photo op of doing something good. If they asked our clients their names or stories, it never felt like it came from a place of interest or caring, but to prove to others that they weren't privileged and viewed everyone as equals.

Not Jamie.

My heart gave more of those stutters that were really getting close to palpitation territory.

"Sierra, is she okay?"

"Yes. Sorry. She's fine." I whirled to face her completely, bringing my left leg up on the bench and knocking our knees. "You and her got me thinking about the clients that come in that like art and how to make things better for them. They need to be able to create. It's part of them." I vibrated on the seat. "With your help I think we could do that. Not you, but the shop. The shop can help." My words came out in such a rush that I was able to listen to the tail end of them as they reached Jamie.

She shook her head, and shot me an apologetic look. "Sorry, I'm not following. I'm going to need you to back up. What is it you want the shop to do?"

Well, that was a letdown. I curled my hands on the seat. Slow down. Explain. But I didn't want to, I just wanted to get to the part where she got excited with me. "I want to get art supplies for the center."

Jamie smiled, a hint of her top teeth showing. "That's not going to be a problem. I'm sure we can find things to donate. When do you need them by?"

"No. I mean, that would be great and thank you, that's generous. But a fundraiser. I want to hold a fundraiser." My voice pitched higher and there was no stopping the speed with which I said the last sentence. I just wanted to share it with her. With everyone.

It'd hit me last night when I'd been marveling about how quickly Jordan and Jamie had connected over art. Jordan had let Jamie see the pain she felt at not being able to do it. Pain that had not been alleviated while she was at Haven Bridge and obviously not after. Art was something essential to her life, but we didn't focus on it at the center. And there had to be other kids at the center who felt the same way. I wanted to focus on them.

Talk about nailing the win-win situation. Art supplies for the kids, and me impressing Wendy by taking the initiative to put together a fundraiser. I mean, were there two better words for a boss than *initiative* and *fundraiser*.

Jamie stared at me unblinkingly. "And that's why you're here? To talk to MJ?"

"Yes! I want to do a fundraiser for art supplies."

"Hm." She nodded and scratched her chin.

Not the reaction I'd been hoping for. As one of the inspirations I'd thought she'd be right here with me. Okay, so she didn't have to go full-out and vibrate like me, but at least a fist bump, a high five, something.

"And you'd pair up with Thorn & Thistle?"

"Yes. You guys would be perfect to work with. Who better to know how important art is?"

"MJ can be a bit harsh." Caution rang in her words.

"I know. I was around her the other night."

"That'll be nothing like now. You weren't asking for favors."

I blew a deep breath out my nose. I would pretend like her words were given out of concern for getting MJ's agreement—not those of someone who was older and wise and schooling a youngster who obviously didn't know better. But it felt a lot closer to the second.

That she was right made it worse. She was pointing out things I hadn't thought of yet, because I was too excited at the possibilities.

I probably just lost any respect I'd gained at the center. And again, why did I care?

The alarm on my phone dinged. I was up.

"I appreciate the warning," I told Jamie genuinely. Now I knew I had to make up for my lack of forethought in other ways with MJ. "If you're not too busy when I'm done, I'll stop by and let you know how it went."

Jamie rose as well. "My next appointment isn't for another thirty minutes, I'll go with you. Maybe I can help."

"That's okay. This is my thing. I should do it on my own."

"Oh, okay." Her face fell and she stuffed her hands in her pockets. "Well, no matter what MJ says, I'll gather some supplies over the next few days and then drop them off at the shelter."

Of course she would. She was good and kindhearted and that was one of the things I liked about her. "Thank you. That's very nice of you."

Her gaze traveled over me, down the length of my long skirt and blouse to the top of my hair that I'd put in a messy bun. This wasn't a pass like she was checking out the size of my breasts or the width of my hips to cup them. No, this was more an assessment of how much pushback I could take.

Once she was done with her little inspection she nodded. Guess I was deemed sufficient to take on MJ. "Go get you your fundraiser."

"On it."

I made my way to the back of the tattoo shop. I crossed past the part that was "employees only" and walked into a… Oh, a break room. It was pretty standard fare and not what I would expect from here, but there was no doubt with the metal lockers and round tables with chairs. We didn't have a break room at the center. Most of us ate at our desks, or if we wanted privacy and quiet we went to our cars.

I continued on, passing walls that were sparse and

painted a dark blue. Then I was in front of a single door. MJ's office.

All right, I was ready to do this. I knocked.

"Come in," a voice called from behind the door. A grumpy voice. Even more so than the night at the trampoline park.

Oh well. I dealt with overworked judges on the regular and sometimes abusive parents whose kids needed to be taken away. Grumpy was cute in comparison.

I turned the handle and stepped in.

MJ looked away from her computer straight at me.

Not waiting for the invitation I was pretty sure wouldn't be coming, I sat in the lone chair in front of MJ's desk. It brought me eye level with the mass of papers and piles on the surface.

MJ's brown eyes sized me up. "So what'd you want?"

Getting right to it. I could respect that. I scooted to the edge of the chair. "I want to enlist your help."

"I know by looking at me that it's hard to believe, but if you're hoping to recruit someone for a beatdown or get you out of a tight spot, Cassie's the scary one. She's got the record to prove it."

Oh-kay. "I'll keep that in mind, but I'm not looking for that kind of help. I'm looking to get you to sponsor a fundraiser."

MJ groaned and started to turn back to her computer.

"I know. I know. But I'm not here to just beg money off of you. It would be great promotion for Thorn & Thistle. I will personally contact all the local papers. Plus, I think this fundraiser will be of personal interest to you."

"No."

"Did I mention it's for art?" Should have probably led with that. "I work at a crisis center and we deal with a lot of kids, some of them artists. Good ones. But we don't have the money for supplies. They're going through what's often the most difficult times of their lives and they're having to do it without art." I put my hands on top of MJ's desk. "So I want to raise funds to get them supplies."

MJ made a sound that was part growl and part sigh.

Hm. I'd thought that would do it. I mean, art kids in need. Who could deny that?

The grumpy was still in full force.

Her lips parted.

I sprang from my chair and held up my index finger. "Hold that thought." I paused at the door. "Actually don't. I'll be right back to get you to say yes."

Jamie

She hadn't wanted my help. She'd said no.

That was a first. It hadn't even entered my mind that she might say no. My mind had been all about thinking this was my chance. And best of all, this chance included being able to do something for her.

After making the decision to contact her, I'd searched her social media, since it didn't feel right to use her email or phone number, both of which she'd given me in a professional sense to discuss tattoos. Going to her work again beyond crossed the line of creepy. So I'd resorted to contacting her on social media. Well, until I'd seen many pictures of her out with groups of other women who looked to be her age, usually at bars, but sometimes at the park and once in a pool. The thought she would friend me back and see pictures of my daughter, tattoos I'd done, and my top scores on some video game had stopped me from hitting the request button.

Yet here she was before I could come up with a new plan. Well, there she was, marching her way down the main aisle of the shop, her skirt swishing with every step.

I didn't want this to end in disappointment for her.

MJ didn't like things sprung on her. You had to ease her into an idea and "no" would always be her first answer.

It was obvious Sierra was enthusiastic and passionate about this. It was equally as obvious she didn't have a concrete plan and once MJ knew that there was nothing to back that enthusiasm she was going to eat Sierra alive, one gorgeous curve at a time.

I looked away from the now empty aisle. A quick glance around the shop showed everything in order. Everybody was working, clients looked satisfied. Guess that meant I should be the professional I was and prepare for my next appointment and cut the staring after Sierra like a pound puppy left behind.

I laid out my inks and got my pile of towels ready. Footsteps rushed toward me. I turned, ready to take on whatever it was, maybe even a little grateful for the distraction. Sierra careened around the corner of my station and slid to a stop in front of me.

She grabbed my hand and tugged. "Come on, I need your help."

I popped up. "You've got it."

She kept hold of my hand and dragged me through the shop to the back. Not that I minded one bit. Nope, I believe my walk could be termed peppy.

"Okay," Sierra said, striding into MJ's office in a way few people dared. "Here's Jamie. She's seen the center in person. She can vouch for it. And pictures, I can pull up some pictures on my phone."

I took a second to get my bearings and try and figure out how far Sierra had gotten and how it was going.

There was no cussing and threatening to throw us out, so that was something, but MJ's flat expression was far from encouraging.

I stepped forward, drawing that hard stare. "I've been there. It's amazing all the things they do, the people they help. I met a girl, Jordan, who's really interested in tattoos. Knows all the different styles. She could have a real future. Is looking to get into illustrations but is afraid that she'll get left behind in such a competitive field."

MJ's look promised she would be paying me back for what she deemed my traitorous appearance, probably in the form of unorganized receipts.

Her expression not easing in the slightest, she faced Sierra fully. "So what do you want from me?"

"To host the fundraiser. Which would require the use of your shop and a small budget for advertising."

Uh-oh, MJ was not a fan of the A word—advertising.

Sure enough she scowled. Harder. "Oh, is that all?"

I moved to stand next to Sierra.

"Yes." She swallowed, but the sideways glance I got of her face showed nothing but determination. "I'll make it as painless as possible for you. I'll do all the work. As much as it takes."

There was that passion again. My daughter was the only thing in my life that inspired anything close to that. I had no special project or cause that I believed in so deeply. Keeping my parents from hurting themselves or someone else just didn't inspire the same enthusiasm.

I wanted to feel what she was feeling. I wanted to experience it with her.

When I'd first offered to join her in the meeting, I'd

only intended to make sure she could get her spiel out. But now I wanted more.

I'd gotten in touch with my parents' creditors and set up payment plans. I'd secured their promise to look at the information I gave them on seeking help. Things were stabilizing on that front. I could do this. I could take this opportunity to see Sierra more. If there were two things I was good at it was taking care of things and stretching a dollar. Maybe not exciting traits, but surely useful for a fundraiser.

I put my hand on the back of Sierra's chair. "We'll do all the work."

Sierra whipped her head my way. Her eyes were huge and incredulous.

Right. We'd just been through this. She didn't automatically want my help, wasn't waiting for me to sweep in. "If you want my help, that is."

Her pause went on and on. Longer than when I asked Riley if she'd finished her homework. Finally Sierra nodded. "It's for the kids after all."

For the kids. Message received.

I hoped to show her that my help was good for her too, not just the kids.

Over Sierra's head MJ searched my expression, asking me with a raise of her brows if I was sure I wanted this. I nodded. I did. I really did.

Seeming unaware of what was passing between MJ and me, Sierra put her folded hands on the edge of MJ's desk. "*We'll* work. In return, not only will you be helping people, which I mean is reward enough, but you'll also get a load of good promotion for the shop."

"With Cassie's work and then this we'd have a reputation as some bleeding heart charity shop."

"Oooh, another bonus."

MJ gave a huge sigh that sent the top pieces of paper fluttering across the desk. "How much are you wanting and what are you going to do with it?"

"I don't know yet. I had to get your agreement first." Her leg bounced, causing the whole chair to vibrate. "The second I thought of it, I knew I wanted you guys involved. There's no one better that'd understand these kids."

She wasn't wrong there. Even my co-workers that didn't particularly like kids and had no interest in having any, would step up with time and money and probably ass kicking for a misunderstood art kid. Most of us used to be that weird, artsy kid.

MJ stared at Sierra for long seconds and then she threw her head back and laughed.

I could probably count on one hand how many times I'd heard laughter coming from this office and almost all of them Cassie had been in here with MJ. Here she was letting loose now, all thanks to Sierra.

"This has got to be the shittiest ask for money ever," MJ said. "I mean, I get not everyone is Cassie and going to have a whole presentation and stuff, but you've got to have a better answer than 'I don't know' when you're wanting someone to give you money."

"I thought you'd appreciate someone who is honest and not bullshitting you. I don't know, but I can find out."

"I'm not giving you shit until I know how much and what you're wanting from the shop. Come back and show me and if I like what I see, then we'll really talk."

That was a yes, grumbled out as a threat, and we all knew it.

"Great." Sierra jumped to her feet. "Thank you."

I nodded at MJ and followed after Sierra. We'd only

made it two feet down the hall, not even close to out of hearing range of the office, before she threw her hands up in the air and whirled in a circle. "Yes! Yes! Yes!"

My eyes didn't know where to look first. There was the joy, absolute joy that radiated from her face and gave it a glow. It captivated me. But she was circling and all of her beautiful curves were in motion and I wanted to watch every single one.

"We did it." She shimmied back to me, her smile lighting her entire face. "Whew. I wasn't sure that was going to happen for a minute."

"But it did." Now that it had, my mind was already moving on to all that would need to be done. "Do you have any plans yet? Any idea what you want to do?"

"None."

I glanced at the clock. Dang. "My appointment is going to be here any minute. Maybe we can get together to go over some ideas."

She leveled me a look that was surprisingly serious from someone who had just been dancing around. "I'll behave and be completely professional."

I'd be subjected to more of the looks like I was receiving right now. Friendly. But there was no spark, no passion. That was gone when she looked at me. My fault. But god did I miss it.

"That's not what I want from you."

Sierra's beautiful mouth actually fell open.

Turning to get to my client, I smiled. Was that flirting? No wonder people liked it so much.

Chapter Six

Sierra

I walked into my uncle's house, the beat of '80s pop greeting me. My hips automatically started to move as I made my way down the hall. When my hearing started to go it would be all his fault. Okay, maybe not all. I did like to hit up nightclubs. But I'd only been able to do that for four years. The rest—all him.

"Where you at?" I called out.

"In here, Sunshine."

I followed his voice to the kitchen and found him leaning over the counter, magazines and his laptop spread around him. He had a beautiful office designed by none other than himself that he never used. He preferred to change locations, swearing it got his creative juices flowing.

I didn't really understand it. Not having an assigned office or workstation at the center left me low-key unsettled. I just wanted to go somewhere and know when I came back it would be the same.

I wrapped my arms around his waist, giving him a hug from behind.

"Hey." He squeezed my arm and then went back to typing.

While he finished up, I went around to the other side of the bar and helped myself to the tortilla chips and salsa he had out.

When I'd first come to live with my uncle after my mother died, the food had been one of the biggest shockers. The cabinets and refrigerator had been full of things I'd only seen in commercials. Fruit snacks and juice boxes and the yogurt in the tube. It'd been hard not to gorge myself in case I never had the chance to eat them again. Only the worry that he'd think I ate too much and my upkeep was too expensive had stopped me.

"So what are you up to?" he asked, still typing.

"I'm going to meet up with the woman who does my tattoos."

"Another one already?"

"Nope. She's agreed to plan a fundraiser with me for Haven Bridge."

Something I still wasn't sure about. I didn't regret accepting her help. It had been obvious that was the only way MJ would say yes, so she was a necessity. But now I'd be working on a fundraiser that I desperately wanted with a woman I was attracted to. One who'd implied she was attracted back.

Usually that meant a visit to the bedroom or the back seat of a car in a pinch, and then we could move on to the fundraiser. But that didn't seem to be the way things worked with Jamie. Was she waiting for me to make another pass? Was I supposed to wait on one from her?

Ugh. I was afraid to make the wrong move. I didn't want to mess up the fundraiser and I sure as hell didn't want to have to find a new tattoo artist after this was done. It wasn't worth the stress. I should move on. Yeah, like that'd be happening. The woman would not leave my mind.

"There." Uncle Drew snapped his laptop closed. "Thanks for coming over."

His text asking me to stop by had been a relief. Anything to stop the thoughts about meeting up with Jamie. I was not this person. The one who obsessed about a woman.

"No problem," I said around a chip, my hand under my chin to catch any crumbs. Satisfied that I hadn't messed up his showcase kitchen, I glanced up and got my first look at his face.

The pieces of chips lodged in my throat.

My normally on fleek uncle looked awful. Stubble covered his cheeks and there were dark rings under his eyes. Visible rings. Odd hours weren't new for him. Being an interior designer, he'd been known to do all-nighters before a client's reveal, but he was always quick to cover the evidence with concealer.

My heart jackhammered as I looked into his eyes. Eyes that looked like my mother's, looked like mine. For a split second I was taken back to when I'd first arrived at his home and I'd feared he'd sit me down to tell me that he couldn't be my guardian anymore, and that I would have to go back into foster care.

But that moment had never come. Not even close.

I dropped the rest of the chips back into the bag. "What's going on?"

"We're just going to get right into it, huh?"

"It must be important for you to let that hair see the light of day."

"Ouch. Harsh. Justified, but harsh." He put his elbows on the counter and leaned toward me. The kitchen lighting caught the grays coming in his stubble. "So I found out some news today."

"Okay."

He stretched his hand on the counter toward me. I immediately put mine in his, my stomach twisting tighter with each second that passed.

"My cousin Henry called me today." His hand gripped mine tight. "Grandma died."

She was dead. My grandmother was dead.

I should feel something shouldn't I? Something more than this emptiness.

Uncle Drew looked tortured in a way I'd never seen. Not when Sergio broke up with him after four years because he wanted no part in raising me. Not when he was let go as creative director from the home decor company during the recession.

He looked this way for her. For that woman.

Now the feelings were hitting.

The wrong ones. Anger. Resentment.

That woman had shunned him, us, for fifteen years. Why did she have to come haunt us now?

"I'm sorry" wouldn't come. I didn't know if I was sorry. I didn't know if he was.

"Wow."

A scratchy sound came from his throat as he pushed away from the counter. "Yeah."

He paced to the other side of the kitchen. He opened the fridge, but didn't take anything before closing it again.

I curled my now empty hand. "How are you taking it?"

"I don't know."

He stopped to stare out the window, but I knew it wasn't the yard, or his neighbors' urban chicken coop, he was looking at. It was his past. The same past I was now thinking about. At least mine had happy memories attached to it.

"She hasn't been in my life. If I hadn't got the call, I never would've known. It doesn't change anything for me." He sighed, his whole body moving with the release. "But she was my mom."

I didn't think the woman deserved the use of that term. I'd had a mom. Someone who loved me and made me feel safe and I knew I could count on. My grandmother was—had been—none of those.

The day my uncle came out to her was the day she said her son no longer existed. She'd kept true to that promise.

No, the grief would not come.

Uncle Drew laid his top half over the counter and pressed his cheek against it. "I can't stop thinking about her. She's gone."

I got up and walked around the island until I could hug him from behind again. "I'm sorry." And I was. I was sorry that he was going through this. That *he* was in pain.

"Me too."

"Is there going to be a funeral?"

"Yeah. Monday."

"Are you going?"

He stiffened, almost throwing me off. "She wouldn't even want me there." He let out a laugh that sounded wet and soggy.

I pressed against him as tight as I could, covering his back. "Then don't go."

"How would it look if I didn't go to my mother's funeral?"

I didn't care. All I cared about was how haggard he looked at the news. How bad would it be if he went back there?

"It doesn't matter. You don't owe her or anyone

anything. Don't go if it's only because you're worried what other people think. Their thoughts aren't worth anything anyway." Not if they thought my uncle was disposable.

He huffed. "I'm surprised they even bothered calling me at all."

Me too. From my memories, which admittedly were from a young girl, my mom and uncle were the only good things to come from that family.

"Do what's best for you."

"You're right." He slid out from between me and the counter. Turning, he kissed my cheek. "I'm not going. There'd be no point."

Well, there was closure or revenge or acceptance of the death, but I was glad he didn't seem to need those.

"I support you whatever you decide."

"I know," he said.

I was proud of the certainty in his voice. The certainty that I would be there for him.

"I'm here for you too." He squeezed my shoulders. "If you need to talk, I'm here."

I smiled reassuringly. I didn't need to talk about her. Yes, she'd had a big impact on my life when she refused to take me in after my mother died, instead letting me go into foster care. She'd been quick to tell me I'd be too much work for her. She seemed to get cruel joy out of revealing to me how she'd told my mom that she'd regret getting pregnant so young. But I hadn't let that ruin my life, weigh me down. The opposite. It made me do what I do.

She was the reason I kept my social media set to public so that if she ever chose to look me up, she could see all that I did. Heck, right now my only regret was that I hadn't updated it about plans for the fundraiser. I'd been too hung up on Jamie.

"I'm fine. It's you I'm worried about."

Leaning across the counter, he grabbed a handful of chips. "I'll be okay. I'm actually surprised how hard it hit me."

"I'm not. You're a good guy. The best." One who would jump on a plane after hearing about his sister's death and go back to the place he'd sworn never to return, the place he wasn't welcome, all to fight for my guardianship. He hadn't even met me. My mom had sent him a picture in their irregular correspondence. That hadn't stopped him from dropping his life in Oregon to go back to Bennet, Missouri, when an old school friend had emailed him about my mom's death. I'd been in foster care for three weeks by the time he was allowed to take me.

My phone buzzed in my pocket.

"Get it." My uncle waved his hand. "I really am okay."

I exited out of my friend group text and checked the new text that'd buzzed.

Jamie: I finished my client early. I am ready when you are.

The pull of the past lessened. I stared at this connection to Jamie, charmed with the periods and formal language.

Should I respond in emojis and abbreviations just to mess with her? No. I didn't want to reinforce the image of someone just out of puberty in need of mentoring, which she seemed to have of me. That was not the direction the night would be going.

I looked up and thoughts of a teasing reply fled. Reality hit me again. Uncle Drew had lost his mother. Just because I wanted to focus on the now, didn't mean my uncle could, or should.

He might need to talk, or some company.

Sierra: Something has come up. I'll need to reschedule.

"Do not send that." Uncle Drew had his head tilted down and was reading my screen. "I'm all right. Really. You can go."

I shook my head. "No. I'll stay. We can watch a movie or—"

He nodded at his laptop on the counter. "I still have work to finish up."

He gave me his learned from detective shows look that was supposed to make me spill my guts. "I'm serious. If you need to talk or if this brings some stuff up, you can come to me. Doesn't matter that she is—was— my mother." He smiled and it crumbled at the corners.

"That's it. I'm staying."

I'd watch him work and be here when it inevitably hit him. Jamie and I could meet another time or text our ideas. A pang hit my chest at the thought of not seeing her. More days without answers about what the heck was going on between us. More days spent dwelling on it.

"No. Go. Do your thing."

I bit my lip and searched his expression to see if he truly didn't want me here. He had plenty of friends he could call up. Sympathy and comfort weren't what we turned to each other for. We saved that for other people.

"The same goes to you," I said. "You can call me, come to me, whatever, anytime. I'll be here."

He nodded and stuffed a chip in his mouth. He chewed but it looked reflexive and I doubted he tasted a thing.

He held open his arms and I went into them. He smelled faintly of oranges and wood which must have been yesterday's scent. There wasn't a particular brand I associated with him. His cologne changed depending on his mood, the season, and what was trending.

I still remembered the scent of White Rain shampoo from when my mom would wrap me in her arms. And then there was the corn chips that my grandmother had always smelled like.

"I love you," I said, rubbing my cheek against his unshaven one.

"And I love you."

I made my way out to my car, not quite running, but walking fast enough that I probably should have done some stretching beforehand. Huh. Was the reaction hitting now? I did not like how unsettled this news had me. And I really didn't like how much it had me wanting to rush to Jamie.

No, not to Jamie specifically, but to her to work on a fundraiser that would help people go after their passions. Just like I did. My grandmother, as unworthy of that word as she was, might not be able to see it, but I was going to make this fundraiser the best ever.

Instead of her haunting me, maybe I could haunt her afterlife with all of my good deeds and winning at life in general.

And right now that required the help of Jamie.

Chapter Seven

Jamie

After calling my daughter to say good night, I sat and waited for Sierra to arrive. That's all I was good for. As soon as I got Sierra's text that she was on her way, my mind had lost its—well—damn mind. There was plenty I should be doing. Working on client sketches. Grabbing some dinner. Reading more blogs about alcoholics that had sought help and what had worked for them. Instead, I stared at the shop door, waiting for it to open.

And then it did.

Sierra walked in wearing jeans and a sweater with some kind of fringe on the bottom. Fringe that moved with every step she took. Not to be left out, her long, thick ponytail swung with each step. As much as I liked the effect, my head ached in sympathy. I kept my hair to my shoulders and mostly pulled back because I hated anything hanging in my face while I worked, even then, I got an undercut so there was less to deal with.

She spotted me and smiled.

I sat up straighter. The same sense I'd developed as a kid that something was off with my parents even before I understood what caused it was going off with Sierra.

I scrutinized more of her, looking for tension elsewhere in her body. There wasn't any in her walk. And what a walk it was. She bounced with each step, along with other parts of her anatomy that I tried not to stare at. But it wasn't even that. If she had been covered in a drop cloth it would be something to watch. It was as if she had so much energy that it couldn't all be released in a simple step, she had to give it more.

That energy should be triggering more alarms, reminding me that it would take a lot to keep up with, instead of appealing to me.

"Hello," she said, stopping in front of me. Her smile was wide and beautiful and showcased those lines around her eyes that I was so fond of. "I am beyond ready to plan this."

I heard nothing but genuineness in her voice. Had my parents poisoned me so much that I was always looking for issues?

"Let's go to the back," I said. "It's quieter."

She grinned and I looked away. I didn't trust that prolonged exposure to that grin would allow me to be able to concentrate on the fundraiser. My gaze dropped lower, right to the fringe on her shirt, swaying enticingly. There was no safe place to look with her.

"I like going back there. I feel very VIP."

"If you want, you can walk around to the side and enter through that door to get the full experience."

"No, thanks. I'll stick with you."

She said it like it was some kind of privilege.

Well, I'd said I didn't want her to be strictly professional, and already she was laying it on thick. And I was soaking it up to a ridiculous degree. Before I let it go too far, after we were done with business I was going to have to clear some things up.

First up was to make sure she knew just how old I

was. I didn't think I looked younger than my age. The time I'd spent in the sun on the soccer field when I was younger now showed in the lines of my face and the wear and tear on my body, but I needed to make dang certain she didn't think I was in my twenties.

Next up was making sure this wasn't me just misreading her warm touches and teasing glances. I didn't trust myself on this one.

In the break room, we went to one of the round tables. As I was sitting, my stomach gave a loud rumble. "Ignore that, it's been a long day."

Her lips twitched, but she nodded agreeably enough.

"So first thing it'd be good to know is your vision for the fundraiser. What's our end goal?"

"Art supplies, whatever the kids need to work on what they're passionate about. They tell me what they need and I make sure they have it."

"That's a lot."

"Yeah." Her smile was wide and bright.

And no more words were forthcoming. "Maybe we should narrow it down to a few. There's painting and drawing and fabric. Those don't need a lot of equipment unlike clay or woodworking."

"Hm." She leaned forward over the table. "Yeah, we don't have much room at the center, and it's never good to have expensive equipment around. But I hate the thought of telling someone their form of expression takes up too much room." A tap, tap, tap came from underneath the table. Her shoe against the concrete floors.

She was right. I might be partial to drawing and that's where my mind immediately went when talking about art, but there were a lot of mediums, and all of them were equally important. Even if they did create logistical problems. "What if some of the funds were set aside for classes or studio time elsewhere for those mediums?"

"Oh, I like the way you're thinking."

I couldn't help smiling at her appreciation. Appreciation for my idea—not me specifically. My mind was having a hard time deciphering the difference.

"Good." I made a quick note. "You mentioned using the space of the shop. Is that all you're wanting?"

"All? I want whatever I can get, but definitely the shop. I can't think of a cooler place than a tattoo shop. Plus, tattoos are art." She looked at my arms. I would not flex them. "Beautiful art. They need to be showcased."

"I don't think that's going to be a problem. This fundraiser is something a lot of our clients could get behind, especially if it somehow involves tattoos."

In the face of Sierra's blinding smile, I pushed thoughts aside of MJ's grumbling about how much more involved this was getting. She'd be happy enough when she got to take credit for what was shaping up to be a celebration of art.

Staring at each other across the table, my stomach chose that moment to give another growl.

"Working's hard when you're hungry." She stood. "Why don't we get some food?"

As much as I liked the idea of prolonging things, I didn't like the idea of it being so she could watch me eat. That would be a beyond boring experience for her.

"Nah, I'm good. I can pick up something when we're done."

Her smile dimmed and she lowered herself back down. "Right. Sorry, I didn't even think that you probably have plans and are in a hurry."

Again so genuine sounding. As if she didn't find the

suggestion that I had plans ridiculous. The only time I had plans were for work or family, and since half of my family was avoiding me in case I wanted to talk about their addiction, and the other half had an early bedtime, my availability was gapingly open.

"You don't mind?" I asked.

"Of course not. I love to eat. It's like my second favorite thing ever."

I would not ask what the first was. I would not.

"Okay, then." I pushed to my feet. "I just need to get my bag."

Once I had my backpack we said our goodbyes to MJ and Cassie who were the only ones still left in the shop, and headed outside. Thorn & Thistle was located on a trendy side street with other businesses, but most of the shops leaned toward the "early to open, early to close" variety.

"There's a pub open," I said. "The food's pretty good."

"That works." She turned and headed to the left. No need for her to ask which way. The drone of voices was louder than I ever heard when I ate there in the late afternoon. We crossed the street, a loud laugh echoing down the street. Another followed, louder, sharper than any of the others. I flinched. God that laugh, it sounded so much like the ones my parents' friends would give on their weekend hangouts right when they started to lose control.

Sierra looked at me out of the corner of her eye and then to the pub. "Or there's a place that's not too far and has a crap-ton of options. I guarantee it'll be quieter."

I got a whiff of beer cheese. At night the beer aspect seemed less inventive appetizer and more starter course of all things alcohol. That clinched it. "Let's do it."

"Let's." Sierra pointed to a bright red Mini Cooper. "Do you want to ride with me or drive on your own? There should be plenty of parking this time of night."

"I'll take my own. That way I can head home after."

It wouldn't hurt to have an escape option for both of us. For me, it'd be if I was reading this wrong and needed to go home and lick my wounds. For her, it'd save the hassle of an extra drive if it turned out I was the old pathetic queer hitting out of my demographic.

I followed behind her cute little car, making sure it didn't ditch my dependable mid-sized SUV. But that wasn't happening, not only because she didn't have the heavy foot I would've thought, but because I was not going to let her get out of sight. It'd end my show. In her rearview mirror I could see her singing. Well, it looked more like yelling and there was some seat dancing.

We ended up in a large gravel lot with about a half-dozen other cars.

"Ta-dah." Sierra came around her car and held out her arms toward the row of food trucks set up. "I recommend the Greek. Oh, and the East African too. Soooo good."

So many smells came at me at once. Something made my nostrils tingle and not in a good way, but others, mm-hmm, they were interesting. I would be hunting down the one that smelled like fried dough.

Trying to see the writing on the side of the trucks, I squinted. Next to me Sierra didn't seem to be having any trouble reading the menus. Just wait. Thirty-five had hit me and suddenly I couldn't read the street signs or see the score on the television.

"What are you getting?" she asked, turning toward me. Somehow over all of the other smells, I could still make out her lemon.

"I don't know what to choose. There's so much."

Her eyes widened and then sparkled like she'd been struck with a great idea.

A great idea that required accomplices.

"Why don't we each grab some things from a few different trucks and then we can share? Instant variety."

It sounded like heaven to me. The shocker was it did to her too. "You're just full of good ideas tonight."

"I know, right? I think that's a promising sign for when we brainstorm some more." She pointed to the left. "I'll take this half."

She bounced off in that direction, drawing my gaze down to her ass.

My pleasing view came to an abrupt halt.

"Is there anything that is a no-go or you're allergic to?" she asked.

Tomatoes didn't sit too well with me anymore and the sriracha sauce that was so popular left my mouth burning for hours.

Screw the probable heartburn and stomachache. Tonight I was going to eat like I was in my twenties. "Nope. Pick whatever looks good. You?"

"I'm open to whatever."

Not even a second to have to think about it. Again, just wait.

I hit my side of the trucks.

In ten minutes I was forty dollars poorer and without a single regret. This was the kind of adventure I could get behind. No travel or stress.

My hands were full with everything that'd looked good and some that sounded so odd—golden raisin curry—that I needed to try them. I made my way over to a picnic bench where Sierra already waited.

"Dig in," she said, handing me a fork like it was a tool to help me complete a quest.

We grinned at each other across our mountain of food and did just that. Only an occasional happy moan or me hacking when a spicy noodle dish she'd chosen proved too hot for me broke the quiet.

Twenty minutes later I stared at the remnants on our plates. All that remained were a few of the pot stickers that I'd loved and one samosa.

I groaned and slid down the bench so they weren't directly in my line of sight. "No more. I'm going to burst."

Sierra laughed. "Yeah, but it was the best meal ever."

"The best." I rubbed a hand over my stomach. "I'm going to have to do this with Riley sometime."

I flattened my hand on my stomach.

And now we'd see how much the separate cars were needed. I knew for some women kids were a deal breaker. That might be especially true for a young one.

"You should," Sierra said, not looking thrown by the mention of Riley. "It's the best. I still remember when my mom did something like this for me."

Relief had me relaxing even more than the good food already had. "Yeah?" I'd never heard her mention her mother in any of our sessions. She'd talked about an uncle, but I couldn't recall any other family. Of course, as it'd become apparent, I didn't know jack shit about her. I'd purposefully engaged as little as possible with her tempting presence in my chair. Now I wanted to make up for it and learn everything I could.

"Yup." She ducked beneath the table and when she didn't come back up, I peeked under to see her lying on her back, stretched out on the bench. She turned her head and smiled at me.

There was an idea. After a day being bent over clients, I bet my back would be happy to have some support. I lay on the bench. Above me was the night sky and to the left was Sierra's silhouette. So long as I didn't look the other way, we were in our own hideaway.

I turned my head completely to the side to take in Sierra. Somber lines dissected her face. My immediate inclination was to make them go away, but no, here in our secluded picnic fort felt like the place to learn what caused them.

"My mom and I used to go on picnics. It was our thing. On payday she'd take me to get fast food and we'd order as many of the cheapest things as we could. Then we'd pig out, sitting in the grass in the park." She smiled but it did nothing to erase the sadness, if anything it highlighted it. "They were my favorite meals ever."

"That's parenting goals there. Those picnics sound amazing." I turned my head straight up to the night sky. Clouds blocked everything but the moon.

My mom had taken my brother and me for fast food when she didn't feel like cooking, but the memories weren't good ones for me. While my brother had reveled in being able to scarf down whatever combo he'd chosen, I'd always gone for the least expensive thing on the menu, worried my mother was using money that should be going to pay a bill.

Those times had made sure Riley never had to think about where her next meal would come from. She would never associate a hard knock on the door with someone threatening to turn off a utility. I was proud of that, seeing it as the fulfillment of a promise I'd made to myself.

But hearing about Sierra's memories of her mother, seeing how much they still affected her, really had me wondering if, while I was busy providing, I was doing enough to make memories that Riley would look back on years later.

I'd been rightly schooled by a childless twenty-five-year-old on the importance of how I spent my time with my daughter.

"Have you brought your mom to experience this food cart version yet?"

"I wish. My mom died when I was ten."

Ten. So young. Younger than Riley. At that time I still had a full-time mother, only beginning to notice that she acted different on the weekends. My mom might not have been involved all the time, but she'd been there. It was something. "I'm sorry. I can't even imagine."

"Thanks. Luckily my uncle came to the rescue." The side of her mouth that faced me lifted in the barest hint of a smile and this time she did brighten. "He was living the bachelor life and had no idea what to do with a girl, but he still took me in."

What must it have been like for an unsuspecting person to have a little Sierra? I'd bet she'd stared around her with wide-eyed interest and asked a million questions and her laugh had filled his bachelor house. "I'm glad you had him."

"Yeah, me too. I'll never be able to repay him."

I turned my head more fully to her, struck by her phrasing. "Without even meeting him I'm pretty sure that having you in his life is payment enough."

Sierra's throat bobbed as she swallowed. "Thanks."

"Is he your only family?"

"I had a grandma."

I swallowed down the need to tell her my grandparents were gone too, afraid that instead of it being a chance to connect, it'd come off as me turning it into a one-upmanship of hard life experiences.

"She doesn't matter though. I didn't know her and I'm better off for it. I have my uncle and he's awesome."

"I'm gl—"

"All right, we have a fundraiser to plan." She clapped her hands like a coach that had just laid out a play drive. She sat up.

Not having much choice, I joined her, sitting at the table properly.

The light coming from the trucks was glaringly bright. The hum of the generators in the background was a distracting annoyance following the dreamlike haze of our picnic. When was the last time I'd had a personal conversation that hadn't been me having to solve something or offering advice?

It'd been surprisingly nice.

Sierra

And I'd officially killed the mood. But I couldn't go there. No more talk about my mom, especially not on the day I learned my grandmother died. I mean, not a day went by when I didn't miss my mom, think of her, wish she was here. But sitting in nature, having a great meal, being in Jamie's calming presence—it was too much. Too close to what I used to have.

"Okay, enough talk about my past. I know you've probably had a long day."

Jamie didn't look fooled by my words or light tone, but she huffed. "Are you saying because it's nearing eleven and I'm old that it's getting past my bedtime?"

I laughed, delighted that she was playing. She was

acknowledging that I might—gasp—realize she was alive before me. "No. I'm saying because you worked all day, you're probably tired."

When I looked at Jamie I didn't see her age. I saw a woman who was calm and so very, very talented. Not to mention confident and sexy as hell.

"Mm-hmm. You wouldn't be that far off, so we better get started."

I pulled up the Notes app on my phone, lowering the brightness on the screen. "I'm ready. What do you want to talk about next?"

"Well, we agree that it needs to involve tattoos."

"Already going to be the best fundraiser ever. No charging per plate dinners or an auction. I mean, those are fine, but this, this will be epic."

"Yeah, dinners and auctions are not Thorn & Thistle. It's all about the tats. Easiest option would be donation jars around the shop with a description of what it's for. We could offer a discount on their tattoo if they drop some money in." Jamie rubbed the back of her head. "That could be a problem with MJ. Discount is a four letter word to her."

"Oh." Donation jars didn't exactly scream best fundraiser ever to me. They didn't even whimper it. My finger hovered over the screen. I couldn't even make myself type that.

"Buuut—" Jamie drew the word out.

I snapped my head up.

"That's boring and Thorn & Thistle isn't boring."

"No. No you're not. Tell me."

"So what if we did themed tattoos—something to do with art? Like an easel or a cool paintbrush. We'd have to get the agreement of everybody, but I don't think it'll be a problem. The proceeds from the themed tattoos go to Haven Bridge."

"Yes." I slid forward until the table dug into my stomach. "That's what I'm talking about."

"Yeah?" Jamie pulled a notebook from her backpack. "Were you thinking something like that?"

"You have no idea. I was going to try and talk you into having a specific tattoo only available to those that donate."

"Ooooh." Jamie's pencil scratched faster on the paper. I preened.

"So you're thinking an exclusive?" she asked.

"If that means it's used for the fundraiser and only the fundraiser, then yes."

"A collector's tattoo. I'm liking this." Jamie hit the end of her pencil to her lip. "So should we go with one tattoo? Have MJ create a Flores original? Or should each artist design their own?"

Oh god, multiple specialized tattoos sounded so amazing. Amazing and like a lot of work. Exactly what I promised MJ this would not be. I knew what I wanted, but I had to be realistic too.

"That sounds like a lot for you guys."

Jamie shrugged. "I mean, I'll ask, but everyone will be in. Not only because it's a good cause. We're a competitive bunch. We'll be tracking who can raise the most. I bet Gina will even find a special piece of jewelry only offered for the fundraiser."

I squeezed my thighs together tight. "Then, hell yeah, we should have multiple tattoos."

"It makes the most sense. That way we can draw more people in, because there'll be different styles to choose from. Or even better, people can get multiples. More money for the supplies."

She was making it sound so reasonable. That's what my pitch to MJ had been missing. "Right, money for the supplies. Probably a better reason than 'I just want to see all the cool tattoos you guys create.'"

"Probably. Not that I don't appreciate your excitement to see them."

I bounced on the bench, squeeing. "Oh, this is going to be so good."

"It really is," Jamie said, closing her notebook and then flashing a smile.

Smiling and I couldn't see it properly. Only places with bright lights from here on out.

"So have you heard anything about your review?" she asked.

We'd already talked about so much tonight, crossed so many lines and now we were going to bring work into it too? I had to be careful of how much I shared with her, how many ways she was taking over in my life. You got used to a person and then when they were gone you were left with a huge hole and all the spaces they used to fill. It was better for friendships to fill different roles. Except I'd already done that when I'd mentioned it in the chair.

"I already had it. Guess who nailed it?"

Her hand shot up, palm ready. "That's great. I knew you would."

I smacked my hand against hers. Should I tell her, that yeah, my review had gone well, but I couldn't really celebrate it because my job was still very much in jeopardy?

No. I liked seeing her happy for me. Liked her looking at me as a capable adult.

"Thanks."

"So I'll check with everybody and once they agree

we can go back to MJ." She tapped her knuckles to the notebook cover. "This won't cost much up front, which MJ will like."

We did have a lot to do still, but Jamie's low voice and the way her words were so evenly spaced kept me from getting more amped up. Her way of speaking was the opposite of my get-it-all-out-in-one-breath. It was a lot like her smile. Slow, beautiful, but not overpowering, more like prolonged seduction.

There was something so comforting in that.

"So what do you think?"

I blinked and dragged my attention away from watching her lips form the words I should have been listening to. "Um, sorry. I missed that last part."

"What do you think about talking to some of the kids who the supplies are for? Get in their own words what this means to them and why it's so important."

I sat up straight. Oh, another good idea. People liked to know where their money was going, and if they saw a picture and heard a firsthand account, even better. Plus, I was always down for spending time talking with the kids in our care. I just wished I'd thought of it. I'd been all set on showing Jamie just what I had to offer. Not sure I was doing so hot beyond the food trucks.

Jamie rested her foot against my tapping one. She didn't cover it, or make it stop, just kept it against mine.

It was such a small move. Simple really. A touch of her foot. But it was as if she was trying to reassure me with that one move. And it was working.

I moved my foot away, my heart starting to pick up. Unh, unh, unh. I didn't need her to soothe me, no matter how effectively she did it. My work, this fundraiser, heck, our meal—that could do it.

She searched my face and I wasn't sure how much

the darkness hid against the strip search she was doing. "Unless you can't do that because of privacy rules."

"Nah," I said distractedly. "It should be fine so long as everyone knows exactly how it'll be used. I'll only look for volunteers. We've had stories on our website and done media interviews before."

The feel of her foot pressed against mine lingered like a phantom touch. Maybe this had been the wrong night to do this. Maybe my grandmother's death was messing me up more than I thought. It was a bad night to test myself with Jamie's company.

"Well, this has been fun." I wiped my hands on a paper napkin. "I'm glad we did this."

"Yeah, me too." Jamie slid out of the bench and started gathering our trash.

Hands full, we headed toward the entrance by the parking lot.

On opposite sides of the trashcan, our gazes met while the leftovers of our exciting, exposing, enticing—all of the E's—meal dropped to the bottom.

"Well, as you know, it's past my bedtime."

An image of Jamie in bed flashed in my mind. It wasn't a fantasy of us naked and crawling all over each other. What was different, scarier, was that my mind went to a place where we were in bed together and I was tucked against her, my head on her shoulder, as we watched something on TV.

Whoa. No. No. Us in bed, her legs wrapped around me, squeezing tight—that's what I wanted.

Damn it, now it wasn't only my mind she had confused, but my body too.

Jamie crossed around the trashcan and stopped in front of me, tipping her head until our eyes met. "I don't want this night to end."

I sucked in a breath. Her tone was as good as a brush against my core.

Her gaze boring into mine. "Do you?"

Chapter Eight

Sierra

"Wait. Hold up. Are you seriously coming on to me right now?"

Even in this lighting I could see how red Jamie's cheeks went. "Apparently not very well."

I took a step back, shaking my head. "I thought my generation was the one that supposedly can't make up its mind. I've offered twice now and you've turned me down flat."

She made a face, bringing her hand up to rub the back of her neck. "In my defense, it was never because I didn't want you. I just couldn't believe that you wanted me like that."

Say what? Should I have given in to the urges and dragged her to the back room in the center? Maybe then she wouldn't have had any doubts.

Those cheeks of hers stayed on red alert and she looked so damn uncomfortable. Okay, well, with her like that, I didn't feel strung along.

I stepped up to her and promptly ran into the hand she held out, stopping me.

My gaze snapped to hers. "Oh no, you didn't."

She made a calming gesture with those hands, that

was pretty much guaranteed to get any breathing person to do the opposite.

"Just one more thing. I want to make sure you know how old I am."

Really? Still with the age thing. I reached out and grabbed the hem of her shirt. Instead of rubbing the yellow and gray plaid fabric between my fingers like I'd intended seconds ago, I gave it a hard yank. "I don't really care."

She licked her top lip, right over that little scar. "I do."

"Yeah, I've noticed."

"I'm thirty-seven," she said like she was at a confessional.

"Okay."

"There's twelve years between us."

"Yup. Didn't even have to break out the oh-so-useful algebra for that one." Since her grave expression wasn't leaving, I put more effort into reassuring her.

"Pfft. That's nothing. I have phones older than that. It's one of those that was a pain to text on because you had to hit the seven four times to get an S and couldn't connect to Wi-Fi or anything."

"Yeah, try pagers for me. No. Car phones that plugged into the lighter."

"I might have seen one of those in an old movie." I waved my hand. "Okay, maybe that wasn't the best example."

"I have a feeling we're gonna run into a lot of those. Because that's a big difference. I'm on my second career. I'm divorced. I have a daughter. My partying days are behind me. Breaking news from Rachel Maddow is an exciting night."

"Are you done there, Boomer?"

Jamie jerked and then frowned.

"Too soon?"

"That will always be too soon."

I chuckled because I thought I was damn funny. Her lips twitched and the subject seemed to lose interest with her. Thank god. Her gaze dropped to my mouth and stayed there. It was like we were right back there in the dark, away from everyone else, the only two people. Testing her, I slowly ran my tongue around my lips.

She drifted closer and my pulse thrummed merrily at my neck. "Would it be all right... I'd like to kiss you, if that—"

I beckoned her with my fingers. "Well, come on now."

The last of my words hit her lips in a breath, but then it became more, a sigh, as our lips touched at last.

My eyes slid closed, a happy moan escaping. Her mouth was warm, her lips soft and plush and receptive under mine in a way that my imagination couldn't do justice to. Her tongue swept out and I eagerly opened for her. Another moan rumbled from the very depths of me. I could feel the power of her, of our kiss.

Her body pressed me back against my car. She was letting me know with the way her tongue was stroking and swirling against mine, the hard rock of her hips against mine, that she was as into this as me.

As we kissed my mind blessedly went empty except for the wonders of being trapped between my car and her sturdy body while our tongues flicked and licked at each other. Jamie showed me that thoroughness I so admired in her as my tattoo artist was even better when she focused on discovering my mouth.

Tires crunched in the gravel not far from us.

Jamie stiffened and pulled away. My lips followed, a protesting mew emerging.

Hands on my shoulders, Jamie held me back, and

kept them there while she turned and watched the car pull into a spot next to her SUV.

I sighed and licked my lips, gathering the last traces of Jamie and the cinnamon sugar waffles we'd finished with.

Ending the kiss had probably been a good thing. Yeah, we were in Portland and I'd never experienced a problem, but that usually involved a quick peck and my hand around their wrist as I led them toward my car. Not me putting my tongue down their throat. That might be pushing it.

Two women around my age got out of the car. They gave us the assessing ever vigilant women-out-on-their-own-late-at-night look that we were giving them. Once we'd all deemed each other no threat, they headed to the food trucks, talking quietly.

Jamie stuffed her hands in her pockets and rocked back and forth on her heels. "So that was...wow."

I stepped up to her and hooked my fingers into her belt loop. I pulled her shirt up enough so that I could glance at the very respectable brown leather belt with a plain thin metal buckle. I wasn't disappointed to discover she didn't have something flashy under there. She didn't need flashy. She was potent enough on her own. So very potent.

"Do you have any free time this week?" she asked. "I'd really like to take you on a date."

Um, what? A date. More of what happened tonight?

Not a good idea. That's how it started. Getting caught up in someone. I couldn't do that.

"That's not necessary." I ran my finger down the seam of her shirt. "I'm a done deal." We could go to my bed right now. We didn't need the other.

If I hadn't been watching her eyes, I would've missed

it. But now that it was gone, I knew she'd been looking at me with hope. She'd been hoping I'd say yes. Yes, to spending more time with her.

Ugh. Fuck.

It was just one. One date. It wasn't like she'd suddenly become my whole world and make everything better.

My pulse whooshed so loud I didn't know if I shouted or whispered my next words. "If you wanted to do that, I guess we could, yeah."

A small, satisfied smile curved her lips and somehow it was better than any blinding one I'd ever received. "Good."

Her gaze returned to my mouth. Slowly, her head lowered, coming closer.

Oh, thank god. Yes, let's get back to kissing. No confusion in that.

I assumed the position, chin lifted, eyes closed.

Her lips brushed my cheek. "Thank you for the good-night kiss." She stepped back. "I'll call you for that date."

Jamie

I knocked on the front door. Would a time ever come that it didn't feel weird to do that? Nicki was fine with me using my key and told me to just come in, but this was no longer my home. I might pay half the mortgage because even with what I paid in child support Nicki couldn't afford it on her own, nowhere close with the pay in retail, and there was no way I was going to have my daughter uprooted, but I didn't belong here anymore.

The door opened and Riley stuck her head out. "Hey, Momma J."

"Hey, Jelly Bean." I waited until I was inside and the door was closed firmly behind me before hugging her. Hugs only happened if there was no chance of witnesses.

I inhaled deep the same way I had since she was a baby, and just like then I got an overwhelming rush of love and rightness.

Riley tolerated it for all of a second before she ducked out. She didn't have far to duck. This last growth spurt had her almost at my shoulder.

I backed up even more, giving her space. Affection wasn't something I wanted to force. Not quite true, I wanted to grab her to me and squish her and plant kisses all over her face, but what I really wanted was her to want that back.

"Grab a sweatshirt, you might get cold."

Riley made a face, but at least she didn't argue, just headed toward the living room, her long ponytail swinging behind her. I swear even her ponytail had developed attitude this last year.

"Oh, hey, I thought I heard the door," Nicki said, coming into the room.

My heart might no longer soar when she entered a room, hadn't since she'd asked for a divorce saying that she needed more in her life, but I was still glad to see her. Would always be glad. She'd shared her precious baby with me, only two months old when we'd met and she was trying to get out of a bad situation with her ex. She let me be part of her life and raise Riley until she became mine too.

Now that some time had passed I could see the divorce was a good thing. I was happier too. I didn't have to keep going places I didn't want, all to keep her happy.

"Hey," I said giving her a quick hug.

She leaned back, her blue eyes traveling over me, no doubt noticing I'd ditched my joggers for a nicer pair of jeans, and wore the peach button-down she'd once told me brought out some pink in my cheeks. Sierra seemed to have a thing for my cheeks. Her hands had cupped them enough when we'd been kissing.

"Not going with the normal of video games and Thai takeout?" she asked.

That was me. Predictable. Boring. Pad Woon Sen— the most exciting thing about me.

Except Wednesday night. I'd eaten food I'd never heard of, flirted with a woman who made me feel like the adolescent I'd never really been, and hadn't made it home in time to catch the news. Best of all I'd be doing it again. She'd agreed.

In my future was the chance for more kisses that left my body vibrating long after—like when I did an extended tattoo session and could still feel the vibrations from my machine even after I stopped.

The thought of going back to a normal Sunday of running errands with Riley and then sitting on the couch after the high of Wednesday night was a letdown.

"Not today," I said. "Maybe next week."

Nicki shook her head and smiled at me fondly. "I'm sure." She patted my shoulder and then headed further down the hall. "I washed your blue one. Take it," she yelled up the stairs.

She left a trail of Daisy in her wake that I'd no doubt purchased. That'd been predictable too. A bottle every birthday, along with dinner at our favorite restaurant and a trip to Salt and Straw ice cream.

My brain immediately went to Sierra. What would she think of a birthday like that? Would she want to be surprised? Before our meal together I would have said yes, but now I wasn't so sure. In the quiet moments when she talked about her mother and their fast food picnics, it'd been obvious traditions meant a lot to her.

I wasn't sure of anything when it came to her, including if I'd made the right choice in stopping anything from progressing between us and leaving when I had. But Wednesday had been about trying new things and hookups were not new for me. I'd had them on the regular in my teens. They'd served a purpose then, but as an adult stress relief and getting off weren't as important as knowing someone. I didn't like knowing that my only use for someone was an orgasm.

And I did not need to be thinking about that with my daughter and ex-wife in the same room.

"Riley, pack it up. We need to get going. I'll be waiting in the car."

Coming in her own sweet time, Riley threw her bag in the back seat. "We're just going to the shop," she said, buckling her seat belt.

"Actually we're not."

That got her head up and looking at me.

"I'm helping with a fundraiser and we're going to meet up with the other person that I'm working with."

Sierra. I was going to get to see Sierra. Fifteen minutes and counting. I was going to introduce the woman—who'd been cagey and hard to nail down when I called to set up anything outside of the fundraiser—to my daughter. Not the normal progression of things. But today was my day with Riley and I refused to leave her behind. Besides Sierra seemed okay when I brought up Riley at the food trucks.

"Mm."

"We're meeting at West Corner park." I announced

it in the same tone others would use for a surprise trip
to Disneyland.

"Oh." Riley pulled out her phone.

Oh is right.

Originally I'd planned for us to meet at the shop,
but I'd been inspired after the food trucks and upped
my game by choosing a park with a pond and picnic
benches for us to work at.

I pulled into the parking lot next to Sierra's bright red
Mini. I spotted her right away, sitting at a table under a
shelter, Jordan next to her.

My breath stuttered and my skin tingled. The ef-
fects of being near Sierra were uncomfortably similar
to heart attack symptoms.

I shook out my hands. I needed to cool my jets. Today
was about helping kids.

"All right, let's go." I grabbed my backpack and a
full shopping bag from the back.

Sierra jumped up and waved.

My shoulders loosened. Surely if she'd changed
her mind about an eventual date, she wouldn't look so
happy. Of course, she might not be so happy if she knew
this meeting wasn't absolutely necessary.

Stopping at the edge of the table, I put my hand on
Riley's shoulder. "Sierra. Jordan. I'd like you to meet
my daughter Riley."

Sierra transferred her megawatt smile to Riley. "Hi
there. I'm Sierra. It's nice to meet you. Thanks for joining in."

"Sure," Riley said, like she'd had any choice.

Maybe now my morning coffee could stop trying
to incite a rebellion in my stomach. Sierra liked kids.
She worked around them. Of course she'd be welcoming to mine.

Riley turned and took in Jordan, who still sat at the table watching us. She thrust her shoulders back and did a little nod of her chin in the direction of the older teen.

Jordan nodded back.

"Thanks for coming, guys," I said to Jordan and Sierra as I slid onto the bench. Picnic benches were becoming our thing. And I really needed to chill with how much I liked the thought of us having "a thing."

"It sounded like you had something exciting to tell us," Sierra said, leaning forward, her eyes wide and sparkling.

"I do. I think you'll really like it. In fact, it might be the best news you hear all day, maybe all—"

"Ugh." Sierra stomped her foot in the grass. "Tell us already. What is it?"

Chuckling, I looked at the other occupants of the table. Riley stared at me like a new, even less cool mom had slid onto the bench next to her, and Jordan looked bored by my antics, but Sierra was all eagerness which made it worth it. She was worth it. Worth taking the chance that it was as she said and our ages were nothing. Or at least testing it.

"So everybody is in to do an exclusive tattoo."

Sierra gasped. "Really? You guys are awesome."

And this is why I didn't want to tell her over the phone. I'd selfishly wanted to see the reaction in person. The way her huge smile scrunched her cheeks and her sitting celebration dance definitely needed to be seen. Even more than the car dancing.

"I told everyone to have their design to me in a week, which means we can expect ten days."

"Ten days? That's awesome. I like working with you guys. You make things happen. Other places we'd still be waiting on approval paperwork."

"No bureaucracies for you to deal with here. Just me."

"I can handle that."

Such energy and enthusiasm. Two weeks to lay the foundation of a fundraiser was not a lot. There would be so much that needed to be done. Yet instead of being wary of adding another thing to the pile of responsibilities I carried and managed, I felt like I'd been injected with a shot of life. This was the kind of work I could get behind. It felt good. And the company, well...

I turned to look at Riley, expecting to see her on her ever-present phone, watching videos of an engine being taken apart. Instead her gaze kept darting from the table to Jordan.

"Up next, I have to design my tattoo."

Sierra's attention shifted to me. "Have you decided what you're going to do?"

"No. I was hoping we could get together this week and work on it."

"Me? You want my help?"

"Of course. This is your idea. You should have input in the design." I looked away from Sierra's incredulous expression to Jordan. "Actually I was hoping you would too."

Jordan's blue eyes got huge, giving me a glimpse behind her front. "Hell fucking yeah." Her gaze shot to Riley. "Sorry."

"Oh, it's okay." Riley shrugged. "I hear it all the time."

Of that I had no doubt. Things couldn't have changed so much since I was that age that throwing some random fucks and shits didn't up your cool factor. As long as Riley didn't start throwing them in public or around adults, I'd call it good.

I put the bag I'd brought onto the table in front of Jordan. "I thought these might help you get some ideas."

The teen bent forward and pulled the handles of the bag apart to look inside. Her head snapped back to look at me. "Are you for real?"

"I am."

"Oh my god." Jordan reached in and grabbed a set of Derwent graphic pencils.

"I gathered some things I thought you could make use of." Actually I'd done some research on what exactly an illustrator needed and made a stop at my favorite art supply store.

Absorbed in looking at her new goodies, Jordan was lost to us. Smiling, I glanced at Sierra.

She'd been excited when I'd asked for their help, but now she was at the next level. She looked like she could levitate off the bench and bounce around like an old-school Sonic, collecting rings.

"I take it you two are in?"

"Are you kidding?" She leaned halfway across the table and for one lung-hitching second I thought she'd grab my shirt, haul me closer, and kiss me. And I'd let her. Right here. With witnesses. Including my daughter. Jesus, I needed to get a grip.

"Tell me when and I'll be there."

I bent and snatched my bag from the grass and pulled out my calendar. Maya and Vivian—hell even MJ—gave me crap about being a dinosaur and not using my phone but I liked a written record. I didn't trust my phone wouldn't reset or some crap.

I flipped to the weekly schedule. All right, today was Sunday so I'd want something as— Today was Sunday. Sunday. Today was Sunday.

Well, hell.

I was supposed to be letting the janitorial staff into the shop.

It wasn't in the calendar because it didn't need to be. It was part of my job. I did it every week.

Yet, I wasn't there. Where I was supposed to be. I was here because I had to go to a park to be more adventurous.

Since the shop was closed, Sunday was the day MJ had a cleaning staff come in and deep clean. She refused to give them a key to the shop, so I'd volunteered to let them in. I didn't live far from the shop and almost never had anything going on. Except today.

"Everything okay?" Sierra asked.

I stared at her face. A face that had been smiling a few short minutes ago and was now staring at me in concern. Whatever I'd been trying to prove here had failed. "It will be."

Searching for an opening for Sierra, I stared down at the pages of my calendar, at all the other entries penciled in. At least four on each single day. And I'd gone and let this one slip through the cracks. Something so small that I did every week. "How about Wednesday? My last appointment is at four so I should be done by eight."

She did a quick look at Jordan and then they both nodded. "That works."

"But I won't be there," Riley said, folding her arms over her chest.

No she wouldn't be. My nights were Sunday and Monday, though I watched her whenever my and Nicki's schedules allowed it. And here Riley was actually having fun, which by extension meant with me. "We'll figure something out, but we have to go now."

I ignored her bitching and pulled out my phone, scrolling for the number of the cleaners. Jesus, I hoped they hadn't left yet. It was almost ten. I was half an hour late. If I thought Riley was complaining now, just wait until I said that we'd be the ones cleaning the shop because I'd screwed up.

I didn't look toward Sierra as we left, not even as we pulled out, no matter how strong the pull was. That one look of disappointment on her face as I said we had to leave was enough.

I'd screwed up. I couldn't afford to screw up. Too many people counted on me. And I counted on that. I needed that, not parks and food trucks and kisses.

There was only one way for me to make sure this didn't happen again. The hope that had been building inside me, making everything lighter, deflated.

Chapter Nine

Sierra

Once again Jordan had come through with the good intel. Trey, the client I wanted to talk with, was chilling in one of the large rooms we had reserved for teens to use, just where Jordan said he would be.

I approached Trey who sat watching TV in one of the maroon love seats that'd been donated last year. He'd been assigned to me a few months ago when his mom had hit a rough patch and stopped taking care of him as she should. I'd arranged court ordered counseling for her and he was staying in our boys' housing program.

"Hey, Sierra," he said, looking up.

"Hey, Trey. Okay if I chat for a sec?"

His expression immediately went wary. I hated that. I hated that a visit from me, a request to talk, had him already thinking it was bad news. I hated it—but I understood. There was always a small part of me—no matter how many good years there were, no matter what I did to make sure it stayed that way—waited for someone to come and tell me that it was all collapsing again.

"Don't look like that. It's a good thing. At least I hope."

"Yeah, okay." He tossed the remote on the cushion

next to him and then pulled his sweatshirt sleeves over his hands and started to get up.

"We don't even have to leave," I said, motioning for him to stay. I took a seat on what was supposed to be a coffee table but in reality was a cheap bookshelf placed on its side. "When we were doing your permanency plan I remember you mentioning that you like art."

"I do some sketching."

"That's what I'm wanting to hear. So I don't have all the details yet and it's not a sure thing, but I'm working on something to get some art supplies in the center."

He shifted in his seat, his eyes meeting mine. "Really?"

"Yeah. I'm looking for volunteers who'd be willing to talk to me about what art means to them and how not being able to do it affects them. Anything that's said might be used to promote the fundraiser, so I'm only looking for people totally comfortable with that."

"Do you want me to do it?"

"If you want to, great. If not, no pressure."

Trey leaned forward and pushed his sleeves up. "Yeah, I'll talk."

"Awesome."

I whipped my phone from my pocket. He took one glance at it and started straightening his hair.

"All good?" I asked.

"Uh, what was it you wanted again?"

"What art means to you, what it's like not being able to do it, whatever you want to tell me."

He nodded, his eyes getting a far-off look. He bit his lip. "Art is like peace for me, ya know? It's just… Everything makes sense when I do it. In my head, around me, whatever. And now I can't do it. It's not the same on some notebook paper or here where you don't know what'll happen to it. I'm lost without it."

Jesus. He needed his art. He didn't have it through no fault of his own, but because his mother had lost her job and fell into a depression so deep she couldn't take care of herself or her son.

I knew that helpless feeling of things happening to you that were out of your control. Decisions being made without your say. For me it wasn't art that had kept those feelings in check—when other kids were bringing home drawings of animals, mine had looked more like something you'd find on the walls of prehistoric caves—I'd been rocking out to empowerment anthems.

I knew he recognized that shared experience in me. It was the same recognition I'd found with other queer people.

"Thank you. That's exactly what I needed." I stood, putting away my phone. "It's not a secret but if you could hold back on telling anyone until I know for sure it's a go, it'd be appreciated."

"Sure. No prob."

Jamie was brilliant for wanting me to get that kind of thing. Donations would pour in after the pull on their heartstrings. I could feel the tugs on mine with every step away from him.

I had known this fundraiser was a good idea, had seen how important it was to Jordan. But until this moment I hadn't realized just *how* important. It should be right up there with job training with regard to preparing them for the future. The future had to be more than keeping a roof over your head and food. It had to be about finding some joy and doing the things you like.

That would be something I would start focusing on

when it came to our cases and hopefully getting them—and the center—to focus on it too.

A rush of longing to see Jamie slammed into me. I wanted to share what had just happened, being sure to credit her "wise wisdom" so I could get a glower from her for implying she was old.

Not much longer. I'd see her soon. Just a few more hours in fact. For now I needed to focus on my work.

A flurry of cases and calls later I was finally headed to Thorn & Thistle. Jamie had asked me to stop by so we could talk. Since designing the tattoo was set up for tomorrow, my hope was "talk" was some old-school way of saying I want to kiss the hell out of you.

I turned and scored a nice parking spot almost directly in front of the shop. Before I could even turn off my ignition, the door to the tattoo shop opened and Jamie stepped out.

She'd had to have been watching for me.

Nice to see I wasn't the only eager one.

Disappointment was too mild for what I'd been feeling when she left. It wasn't like anything would have happened. She'd had her daughter there. A sweet, awkward, beautiful preteen. Not to mention Jordan, who'd rather stab you than watch you make googly eyes at each other. Even without the promise of kisses or sex, I still wished it could have lasted longer.

But tonight, tonight I'd take the kisses. I'd even stop stalling on the date to get to them. I'd been trying to figure just how many roles she would be in my life and how to keep her from taking over any more before I chanced it.

I hit the button to roll down the window as fast as my finger could press it.

"Hey, there." Jesus, my voice sounded like I was trying to pick up a sex worker.

Jamie bent and draped her arms on the open window. "Hey," she said, sticking her head inside the car, her voice reaching out to me like soothing vapors from a diffuser.

I leaned over the emergency brake, starving for her taste.

"Wow."

I pulled up short.

Jamie looked at the interior of my car with an expression of horror.

Oh, that. "I have a system."

"Uh-huh."

Okay, so if anyone wanted to sit in the back, it'd take me some time to clear off space. But it was a Mini. Not many people wanted to be back there.

She pulled her head outside of the car and took a step back onto the curb as if the mess was a living thing that might attack. Staying a safe distance away, she jammed her hands into her pockets.

And oh, that pulled the fabric tight against the muscles of her upper thighs. I wanted to stuff my hands in there and explore. Back pockets too. I'd sling my arm around her waist and slide my hand down into her pocket, after giving her ass a squeeze of course.

"Thanks for coming by. I was hoping to talk to you real quick." She pulled one of her hands free and massaged the back of her neck.

"And you don't want to do it in the shop?"

"No. Private would be better."

That sounded promising. Tucking the seat belt under my arm, I leaned down and scooped up the brochures and flyers of different agencies and nonprofits on my front seat and tossed them in the back. Screw my system.

"There. Plenty of room. Hop in." I smiled at her, trying to make it welcoming and not "I've got you in my car and now I'm going to kidnap you to do wonderful things to your body." She missed my effort anyways. She was too busy trying to get situated. Something crunched and she held her leg up, wincing.

"It's fine. Probably a takeout container."

She nodded and then stared straight ahead out the windshield. Uncomfortableness poured off her, like for once her skin wasn't the perfect fit for her. Aw. I thought I was the one who was all in a tither about this. The woman had no game and it was becoming one of my favorite things about her.

"So you wanted to talk?" I prodded gently.

"Yeah." The car bounced as she turned to face me, a look of determination on her face. "So I know we're starting something between us."

I'd say so. I'd agreed to go on a *date* with her. "The chemistry between us is pretty intense."

"Yeah." She gripped her knees. "That's what makes this so hard."

"Hard?"

She rolled her shoulders and then looked me directly in the eyes. "I'm sorry, damn sorry, but this can't go any further. I can't get into a relationship. I thought maybe… that I could make it work…but no."

Relationship. No, I'd agreed to a date. There was no way I could handle a relationship. I was barely certain on the date.

"It's okay," I reassured her, putting my hand over hers on her knee. Like really, really, okay. "I don't do relationships either." I slid my fingers from over her and to the inside seam of her jeans. "But we could still make something work."

She sighed, the muscles under my fingers tense. "And I don't do casual. Not anymore. I don't like the way I feel afterward. It fills my body's needs, but leaves everything else in me empty." She took my hand in hers, lifting it away. Her thumb stroked my palm, one quick caress before she put my hand back on my lap. "I'm sorry. I don't have anything to offer you."

So that was that then. Right when she'd got me thinking that I could try this, to spend more time with one person, to test myself. Right when I learned that her kisses were ferocious and consuming. Right when she'd confirmed that being around her felt like she'd sat on the other side of the teeter-totter that was my life. She balanced it between going hard and fast to prove myself and that sense I was missing something.

"You have yourself," I said.

The look in her eyes went more miserable. "It's not enough."

She sounded like she really believed that. How? What was it she thought I wanted from her? What had other people wanted from her?

"What does a relationship mean to you?" I asked.

What was I doing? I'd received my answer, no more fretting necessary. But I couldn't let it go. I just couldn't. Just like I'd kept wanting her even though she affected me more than was comfortable.

"It doesn't matter," she said, shaking her head against the headrest, looking like she was going to wear away the upholstery. "I don't—"

"No. No. I get that. I just wanted you to explain a relationship to me."

At first she stared at me suspiciously as if I was

asking to be purposefully difficult, but then her expression softened. "It means spending time with someone. Going out on dates, having meals together. It means being there for them and supporting them."

It sounded scary as shit and yet so amazing. Too amazing. I'd had that before. Someone that supported me and meant so much. And I'd lost her. I'd lost my mom. And I'd promised I would never let someone into my life so deeply that when they left, I couldn't recover.

"So it's time?" I asked. "That's what's stopping you from doing something with me?"

"Yes. There's Riley who has to be my first priority and my parents and work. I messed up on Sunday. I can't do that. I can't let anyone down that's already counting on me. I've reached my limit."

"And I'm not in the place to go all in to a relationship. I've got to focus on work and now the fundraiser. I need and like my independence." It was the only way I stood a chance of assuring I didn't let someone become everything to me.

I finger walked my hand to the edge of my seat and held it there. "So what if we got together when we can? I'm not going to be demanding you spend your time with me, not at all. And I'd never come between you and your daughter. I know and respect how important that bond is."

Jamie's expression was all disbelief. "That's what you would want?"

Did I? Not exactly, but it's the closest I could come to where we each got some of what we wanted.

"Yes."

"I'm going to be tired. I won't be up for always going out and partying is still not my thing and—"

"Independence, remember? I already have people I can do that with."

"So like a part-time relationship?"

"Exactly. Less pressure." I trailed my finger against the edge of my seat and ran into the pinky she had there. "We still live our lives but also enjoy the time we have together. When we're busy or can't meet up, no guilt."

"No guilt," she repeated like it was a foreign word.

"And no pressure. Don't forget that, it's an important one."

Her lips twitched. "I'm seeing that."

Did she? Here I was trying to talk someone into dating. No, I was going even further. I was practically begging for a relationship. But not a full one. One with training wheels.

"So what do you think?" I asked.

She clasped her fingers over mine. "I think I have some free time right now."

There was no missing the testing edge to her voice, which I guess meant she was sticking to "no casual" and "I like dates."

I had this. Because even though I was freaking out some, I was also in her company so it all kind of balanced out.

I swallowed and met her gaze. "If you haven't had dinner yet, maybe we could go get some food."

Was that what she was looking for?

Her instant smile said it was. "I'd like that. A lot."

I let out a breath. I was going to do this. *We* were going to do this. I leaned over and gave her a quick, smacking kiss.

Before I could pull away, her hand caught the back of my neck, deepening the kiss. Oh god, the taste of her. There was a hint of coffee, but something sweeter too like caramel, and the combination was so soothing and comforting.

It would be okay. It was a meal. We'd already done that. The shocking effect of the last one wouldn't be as potent.

We eased apart. I didn't go far, staying close, feeling her breath hit my face and staring into her eyes.

"I still don't want this to be all about sex," she said against my ear. "But how about we make the food to go?"

Jamie

As Sierra drove to her apartment I buzzed with energy. What even was this? Nervousness? Excitement? A crazy combination of both?

The surprises just kept coming with Sierra. Waiting for her to arrive, I'd been so certain I'd have to bail on this thing between us. Instead I sat in her car, on the way to her place.

To do what exactly remained a bit of a mystery. I didn't even care. I cared that she'd worked to find a way to make this happen. I wasn't used to that. Coming up with solutions was my job. Except I wouldn't have come up with this because a solution was supposed to be good for both parties and I didn't see what she got out of it. I wasn't doing anything for her.

Sierra pulled into a covered, numbered parking spot in a well-lit apartment complex. The opposite of mine. We did not have designated parking spots and definitely no guest spots with fancy wooden signs.

Carrying our take-out bags, I followed behind her on the landscaped walkways to a first floor unit.

One foot in and I immediately stepped back to slip

off my shoes. Wow. Starter apartments had changed a lot since my time. This looked like something I was still aspiring to get. Making sure nothing was leaking out of our bags, I walked off the linoleum entryway and onto light beige carpet.

A large gray sofa with pillows of colorful flowers took up most of the room. On the walls were prints of meadows and more flowers. A bright lime green rug lay under a white coffee table.

"Your place puts mine to shame." Mine was all about comfort. Comfortable couch. Comfortable chairs. Coffee table to kick your feet up and put your drink down. It didn't have any of the personality of her place.

"I doubt that," Sierra said. "Besides, as long as you like it, that's all that matters. It's for you, not anyone else."

It should've sound so corny, especially coming from someone her age, but it was nothing but the truth. I'd discovered that once I moved out of the house I'd been so proud to purchase for Nicki and Riley. The blue Craftsman had been all about a symbol that I was taking care of my family, not because I needed two stories and a separate dining room. All I needed were my bed, my couch, pictures of Riley, and my old gaming system.

"So this is what you like?" I asked, taking it all in. It was bright and colorful and nature-y—yes, I could see how that would fit her.

"I do like it, but this is shared space. So I guess it reflects me and my roommate. My room—that's all for me."

And now that's where I wanted to be as fast as possible and not only because of the warmup kiss. "Are you going to take—"

"Hi, there." A pale young woman with black hair walked down the hall, smiling.

Sierra whirled around. "You said you weren't going to be home tonight."

"Plans changed." The newcomer gathered her hair and twisted it up at the top of her head, securing it with a large clip.

Her roommate. It's not like Sierra had hidden the fact—heck, she'd mentioned her only seconds ago—but seeing her struck me how young they were. This was the beginning of their lives, where they were still figuring everything out. Me, I was in the process of trying to juggle everything I'd thought I'd figured out.

"Ashley, this is Jamie. She's the one responsible for my awesome ink and also who I'm working on the fundraiser with. Jamie, this is Ashley my roommate."

Ashley put her hands on her hips, the oversized shirt she wore over her sweatpants sliding off one shoulder. "Really? That's the introduction I get? She gets an ode and I get roommate."

"I share a home with you. That's no small thing."

Ashley rolled her eyes—I would not think how young she looked doing that—and held out her hand. "Hi. It's nice to meet you. I'm Ashley, technical engineer in training."

"Jamie. Tattoo artist." I shook her hand. "Technical engineer. That's something you have to do extra years of school for, right?"

"Yup. I'm going to be a million dollars in debt and thirty before I'm finished."

"Right." I smiled tightly. "Thirty—the horror."

Sierra knocked her shoulder into mine. "Don't listen to her. There's nothing wrong with thirty."

"That's good because I left it behind quite a few years ago."

Ashley waved her hand. "You're killing it. It's like if you've got your career and can actually live off of it by thirty, you're a damn inspiration."

An inspiration. Divorced with a daughter pulling away. Monitoring my parents for more signs they were progressing. Currently on my boss's shit list. I had double the amount of work I'd had in my twenties, with half the energy to do it.

At least she didn't seem thrown by my age. Then again she thought Sierra and I were client and artist working on a fundraiser. I hadn't been introduced as anything more.

Ashley pointed to the bag dangling from my wrist. "Whatever is in there smells delicious."

"If I'd known you would be home, I could have brought you some." Sierra gave her a pointed look, but any sharpness in the look was tempered by her freckles. It was hard to look intimidating with those kisses of sunshine on your face. "You were supposed to be in study group."

"Well, I'm *supposed* to get this paper done. It's twenty percent of my grade. That wasn't happening if I went there. It's social hour central up there."

If she thought twenty percent was bad she would have hated both my test to get my license to be an insurance agent and a tattoo artist. They were pass or fail. That was it.

After that there'd been my apprenticeship. Not much you could study for there. You did what you were told when it was demanded of you.

I'd apprenticed under Hugh Dewit. He'd been hard, but fair. He'd taught me not only the ins and outs of

tattooing, but probably the lesson I needed the most—
that you couldn't let anything interfere with the art. No
matter what else was going on in your life when you
were creating, you gave it the respect it deserved and
focused on it.

I'd always been artistic and enjoyed coloring and
drawing, but it became vital to me when I'd hit my early
teens. With art I could lose myself in it. Forget about
everything else that was going on around me and make
something beautiful. I'd always been intrigued by tattooing, but hadn't pursued it because I'd needed a job
right out of high school to be able to support myself,
not somewhere that needed schooling and an apprenticeship and then had no guarantee of income. But I'd
never stopped longing for it. I'd saved and scraped—
not easy with a wife and a child—until I could go for it.

"Well, we'll leave you to study," Sierra said.

"It looks like you've got a lot of food there."

I curled my fingers tighter around the bag. Which
was rude. We did have a lot, easily enough for a third.
But this was our first meal as…people who would spend
as much time together as we could when we could find
it.

"Hm." Sierra walked into the kitchen that was right
off the living room. She opened a cabinet and looked
at Ashley over her shoulder. "Would you look at that?
There's a lot of food there too."

"Bitch." Ashley laughed and went and bumped Sierra with her hip.

It was official, I felt twenty years older since Ashley
stepped into the room.

I tried to picture MJ and myself acting like this. I
couldn't. If MJ giggled at me I was pretty sure it'd be her
version of blinking in code and I needed to call 9-1-1.

"Come on," Sierra said, grabbing my wrist and pulling me after her.

And now a blush was heating up my neck. There was no doubt where she was dragging me and Ashley was witnessing it.

"It was nice meeting you," I said, trying to sound like this was as normal an occurrence for me as it obviously was for them.

"You too," she called after us, her tone standing in for a knowing wink.

Sierra stopped at a closed door on the left of a small hallway. "You still okay being here or did you want to go somewhere else?"

Other desires might have abated with the reminder that we were in very different phases of our lives, but not my desire to see the space she felt most comfortable in. "No. This is fine."

"Okay." She took a deep breath and then opened the door. "This is my room."

Chapter Ten

Sierra

"Wow," Jamie breathed out.

"Is that a good wow?" I asked, watching her expression. I didn't know why, but her seeing my room, my sanctuary, felt bigger than with other women I brought home. Maybe because there was every likelihood she'd be back. And she was looking around in interest at more than the bed.

Jamie immediately headed for the right side of my room with the east facing window. "It's like I've walked into a terrarium."

"That's a good word for it."

Plants hung from my ceiling, sat on shelves next to the window, and any flat surface. Green everywhere.

It'd all started with a simple dracaena plant. I'd liked how calm I'd felt looking at it and taking care of it. When I watered it, I'd gotten the same feeling as when my mom would brush my hair before bed, the action seeming to soothe both of us. So I'd gotten more. And even more, wanting to replicate the feeling. Unfortunately, when I walked into the room it didn't have the same impact. I'd gotten used to them, my eyes not catching on them like before, but I kept adding and trying.

In keeping with the chill vibe my comforter and pillows were also in shades of green. My accents were pieces of wood.

"How long does it take you to water all of these?"

I laughed, not at all surprised that would be Jamie's first question. It was a down to earth concern for a down to earth woman.

"Not that long. During the summer I only have to do it once a week. In the winter sometimes I can go three."

Jamie stepped closer to one of my fittonias and very carefully ran her finger over a pink veined leaf. "It's so peaceful."

"It is." I loved them during the day, but my favorite part was at night when I was sleeping. It felt like my plants were watching over me.

"I wasn't expecting something like this," she said, doing another slow circle. "I like seeing this side of you."

"And what side would that be? The glitter-free side?"

"The peaceful, relaxed, restive one."

That's exactly how I felt in here and now I'd invited her into it.

She stopped at a bromeliad, leaning over its bright pink flowers. "Riley would love something like this. We plant sunflower seeds in the backyard every year. But having something like this around all the time, she'd love."

"I knew I liked her." I tested the moisture of the soil in the pot with my finger. "I really liked watching you guys together."

She looked at me out of the corner of her eye. "You don't get weirded out by it?"

I cocked my head. "That your daughter looks at you like you're the most embarrassing thing in the world?

No, I think it's pretty normal. I never got to that stage with my mom, but I'm sure I would've."

Jamie huffed. "Yeah, that look—not one of my favorites. But I meant that I'm old enough to have a teen and you're not much older than one and—"

"Oh my god," I wheezed. "My teens are way behind me. Years. So no I'm not weirded out by it. I like you for you and a mother is *one* of those things. I think that might be one of my top five favorite things about you."

Her cheeks flushed.

I wiped my hands of any lingering soil on my pants and then reached up and stroked the warmth of Jamie's cheek. "This is in my top three." Her skin burned hotter against my fingers.

"Now you've got me worried this is some mommy kink." There was a twinkle in her eye so that was a good thing.

If she could see in my head—bad thing.

No, I wasn't looking for a mommy. She was safe in that area. But I had taken enough human behavior courses to know that deep down I longed for the feeling of safety I'd had with my mom. No matter how many questions I asked, movies I talked through, times I wanted to play cloud shapes—the look of love in her eyes had never changed. There was something about Jamie's steadiness, her calmness that appealed to the same part of me.

"I want you for you. I don't want you as a stand-in. I'd want you if you were younger than me. The traits I'm interested in with you have nothing to do with your age and everything to do with you."

"Yeah?" She searched my face and then nodded and faced my plants again. "Okay."

"Okay." I stepped up right next to her and then slid

my hand down into the back pocket of her jeans. So tight and firm against my hand. And squeezable, so very squeezable. The perfect palm rest. "Now getting back to Riley—who I'm totally not weirded out about and actually liked—and flowers. Let me just say I totally approve of sunflowers. They're such a happy flower."

She turned her head to look at me, a small smile on her lips. "Yeah, it doesn't surprise me that you'd like them."

"If you want to get her a plant for indoors that will last all year, a pothos is one of the easiest. If you want a flowering plant, I'd go with an African violet. You have to make sure they get enough light, which can be tricky in the winter, but otherwise they're not demanding."

"Thanks. I'll have to look into that."

My insides went all soft and squishy.

So many times around Haven Bridge and during my field placement, I'd heard parents promise things. What they would do, what they would look into, and they never did. With Jamie I believed her. Her words weren't to appease, but intentions.

Cupping the tip of her chin, I turned her head to face me. I slowly rubbed my thumb over the little scar on her lip and then placed a kiss on it.

"Soccer," Jamie said. "A cleat to the face."

I gave it another kiss.

Jamie turned and reached out to a peace lily, touching a brown leaf. "Is this one dying?"

"Not if I can help it. Someone had it at the dumpster, but I think I can bring it back. It just needs some TLC."

She gave the wilted, mostly brown plant a dubious look. "I've never thought of having inside plants. They seem like so much work."

"They can be, but they're worth it." There was nothing like seeing something neglected and being the one to bring it back to life.

Jamie carefully trailed her finger around the edge of the pot, the movement mesmerizing me.

"When I get this one healthy again, I'll give it to you and you can see if they're too much work or if you like it."

In the middle of kicking off my shoes, I felt the stillness in my room. The sudden stillness like you've said one of the things that are supposed to be inside head only. Sure enough a glance at Jamie found her staring at me with a frozen expression.

"What?"

She shook her head. "That's just a very relationship-y thing to offer."

Yeah, I guess it was. Not like I'd offer someone I was just going to sleep with a plant. I cared too much about them, put too much time in them—my plants, not the people I was sleeping with. I wouldn't know that they wouldn't neglect it again. But I knew Jamie helped her parents, I knew how much the people in the shop looked up to her, I knew she stared at her daughter like she was the most incredible being ever made. That was enough to know my plant was safe with her.

Heck, I'd had to place kids for a night with less vetting.

"I guess I trust you." This time I didn't need any stillness on her part to alert me I'd gone too far. My thudding pulse was enough. "With my plants."

Walking over she handed me my container of food. "I'm glad." Her fingers slid against mine in a purposeful caress that made it all the more shiver inducing.

I climbed onto my bed and sat cross-legged. Mak-

ing me very happy, Jamie bypassed the lone chair I had
in my room and came and sat next to me on the bed.

"Don't take this the wrong way," she said as she
stretched her legs out and balanced her carton on her
thighs. "After being in your car, I can't believe how
clean your place is."

"Eh, I don't care what my car looks like. It's not like
I like being in there. Stupid traffic and even stupider
other drivers."

Jamie's lips twitched. "So wouldn't it make more
sense to have your car be all Zen, like your room? Might
help you with that road rage."

"I like being angry in the car."

Jamie paused, her fork halfway to her mouth. "Come
again?"

"Yeah. I can cuss and tailgate and get mad. It's the
only place I can be angry. At work I'm supposed to be
an example."

Chewing, she nodded. "I actually get that. I'm not
like that in the car because Riley could see. Definitely
not like that at work—I'm still trying to tamp out everyone's outbursts. For me, I get it all out with gaming."

"I'd like to watch that."

"I don't know. It can get a little scary." She leaned
closer to me, our shoulders brushing. "I've been known
to throw my controllers on the couch."

"No." I fake shivered. "That's nothing. Just in the last
few months we've had two holes punched in the wall
in the teen room over video games. Things get heated."

"Riley refuses to play on the same team as me."

I settled back further into my pillows. "I bet I'm up
for it."

"I think you're right. I'm guessing not much scares
you." Jamie smiled around her bite.

What would she say to knowing that having her in my room scared me? Would she be back to thinking I was young and immature? It wasn't immature to protect yourself. It was smart.

"I like picturing you all intense and loud. It'll give me a preview of what it's like when you let go." I moaned as I put another bite in my mouth and closed my lips slowly around my fork.

Jamie stilled, nothing moved but her eyes as they traced every movement I made.

Now that I had my audience captive, I licked the prongs on my plastic fork clean with flicks of my tongue, being very thorough.

She blinked and then her eyes narrowed. "Are you trying to make playing video games into a sexual thing?"

"Uh-huh. Is it working?"

"You know, it really is."

Jamie

No longer having to fear I was reading Sierra wrong and she'd catch me being a creeper, I was free to look my fill at her. I focused on the freckles covering the bridge of her nose, looking like a galaxy of stars. All the while her lemon scent filled my lungs, so much richer here, in her domain.

Warned by Sierra's mischievous smile, I preemptively set my fork down. She surveyed me like she was deciding which part to go for first.

"You're done eating, right?" she asked, coming up to her knees, her body coiled tight.

I braced myself against her pillows, letting them cradle my sore back after a long day. "Yes."

"Oh, good." She pounced.

She peppered my face with kisses. Cheeks. Chin. Forehead. Nose. I tried to catch her lips with mine, but she remained elusive. Giving up, I lay there and took it. What a hardship—a gorgeous woman loving on me.

When her lips finally landed and stayed on mine, I licked away what was left of her lip gloss and swallowed down the taste of sweet cherry before getting to her. This is what I wanted to taste, to linger in my mouth until the next time I got to see her.

Her thighs squeezed my hips as she rose up, her breasts dragging against my hard nipples. I shuddered.

"Again." The word scraped across my throat, a commanding growl I'd never used before.

Sierra moaned, her shiver traveling down to me.

She liked that, did she? Well then, I'd be stocking up on throat lozenges, because I would be leaving here with a sore one.

Our nipples slid against each other as she did as I asked. Back and forth. God, I couldn't wait to feel it when we were both naked.

"I'm ready to see you let loose," she said directly into my ear, ending with a nip to the lobe.

"It's going to take more than this." The challenge in my voice shocked me. A fast fuck to get off or a chance to prove a soul connection, those were my two modes in bed. Except apparently when it came to Sierra. She inspired me to tease and have fun.

She pushed back and smiled down at me. "I can't wait to find out how much more." She rocked her hips into me and her bed frame squeaked.

I froze, my tongue still inside her mouth. I strained, listening for any stirring. This time it wasn't worry that

I'd woken up my kid. No, it was worse. Ashley was an adult. She'd know exactly what made that sound.

Sierra's hand slid between my head and the pillow, holding me to her. Her fingers made their way beneath my ponytail to the shaved section underneath, scraping gently.

My muscles were still locked so tight that my shiver couldn't make it through.

"It's okay," Sierra said against my lips. "She doesn't care. She usually has music on while she studies. She probably can't even hear us."

"Probably" wasn't going to cut it.

"Just one second." I slid from the bed.

Sierra's lips, swollen from our kisses and still damp, pushed out in a pout.

Huh. Pouts were usually something that had me gritting my teeth. On her, I wanted to kiss those pursed lips until she had nothing to complain about.

I riffled through my backpack until I found the extra pair of socks I kept in there because I hated wet feet. Turning back to the bed, I wedged the socks between her mattress and the box spring. Satisfied with the placement, I gave an experimental bounce. Ahh, squeak-free.

"Whoa." Sierra knee walked over to me, tipping her head back. Those beautiful lips were just inches away. "That's seriously impressive."

"Just call me MacGyver." Seeing the confusion in her gaze, I shook my head. "Never mind. We're not going there. Instead I'll focus on what I should be." I leaned in, our noses brushing as I hovered over her lips. "You."

I caught her gasp as I closed the last distance between us.

We kissed. One after another. We stopped only to

catch our breath and then we were right back to each other. I trailed my hand down her arms, to her back, and ended on her hip. I discovered the feel of her, imagining what lay beneath.

She shed her jacket and the freckles near her shoulders caught my attention. I leaned down and kissed one and then the next making a path to her elbow. God, were they everywhere? I intended to find out. I got to her forearm in my exploration when she knocked me in the forehead as she continued with the buttons of her shirt, obviously getting ready to slip out of it.

A pang hit my chest. Not quite disappointment. How could I be disappointed when there was a gorgeous woman taking off her clothes in front of me? But this was familiar. I'd done it before. Maybe not with Sierra, but I'd done quick. I'd done follow them back to their place, throw off the clothes, learn what gets them off, but not know their favorite color or food.

"I could kiss you all night," I said.

She nodded, going to the next button, showing me more of her throat. Her freckles weren't as numerous there, but still plentiful enough for me to kiss multiple paths around the area. Her fingers paused on the next button and she cocked her head. "Wait, just kissing?"

I leaned up and pressed my lips to the inside of her neck. Catching the hint of salt, I swiped it with my tongue. I wanted more of this. Of the slow discoveries.

"I've never done just this," I confessed.

Sierra stilled, her gaze going from where mine rested at her third button and then back to my face. "Um, you were married."

"Obviously I've kissed and gotten naked. I've had hookups. And after that I've been in two long-term relationships, one of them my marriage. You know the meme of the lesbian who wakes up and is like 'oh so we aren't best friends we've actually been an item this whole time'—that's me. I've never spent time getting to know someone before jumping into sex. I've never just kissed to kiss as a get to know you. I missed out on the steps." I offered a smile. "It's been nice."

"Yeah." Sierra's skin was losing the flush of arousal.

"You probably think I'm ridiculous."

"No, not exactly." She glanced behind her looking like she regretted taking her jacket off and would like it back for this conversation.

"Is this new for you too?"

She'd said she wasn't into relationships and she'd made it more than obvious that she was down to fuck, but that didn't mean she hadn't been into slower things before.

"Not banging one of the sexiest women I've ever met? Can't say that it is."

I flushed. It defied reality to believe she meant that about me and god did it make me feel good.

But I still didn't have an answer. I'd value that even more than the flattery.

She must have seen what Nicki used to call my "undeterred" face because she sighed. "No, I don't usually take it slow. I'm usually working on a tight timeframe and want to get to the goods."

"Maybe this is something we can experience together."

Her fingers worked through her hair as if she'd find the right response in those fiery strands. "Yes, it will definitely be that."

It didn't sound like she was expecting it to be very pleasant. And here I thought it sounded so very pleasant. "I like the thought of kissing you for so long our lips are swollen and we feel it hours later. Of building up to touching you, caressing you. Of discovering your skin and what makes you sigh. Where I have to touch to get you to gasp. Learning what gets you wet."

Sierra wrapped her arms around my neck. Her fingers immediately went to play at the short hairs at my nape. "When you say it like that, it doesn't sound too bad."

I kissed her cheek. "Up to you. I want to make sure we're on the same page."

"Yeah, we can try it your way."

"I'm not against sex," I whispered in her ear. "I'm just delaying until I've gorged myself on everything else first."

"I expect lots of caresses and moans."

"That's not going to be a problem." I pressed another kiss to her lips and then slid back until I could plant my feet on the floor.

Her bottom lip making a pronounced appearance again, she held her hand out toward me. I grabbed it and placed a kiss on the palm. My cheeks flamed. That'd been a silly action and— And nothing. She smiled and curled her fingers like she was holding the kiss in.

"Thank you for tonight," I said, bending for my bag.

"Not so fast there, slick." Sierra swung her legs over the edge of the bed. "I need to drive you back."

"I'll get a ride." I held up my phone, showing the ride share app. "It's the least I can do."

"For leaving me high and dry." She rocked her hips side to side. "Well, not dry."

I moaned.

"Kidding, except I'm not. I'd rather drive you, at least I'll get another kiss out of it. Then I'll come back and take care of this problem."

Chapter Eleven

Sierra

I knocked on the doorframe of my boss's open door in an upbeat series of raps. She was the only one who had a permanent office. Hers, like the others, had concrete floors, a desk stained with ring marks, and walls that needed painting. Another reason I respected the woman so much.

Wendy looked up from her computer and motioned me in. "Sierra. What can I do for you?"

"I wanted to talk to you about something I'm planning and get your okay."

"Well, that sounds intriguing." She grabbed a notepad she had on the side of her desk and placed it by her hand. "Go for it."

"I'm organizing a fundraiser to benefit Haven Bridge."

She leaned forward, some of the tiredness she wore like an accessory fading. "That's welcome news. What kind of fundraiser?"

"The best fundraiser. The idea actually came after talking with Jordan…" I told Wendy about the inspiration and teaming up with Thorn & Thistle and the plans we'd created.

Blinking, Wendy leaned back in her seat. "That's a creative way to go about a fundraiser."

Creative. That was a good trait in an employee. She should write that down in my file, right under reasons not to cut me.

"With the help from the tattoo artists it should get a lot of traction."

Wendy leaned forward and grabbed a red pen from her desk, clicking it. "I don't doubt it and as you know it couldn't come at a better time." She glanced at her computer screen. "I was just going over some of the numbers and was going to have to talk to you."

My heart galloped. No! I was—

"We're going to be making some changes and re-organizing our resources. Which brings me to the groups."

I was able to relax slightly into my chair, but not by much. "What about the groups?"

"I know that you enjoy participating in them, and we love you for it, but that's one of the changes we'll be making. From now on we're going to have volunteers run them. They'll be trained of course." She shot me a hopeful glance. "That might be something you could be involved in. But with money so tight, we need our caseworkers working, well, on the cases."

I loved leading the groups. Looked forward to seeing the reminder pop up on my calendar each week. It gave me a chance to be with the kids more than just a relay of information about their cases and what was going to happen next. I got to know them. Learn about them and from them.

"So it's all about the money?"

Wendy pressed her lips together. "I'm afraid so. We—"

"I'll keep doing it. For free I mean. You can add extra cases or whatever, but I'd like to keep doing it."

"I can't ask you to—"

"You're not. I'm volunteering. Please, I love doing it."

Wendy looked back at her screen as if she was trying to see if there was a way to rearrange what was there into something she actually wanted. "Um, okay. We can try it out on a trial basis and then you come to me if it gets to be too much or—"

"It won't," I assured her. "I don't have a family I need to run home to. No one waiting on me. Just some plants I need to take care of."

Jamie's face popped into my mind. Not the serious one when she was tattooing me but the tentatively hopeful one when we agreed to try out a part-time relationship.

This would be a good thing. Make sure I rotated my time between all of my interests.

"If you're sure," Wendy said.

"I am."

"Then if there's nothing else, back to work with you."

I did and got a good solid seven hours in before Jordan came and sucked the productivity out of the last thirty minutes as she "kept me company" until it was time leave for Thorn & Thistle.

I pulled up outside of the shop and assured myself that I was not nervous. I was not. I always got a little excited when it came time to see my favorite artist. Which didn't explain why my pulse was so loud I couldn't even hear my music and my stomach was doing full-on whirly-woos.

I was in a relationship. I was going to see the woman I was in a relationship with. Except tonight it wouldn't be about that, it would be the fundraiser. But my body didn't know that. I didn't think my brain did either.

"You ready?" I asked Jordan.

"Are you?" She gave me a critical once-over.

MJ had given permission to have Jordan in the shop. Usually anyone under eighteen was only allowed if they were with a parent or legal guardian, but since Jordan was emancipated it was a grayer area. She was legally on her own but couldn't do anything illegal for her age like drinking or getting a tattoo.

"Yeah, let's do this." The bell on the door jangled as we entered.

"Hey, welcome to— Oh, it's you."

I laughed at Maya's abandoned greeting. "You sure know how to make a gal feel welcome."

"Eh. I'm not wasting my awesome words on some-one who's not here for ink." She shifted her attention to Jordan, who was studying the sketches on the walls. "Unless you're here for a tatt."

The teen turned and swallowed visibly. "Um, no. Not yet."

"Maya, this is Jordan. She's the inspiration for the fundraiser."

The tattooer nodded, her vibrant hair having faded to fuchsia since the last time I'd seen her. "Good, we need more artists in the world."

Jordan's shoulders straightened and she tipped her head back. "Facts."

The look they shared seemed to acknowledge the respect they had for each other for being artists. It was nothing like the harried looks me and the other social workers flashed each other in the halls at Haven Bridge.

Maya angled her head toward the interior of the shop.

"She's finishing up and then you can do whatever it is you're going to do."

I turned and glanced at Jamie's station.

The tip of her head and her eyes were the only things visible over the half wall. Eyes that were locked on me.

My heart gave the skip and jump my body wouldn't.

How could it feel like an eternity since I'd seen her? It'd been all of twenty-one hours. Not long at all, especially when there'd been texts spread in as well. Texts with full sentences and punctuation that only made me miss her more.

I was planning to wait a week before we saw each other again. That sounded like the perfect amount of time to make sure I didn't get too attached.

How would I ever make it that long?

Jamie motioned for us with her gloved hand. I tilted my head in Jordan's direction and Jamie nodded, continuing to wave us over.

"It looks like we're being summoned."

Eyes wide, Jordan's head was on a swivel, trying to take it all in as we made our way down the center row of the shop. Uh-oh, her I've-seen-it-all-you-can't-impress-me mask was already slipping and we'd just got here.

I stopped at the partition outside of Jamie's work area. A blonde woman sat in my sacred space with her inner arm exposed while Jamie worked on her. That's where I went to get my permanent dose of comfort.

I knew Jamie tattooed other people. Of course I did. I checked her website and Instagram regularly to see new pictures of the tattoos she did. Since the food trucks it'd become compulsive.

"I'd hoped you'd make it in time." Jamie kicked out a second rolling stool that wasn't usually there and nodded to Jordan. "Want to pull it up and watch?"

"Oh my god, yes."

"I already asked Misty here," Jamie said to me. Our gazes connected and I could see the same heat from when I'd dropped her off at her car and we'd kissed in the back alley. The woman might be getting a lot of other things in that chair that I got from Jamie but she wasn't getting her smoldering look. "She doesn't mind an audience."

The woman—Misty—smiled at Jordan. "Jamie was telling me about the fundraiser. I'll definitely be back for one."

Jordan tucked the side of her face into her shoulder. "Cool," she mumbled.

It was hard to hate on a woman who was not only letting Jordan get this experience but was also going to come back and support the fundraiser.

Nodding at all parties as if to make sure we were situated, Jamie resumed tattooing. Brows coming together, it took only seconds for her look to be one of complete concentration. Her hand moved in a steady rhythm only broken as she wiped at the woman's skin with the paper towel in her hand.

Occasionally she would explain something to Jordan while she worked. Somehow Jordan restrained herself and didn't ask a million questions, instead watching Jamie's every move so intently that I was pretty sure she'd be able do a play-by-play reenactment.

Me too. Except it was different things that were holding my interests. I loved the way Jamie's arms moved with such purpose and the straight set of her shoulders as she bent forward. Such beautiful shoulders she had. They looked capable of supporting so much.

"There. All done." Jamie pushed her seat back.

As Jamie showed the client her tattoo and then covered it, Jordan came and sat next to me. She practically vibrated. About the only other thing that could shake a reaction out of her was when we got siblings in the center that were going to be placed in different homes. I went to pat her, remembering the no touching just in time so I left my hand hovering. Jordan looked at it and rolled her eyes, but I kept it there so she knew I was thinking about her.

"Okay," Jamie said, tossing her gloves into the trash. "I'm going to walk her out and get Riley from the break room and then we can get started."

My back sprang forward on the seat. Wait. I needed more information. She couldn't just walk away after dropping that bomb on me.

"You okay there?" Jordan asked.

"Yup. Great. Just great."

Though it'd be nice to know how I was supposed to act here.

Yes, I'd been the one to suggest a "part-time" relationship and I'd agreed to enjoy all the "bases" as Jamie called them, but it was too soon for Riley to think of us as a couple. We hadn't discussed her yet. I thought time with Riley would be the part of Jamie's life that didn't involve me.

Jamie came back into her station with Riley trailing behind her.

"Are we ready?"

Maybe.

"Yes." I pushed to my feet, searching Jamie's face for a clue.

Jamie cocked her head the slightest bit. "Good." She put her hand on her daughter's shoulder. "You guys remember Riley."

Riley nodded at me, but her attention quickly went

to Jordan. Riley shrugged off Jamie's hand while simultaneously tipping her chin. "Hey."

Whew. Jamie was keeping to our agreement and keeping the pressure turned low. That was it. I could do this. I stepped up to Riley. "I'm glad you'll be here for this."

Jamie

Riley nodded. "Uh, yeah. I'm glad to be here."

Glad. She was more than glad. This was going to earn me some major points. She hadn't stopped demanding that I make sure she was here for it since Sunday.

Yeah, I knew the surly teenager standing across from me was likely the reason for that interest, but I'd take it.

"All right, why don't we head back?"

I led them to the drafting table set up in the corner of the shop. While they took seats on the metal bar stools, I pulled out some sheets of paper and grabbed a black marker.

Taking the cap off with my teeth, I looked around the table. "What are we thinking of for ideas?"

Sierra and Jordan stared at me with identical wide-eyed looks like I'd sprung a pop quiz on them. They slowly turned to each other. Then looked to Riley. Together they all faced me. The trio shrugged.

I laughed. "It's your fundraiser."

Sierra held up her hands and looked from me to Jordan. "I'm leaving this one to the experts. Only thing I ask is that you guys make it the best ever."

"Oh, is that all?" I turned to Jordan. My fellow artist should be able to help me out here. "Let's back up. What do you want the fundraiser to represent?"

I could practically see her case of hero worship for me wither up and die. "Art supplies," she said. "I thought it was to get art stuff for Haven Bridge."

"Right. So what do art supplies mean to you?"

Jordan and Sierra began to turn toward each other.

I waved my hand between their faces before they started the whole look and shrug process all over again.

"Momma J," Riley drew the J out until it was longer than momma. "You're not making sense."

"I can see that. Let me try this again." I thought for a second. "To me art means passion."

"Oh. I think I know where you're going with this." Sierra slid further on the stool until I was questioning just how much was left for her to balance on. I couldn't check because that would require looking at her ass and I wouldn't do that in front of my daughter.

"To me," she said, "art means being awestruck and a little jealous because I really wish I could do what you guys do."

I wrote that down and then looked to Jordan. Her closed expression had me skipping to Riley. "How about you, Jel—" Oh, no. I would not mess up her wanting to be here with me by using her nickname. Her totally uncool one. "How about you?"

Riley chewed her lip and shot a quick glance at Jordan, but Jordan was staring fixedly at the table. "Color."

"That's a good one," I said as I wrote it down. "Jordan, what does art mean to you?"

"Hope," she whispered.

It might have been spoken softly but it had the power of a shout.

"Nice. Now what are things that come to mind when you think of hope?"

The teenager dropped her gaze right back down, her shoulders hunched.

"I'll start." Sierra held up her fingers and ticked them off. "Sunrise. A plant sprouting. The change of seasons. A rainbow. A dandelion."

My hand flew over the paper. "You're good at this. Keep 'em coming."

"Cures," Riley said.

My Jelly Bean looked pretty pleased with herself. As she should. I couldn't hold back my proud mama smile.

My smile remained as Sierra and Riley's suggestions got more and more ridiculous, until they were giggling.

Jordan let the words flow over her without picking one up.

"An old car starting," Sierra managed through her laughter. "That's it." She plopped her head on her arms on the table. "That's all I've got. My brain is tapped out."

"A home."

My hand twitched involuntarily, but I was careful not to react any other way. Jordan reminded me of when I had the beginning of an idea for a piece and I knew it was going to be good, but if I tried to force it, it vanished.

Sierra stared at Jordan with an understanding expression.

Riley seemed to pick up on the seriousness of an otherwise mundane word, looking like she wanted to go over and give Jordan a hug. That was my girl. She'd always been compassionate and the first to comfort someone. With all that felt like it was changing with her, it was nice to know that wasn't.

"Anything else?" I asked casually, shaking out my hand.

Sierra shook her head and Jordan did the same.

I slid the list to their side of the table.

Sierra leaned forward. Then leaned even further, squinting. "Uh, for someone that makes such beautiful art, your writing is trash."

"It's not that bad," I said.

"Most of these words came from me and I can't make them out."

"It's bad," Riley said. "I always get Mom to fill things out."

Out of all the things they could bond over they were going for my perfectly fine penmanship.

"You too?" I asked Riley, not bothering to keep the smile off my face.

"Uh-huh."

Sierra clapped her hands and oh how her luscious breasts bounced with the movement. Nope, couldn't look. Couldn't enjoy.

"Okay, so now what?" she asked.

"So now we see if any of these words spark an idea. We should probably keep in mind that I specialize in new traditional and anime. I'm willing to do anything for the right design, but we have the best chance of raising the most money by sticking to what I'm known for."

Sierra pursed her lips out as she thought and my mind immediately went to kissing those lips. To feeling them against mine and the way—

"Hey there, Jelly Bean. You ready to go?"

Errt. All my fantasies stopped at the sound of my ex's voice.

Next to me Riley stiffened and shot a humiliated look toward Jordan before whirling to look at Nicki. "Mom."

I turned to face her as well. "Hey."

Nicki bent down and kissed my cheek and then

stepped up behind Riley. "You ready?" she asked, reaching out to run her hand through Riley's ponytail.

"No." Our daughter leaned forward, evading the move. "We're working on something."

"Well, we need to get going. I'm opening supervisor tomorrow and still have to do the break and lunch schedule and you've got to get to bed."

If Nicki wasn't careful, she'd take my crown for most embarrassing parent.

Nicki's gaze went across the table to Sierra and Jordan.

I straightened, my heart picking up. This would be the first time my ex had ever met someone. And though I wasn't ready to make any kind of announcement, I still wanted it to go well. "Nic—"

At the same time I started to make introductions, Nicki nodded to Sierra and Jordan and turned to Riley. "Come on. Say goodbye to your friends."

All that came out was a long groan.

Chapter Twelve

Sierra

Jamie winced, her cheeks sounding the alarm on her internal state.

I burst out laughing. When I felt everyone's gazes on me, I laughed harder. Oh my god. I'd just been called a friend to a thirteen-year-old. By the ex-wife. I was meeting the ex-wife.

I so wanted to introduce myself as Jamie's lover and see Nicki's face. See Jamie's face. But yeah, that would be crossing so many lines.

Nicki had brown hair that was thrown up in a casual ponytail. Continuing the casual look she wore jeans and a purple T-shirt. I guessed her to be younger than Jamie by at least a few years, maybe closer to five.

Jamie got to her feet and put her hand at Nicki's waist, interrupting Riley who was now begging to be allowed to stay "just a little longer."

I stared at Jamie's hand on that trim waist of the very hot woman. A gut check found no jealousy. Not like when I'd witnessed Jamie tattooing someone else. Her client had been getting something from Jamie that I craved. Nicki had shared a child, a marriage, a home with Jamie—all things I didn't see allowing myself, so there was no need for me to be jealous.

"This is Jordan and Sierra," Jamie said. "We're planning a fundraiser."

"Oh. That's awesome." Nicki looked at her daughter. "You got everything? We really do have to go."

"Yeah." Riley got to her feet about as slow as she could without gravity kicking in and keeping her butt planted on the seat. She looked at the papers we had spread on the table. "You've got some good stuff. I'm sure you'll think of something really awesome."

Aw, that was a big case of FOMO she had. "We'll be sure to let you know what we choose and you'll have to tell us what you think."

"'Kay."

Nicki waved. "It was nice meeting you all." She gave Jamie another kiss on the cheek. "See you Sunday."

Riley shuffled after her mother, pausing every few steps to throw a sad, pathetic look over her shoulder.

Jamie sat back down and let out a breath.

The meeting of the ex had gone worse for her than it had me. I patted her shoulder.

"Should we get back to it?" I asked.

We bent back over the list.

I tried to remember the words because Jamie's writing really was unreadable. None of them stuck out as tattoo worthy. Not mine. Not Riley's. The only one that sparked anything was home, but how would Jamie draw that?

My gaze shot to her. "Hey, why didn't you come up with any words?"

"I didn't want to get stuck on one idea, especially if you guys didn't like it. Once something's in my head and I'm picturing it, I have a hard time moving to something else."

Most of the time I saw Jamie as laid-back and unruffled. But after being around her more, I could see hints of her inflexibility once she set her mind on something. Her continued support of her parents. Not stopping until she got me up that rock wall. And of course there was her refusal to do casual.

Yeah, I could see how that stubbornness might mess with creativity.

But we could use some of her words. Mine weren't doing it. They were like my beloved animal tattoos. Too happy. They weren't for Jordan. They weren't for the other kids like her. We needed something to represent what art meant in *their* lives.

They needed more than sunshine and rainbows. They needed a...

"A demon slayer," I gasped.

Jamie's head jerked up. "What?"

Jordan finally stopped trying to become one with the table and looked at me.

"A demon slayer," I repeated. I slid to the edge of the tiny metal seat. "That's a possibility. Art is like a demon slayer."

"Hm." Jamie tapped the marker to her lips. "So you're thinking more anime."

I was thinking bright and bold and meaningful. "I guess?"

"He's done best in black and white and—"

"It doesn't have to be a he. A demon slayer can definitely be a female." In fact, I dug the idea.

Jamie stopped tapping the marker. "You're talking about the game? Demon Slayer?"

"No. I don't think so. I'm talking about someone or

something that slays people's demons. Like a hyped-up version of a guardian angel."

Jamie shook her head like she was dislodging something stuck in there. "Hold on. Demon Slayer was a game."

I slid my gaze to Jordan, who shrugged.

"Was that a thing from the eighties? 'Cause we've never heard of it."

"No, it's not from the eighties." Jamie frowned at us. "More like the two thousands. Closer to your time than mine."

"Yeah, I don't know it. Let's get back to my idea."

"I like it," Jordan said.

Jamie lifted the marker. I bent forward, waiting to see what she would create, but she only wrote a few words down.

"What? What did you put?"

She turned the paper fully in my direction.

"Um, yeah, I can't read that. Don't you have to do quotes and names and lettering?"

Jamie made a face. "I don't free hand. I use a stencil. Warrior. Guardian angel. Slayer." She tapped each word as she said it. "I'm letting those percolate."

Was there a way she could percolate faster?

Now I understood what she meant by being married to an idea. This was it. I knew it. Yes, it might be cliché, but Jamie's design didn't have to be.

"You said you wanted it to be a woman?"

"I think that'd be cool. Seems like that'd be something popular with most of your clients."

She bent down and opened a drawer. Inside were colored pencils.

Both Jordan and I leaned closer. Here it came. The magic was going to start.

A faraway look on her face, Jamie held the black pencil suspended over the paper.

This was a look I hadn't seen before. When I arrived my tattoo was already designed. Right now she stared at the paper as if she were there, in whatever she was imagining in her mind. It made me ready to stand guard over her and make sure no one interrupted this moment.

"I'm not seeing a typical warrior," Jamie said. "I'm thinking something softer, almost maternal. Standing in profile, holding a weapon with blood on the blade and splatter on her gown."

"Oh." Jordan leaned further over the table.

Blood dripping? What happened to the hopeful we were going for? "Does the blood have to be red? Maybe it could be a rainbow or something lighter."

"Hm." She got that far-off look on her face again.

Putting my chin in my hands, I sighed and watched.

"Green? And new growth is sprouting at her feet."

I gasped. "Yes, that one." I pointed to the paper. "Get that one down."

"It's okay. I'll remember."

I grabbed the marker off the table and pulled her chicken scratch toward me. "I'll write it down just in case."

Jamie's lip twitched and then her gaze went very pointedly to Jordan.

Right. This wasn't about me. I turned to Jordan. "I mean, if you like that idea too, of course."

She rolled her eyes. "Just write it down before you burst."

I did just that. "All right, you two, get to work and make our demon slayer."

Jordan walked around to the other side of the table

to stand next to Jamie who rolled the set of pencils so they were between them.

"What are you thinking?" Jamie asked.

Jordan stared down at the paper even though Jamie hadn't drawn anything yet. It must have been an artist thing. "So it's like whatever she slayed is feeding the ground and causing the growth."

"Exactly."

"I like it."

Jamie pushed a paper to Jordan. "You good with doing the growth and I'll focus on the slayer?"

"Really?"

"Yup."

Oh, Jamie. Jamie. Jamie. She'd just given Jordan that like it was nothing and to the teen it was everything.

God, how I wanted to grab Jamie's face and kiss her.

Since we were in public and that would take away from this moment for Jordan, I made do with slipping off my shoe and stretching my leg out until I reached the bottom of Jamie's jeans and could wiggle my foot underneath.

She twisted her head enough to look at me, a glint in her eyes. We held the contact for a few of my increasing heartbeats and then she cleared her throat and focused on her drawing.

Occasionally Jamie pressed her foot against mine, almost as if letting me know that she wasn't completely lost to her art and she remembered I was there. When she did it again, I couldn't resist pushing my foot higher up over her calf. Her hand faltered and her gaze flicked to mine.

"Um, can you guys not. I'm trying to draw here and you're being all disgusting."

Instead of the instantaneous pull back and blushing, I'd expected, Jamie smiled at Jordan. "And here I thought I was being all discreet."

"Yeah, no."

"Hm. Well then, since I'm being disgusting anyways." She pushed up and leaned across the table. She kissed me.

She was gone before I could do more than breathe. No slipping my tongue inside and tasting.

The ex, and now kissing at her work. What happened to the slow operator? Next there'd be a U-Haul outside.

Putting my fingers to my lips, I slid back all the way onto my seat. Over the sound of Jordan's fake retching, I tried to decide how I felt about Jamie's progression of things. That was the thing about Jamie's kisses—they made it all seem worth it.

Once the outline of our slayer was done, Jamie dropped her pencil to the table and blew out her breath. "I still have some fine-tuning, but I think this is going to work."

"Work?" Was she kidding? "It's amazing and I'm signing up for the first one."

Her gaze met mine across the table and images of the night before, of our tongues stroking together flashed in my mind. "Consider it reserved for you."

I stared down at the sketch, already picturing it on my body. "When you're done with this may I have it? I want to hang it up at Haven Bridge."

"I'll make you a bigger, better one."

That'd be nice for the center, but if she didn't want this one, I did. I could see the marks underneath of her first attempts and then where she darkened when she liked what she'd drawn. I could remember her face, her very expression, as she made those marks.

"Holy shit," Jordan said, staring down at her phone. "We've been here for two hours."

Two hours. Two hours for Jamie to somehow pluck out what was in my head and make it come to life. It'd been so long since I'd had anyone know me, be close enough to be on the same wavelength, and Jamie had done it. It was powerful and intense and I'd...missed it.

My stomach pitched.

She was making me remember and long for things that I'd purposefully gone without.

"I'm going to grab the bus."

I jerked my head up to look at Jordan. "I'm your ride."

"Yeah, that's okay. You stay. I can't even with your thirstiness."

Jamie stared at Jordan with a little frown. "Do you live close?"

She threw her shoulders back and gave Jamie a challenging stare. "Adult, remember?"

"There's plenty of adults that I worry will get home safe."

"Well, I don't need to be one of them." She flashed a sideways peace sign and then turned away.

Jamie stared after her with a worried expression, looking like she was thinking about chasing after her and giving her a lift home. My stomach settled. God, the way she cared for people.

When Jamie turned back to me, she did a double take.

Oh, yeah, my lust was visible. I waggled my brows at her. "So drop her off and then pick up food and back to my place?"

"I have a better idea."

Jamie

Sierra waved to Jordan, who was entering her apartment. As soon as the door closed, Sierra whirled toward me, and her perfectly pleasant smile went to pure sex. "There. She's all safe and sound. Now tell me what you had in mind."

Not what she obviously did. "I'd like to do something that doesn't involve the fundraiser," I said. "Something where we can hang out and get to know each other."

"Which can't happen in bed."

I gave her a side-eyed look which I was beginning to suspect was the very reason she said things like that.

"Okay, okay," she huffed. "Take me on this date. Let me learn about you."

Well, now I'd gone and put the pressure on. Pondering, I tapped the steering wheel.

There was always dinner and a movie. Boring and expected. That wasn't her. That wasn't what I wanted us to be.

The other place that popped into my mind had more personality, but wasn't exactly a date place. It was where I went to have fun and I liked the idea of sharing it with her. Liked the idea of seeing her response to it.

"You said you'd like to see me play video games sometime. There's an arcade not too far that has all the old-school gam—"

My phone rang, interrupting me.

Heaving a sigh, I fished it out of my pocket. I glanced at the screen and sat up straighter, my gaze snapping to Sierra.

"What? Who is it?"

"My parents' neighbor." I kept my voice calm, but there was no controlling my muscles. They went taut.

Sierra put her hand on my shoulder.

A simple touch. But it was so much more. It was support. It was someone here with me as I dealt with whatever this was going to be.

"Hello, this is Jamie."

"Hi, dear. This is Mrs. Meyer from across the street."

"Hi, Mrs. Meyer. Is everything okay?" A tremor made its way into my voice. I tightened my jaw to lock that down. No matter what it was, I would handle it. I always did.

"Well, that's why I'm calling. I've noticed your parents' cars haven't moved in days and they didn't put their trash cans out this week. I just wanted to make sure everything is okay. I can hear noise inside, but no one's answered when I knock."

"Thank you for letting me know. I'll check on them."

"I don't mean to be a nosy neighbor. I was just worried."

"No, not at all," I assured her as I yanked at my seat belt, it suddenly feeling like it was strangling me, dislodging Sierra's hand in the process. "I haven't talked to them in a few days so I'll go over and make sure everything is all right. Thank you."

"Oh, good."

I thanked the woman again and then hit end. The screen didn't even have a chance to go dark before I was calling my mom. Her phone went straight to voice mail. Same with my dad's. I worked my jaw loose and looked at Sierra.

One uninterrupted date, at an arcade no less, that's all I wanted.

"I'm sorry, I need to go check on them."

And this, right here, was why I couldn't have a relationship. I couldn't be counted on to make plans. I couldn't devote all my time to someone and give them what they deserved.

"Of course."

Caught by her unruffled tone, I turned to stare at her face in the yellow lights of the apartments' parking lot. She didn't look upset. Didn't look much of anything, not even disappointed. That was a good thing. Proof that she didn't need me around all the time. Just as her unruffled acceptance of Nicki was a good thing. There hadn't been a hint of jealousy, a side-eye look, nothing. And I'd looked hard. But you couldn't find what wasn't there. That was fine, good even. I didn't need any more drama in my life. As evidenced by the phone call I'd just received.

"I really am sorry about this. I'll drop you back off at your car."

I went to turn on the ignition, but before I could she grabbed my wrist. "Why don't I go with you? This seems like something you shouldn't do alone."

I froze. All my life my parents had been something to hide away. I'd never had friends come over because I didn't trust what state I'd find them in.

Nicki had never liked going over to my parents' because all it did was get her heated to see how much I did for them. Of course, I didn't allow Riley to be around them if there was any chance they'd been drinking.

I'd always been the one to handle them in secret. And now Sierra wanted to be there.

It already felt wrong for someone to know about my parents' problems the way Sierra did, but for her to see them. Not only see them, but see that I hadn't been able to stop them.

"You don't need to do that."

"I'm not scared of what we'll run into. I come across a lot in my job. I promise nothing will shock me."

Because she was a social worker. One who worked with kids who I was sure came from horrible situations. Why did my brain have such a hard time seeing her that way? Why did I insist on thinking she was young and bright and could be hurt by so much in life, when she was the one fighting those hardships for others? An adult going to check on their parents would be nothing for her. It was me who was making it a big thing.

It made sense for me to have her come along and also for her to help with…whatever state we found them in.

I cleared my throat. "Thanks. That might be a good idea."

The smile she sent me was more subdued than her usual light up the whole vicinity ones. Made sense since we were going to check up on my parents. Still I hated seeing that my life was already affecting her.

In less than fifteen minutes we pulled up to my parents' house. Sure enough their cars were there. Along with the new addition of two large bags of trash thrown in the yard.

A box of cherry cordials during the holidays wasn't going to cut it for the neighbors this year.

I climbed the porch, able to feel Sierra behind me even before I heard her footsteps. Blowing out a breath, I knocked on the door. Not surprisingly there was no answer. I pressed my ear to the door, catching the muffled sounds of a television. I tried knocking one last time.

This wasn't going to happen the easy way. It never did once I turned on Lampson Street.

"The doorbell doesn't work," I explained as I pulled out my keys.

The doorbell hadn't worked for a while now. While I

was fairly handy and didn't mind working on projects, I noped out of anything that involved electrical wires.

When I was twelve I'd given myself a shock after attempting to bake a birthday cake for my brother since it'd fallen on the weekend and stupidly licked some batter off the cord. I still cringed every time I plugged something into a socket.

I put the key in by feel since my parents didn't have any outside lights on or pretty decorative solars like everyone else on the street.

I opened the door a few inches and popped my head inside, keeping my body in the way of Sierra so she didn't see...what, the truth?

Chapter Thirteen

Jamie

"Mom? Dad? It's Jamie. Are you home?"

I pushed the door wider. When only stale air tinged with grease met me, the tight grip constricting my chest eased. No overwhelming stench meant I wasn't likely to be discovering bodies. God, that the thought had even popped into my head.

The TV blared from the living room, so I headed in that direction, very aware of Sierra's presence. I didn't dare look at her. I didn't want to see my parents' place through her eyes. The glimpses of pizza boxes and take-out containers lining the counter that I was getting were enough.

I hadn't been over in days. After talking to the insurance company and mowing the yard, I'd really believed they'd scared themselves with their actions with Ryan. There'd even been a pipe dream that they'd read the pamphlets and decide they need help.

In the living room my mom and dad were on opposite ends of the sofa asleep—or passed out. Beer cans surrounded them. A recent stain that looked to be still wet spread across my dad's once-white T-shirt. My mom wasn't in much better shape in her torn sweatpants. Another open pizza box was on the coffee table and burger wrappers littered the floor.

Was this them hitting rock bottom? Could it only have taken two days? And Jesus Christ how sick did it make me that I could feel pleasure at that. Pleasure that they hadn't been able to cope without me for forty-eight hours.

I ran my hand over my mouth.

"Should we try and wake them?" Sierra asked, startling me. "Make sure we're not dealing with alcohol poisoning."

I spun to her. "Yeah, this happens and—"

Right. I snapped my mouth shut. She didn't look panicked at seeing them like this. No horror at their conditions. No judgments. I let out another breath. I didn't need to shield her from this, and in fact it felt like she was here for me. A real version of the demon slayer we'd created.

"You might want to stay back. They're not always happy when they get woken up."

Sierra stayed on the other side of the trash-covered coffee table. "Yeah, me neither."

"I'll keep that in mind."

We shared a smile that somehow didn't feel wrong, even with my parents out cold mere feet away and the scent of old food hanging in the air. It was strangely hopeful as if we could rise above this and my parents didn't have to infiltrate every part of my life.

I kicked the food debris out of the way on my approach to the sofa. They couldn't afford this. Not the food. Taking time off of work. None of it.

The closer I got, the more potent the smell of alcohol. My nostrils burned and I knew it'd stay with me long after I left, an olfactory souvenir.

It was a weeknight. They shouldn't be like this.

"Hey, Dad. Wake up." I shook his shoulder, the frailty there a reminder that he was getting older. "You okay?"

His eyelids fluttered.

My hands steadied. At least he wasn't passed out.

I'd only ever found him like that once. Afraid they'd take my brother and me away, I hadn't called 9-1-1, instead standing over him to make sure he didn't stop breathing or choke. It'd been two very long hours before my mom had got home.

Now my dad's blue eyes stared up at me. I'd always wished I'd gotten his eyes. They were so pretty even as bloodshot as they were now. It took one...two...three seconds for any recognition to hit.

He pushed himself up until he was sitting, wiping his mouth. His gaze shifted to Sierra. He didn't even react to seeing a stranger a few feet away.

"Hey, honey. What are you doing here?"

Honey. My heart squeezed. That one word. It had so much power over me. "Honey, can you go and get me a snack."

"Honey, I'm in a bind. You think you could help your old man out?"

"You're so good to me, honey." That one. I lived for that one.

And that one word was why I was here, glad they might be falling apart without me.

Fuck.

I staggered back, running into the coffee table.

Sierra pressed her hand against my lower back, bracing me.

"Jamie?" my dad asked.

Steady. This was nothing new.

So why did it feel that way? Why had the addition of Sierra, knowing someone was looking at the same things I'd looked at all my life, make me see things I hadn't before?

"I'm checking on you."

"Oh, that's nice."

Yeah, real nice. I could have been out playing video games and learning more about Sierra and what she wanted and needed in her life. Now all I was learning was that she wasn't freaked out by seeing my parents.

I made my way to the other side of the couch where my mother continued to sleep. It only took one tap for her to jerk upright.

"Hm? What? What's going on?"

"Hey, Mom. I came by to check on you guys."

"Oh." She blinked and desperately tried to look alert, but the sleep just wasn't shaking off fast enough. I was sure that's how I looked to Riley when a movie would end and I'd try and pretend I hadn't fallen asleep.

She sat up straight and fixed her sweatshirt. "You didn't need to do that. We're fine."

So not rock bottom then. We were still going with denial. I shouldn't be surprised. We'd been stuck in this phase for twenty-something years. Two days was a bit optimistic.

But man I was tired. Two decades tired.

"Totally fine," my dad piped in, his eyes glazed enough that there'd be no way he'd pass a breathalyzer.

"Yeah, you look it." I bit my tongue. I didn't do that. Sarcasm. Baiting. This wasn't me.

My mom rubbed her hands up and down from her knees to her thighs. Up and down. "We had a hard day so we're relaxing."

Relaxing. Escaping. Bingeing. There were so many different names for what they did. The only common denominator was that it involved alcohol.

"Have you thought about any of those places I brought you the info on? That outpatient one looked—"

"No, we don't need them. I know you think you're helping, but we don't have a problem."

My dad ran his hand over his face, seeming surprised when he encountered the start of a beard. "Besides, those programs don't even work."

"That's true." My mother nodded.

"But this does?" I slowly looked around the room, ending with the pile of trash I was standing on. Did they not see it? How could they—

Sierra stepped up next to me, snagging my mother's attention. "Hello, I'm Sierra. I'm a friend of Jamie's." She held her hand out.

This close she had to be getting a whiff of the delightful mix of sweat and alcohol and the remnants of my mother's perfume, but she greeted my mom with a warm smile like this was an ordinary "meet the parents" moment.

My mom ran a quick hand over her knotted hair. "I'm Patricia." She shook Sierra's hand. "This is Joe."

Really? She was going to do this? Act like this was normal? This was not normal.

I was so sick of pretending it was.

"It's nice to meet you both." Sierra pushed up the sleeve of her jean jacket and showed her turtle tattoo. "As you can see I'm a fan of your daughter's work."

As expected they gave it nothing more than a cursory glance. They'd never been interested in my art or my career beyond that it had flexible hours and I was finally making some good money doing it.

"Speaking of work. Are you still going to yours?" Did they even have jobs anymore? Would they tell me if they didn't?

My mom waved her hand. "You're allowed to take a few personal days off. I haven't been feeling so well and I think I gave it to your dad."

I rubbed my hand over my face, surprised to feel my fingers flutter against my nose. I was trembling. "Mom, you can't do that. You have to go to work. Those days off aren't paid. You're already behind. You—"

Sierra's palm pressed against the small of my back. And now she probably would feel how damp it was because in addition to shaking I was also sweating.

Why did she have to see me like this? I was trying to show this woman I had something to offer her and I was losing it.

Stepping in front of me, Sierra addressed my mom. "I hope you start feeling better soon. I know how hard it can be to miss multiple days of work. It just starts piling up." She looked around the living room. "You start getting behind on everything."

My head snapped up. I couldn't see Sierra's expression, but it was enough to see my mom's. She stared at Sierra with the rapt attention of someone who had found their savior. A look I'd never received. Of course—Sierra was offering excuses for her.

Why wasn't Sierra telling them they needed rehab or at the very least their jobs were not something to mess with?

"Yes, that's it exactly." My mom's gaze darted to me. "I don't know what you've heard, but we're not bad parents. We're just having a bad month is all."

"I don't know specifics beyond that Jamie is very concerned for you."

My mom shook her head, tugging at her sweatshirt again. "We're not usually like this."

My dad cleared his throat. "I'm sure we'll be feeling

better soon. We'll go back to work." He sent his innocent
expression my way. "Will that make you happy, honey?"

Again with the honey. Like that'd make this okay.
None of this was okay. And I didn't know how to get
it there. What more I could do? How did you break
through when you were trapped in this world of pretending and lies and misdirection?

I needed out.

I needed out of here.

"So, I'm gonna go." Go to work or don't. Right this
second I didn't care.

I walked down the hall, not looking at anything. I
didn't want to see the proof. All these years of work and
effort by me and they were getting worse.

I lunged outside and drew in deep gulps of the cold
night air. It almost hurt, the sharpness and chill. Good.
Let me feel something besides this helplessness trying
to crush me.

Sierra stepped up next to me, but I couldn't look at her.
Not yet. I just breathed in the air, trying to find my calm.

I took off toward the car, Sierra with me every step
of the way. When we reached it she held out her hand.
"How about I drive?"

Not protesting, I put the keys in her outstretched
hand. As if from far away, I watched as she opened the
passenger door and held it open for me. No one had
ever done that for me.

But I didn't need that. I could open a door on my
own. The one thing I could maybe have used, she hadn't
done. At the critical moment she'd left me alone in there.
Yeah, she might've been standing physically next to me,
but I'd been on my own.

I lowered myself into the seat, but stayed sideways

with my feet out of the car. I cradled my head in my hands. "What happened in there? You didn't even try to convince them to get help. Or tell them about what kinds of options are available."

Sierra crouched down on the curb in front of me and I could feel her gaze.

Not avoiding it any longer, I looked at her. My insides shrank. Pity. She was staring at me with pity.

"I could have done all that, but it would've been a waste of time," Sierra laid out calmly. "They're not ready."

"You met them for five minutes and what, can decide that? I've been taking care of them for longer than you've been alive." And fuck, now I was lashing out at the wrong person. Not that there was a right person. There was no one. Ugh. I rubbed my hands over the back of my hair. "I'm sorry. That's not your job. It was nice enough of you to even come."

She put her hand on my thigh, and I looked down at it, wishing I could see the freckles I knew were there. "I can't make them want to change, but I could step in before you got any more upset."

My gaze shot back to hers. "What? You said that stuff for me?"

She reached up and put her hand on the side of my face, cupping my cheek. "You are such a good, kind, patient person, Jamie Winston. Seeing you with them. Knowing that you've taken care of them for so long when they should have been doing it for you." She clutched her free hand to her chest. A tear ran down her cheek and then another. "I couldn't stand it."

Crying. She was crying for me. I reached out and caught the evidence with a trembling finger.

I swallowed against my tightening throat that was

preparing to join in with her. "I don't know what to do," I confessed. Confusion rang in my words. A foreign sound. "They're getting worse and I don't know what to do, how to make them see it. But I have to do something. They're my parents." Parents. Why did that word have so much power over me? They didn't act like parents in most of the traditional ways, yet just knowing they were my parents fostered a connection I couldn't break.

"I know. I'm sorry. I can't imagine how hard this is for you. And there is no easy answer. No step you can take to make it better." She looked at me with something I'd never seen in a situation that involved my parents—concern. Concern for me.

I wrapped my hand around her wrist, and pressed my face into her anchoring touch. "Thank you."

Thank you for coming. For understanding. For caring.

I'd been mad that she hadn't done enough, and instead she'd done everything. She'd stepped in, distracted them, to try and protect me.

And what had I done for her? Never had I felt like I brought less to the table. I needed to up my game if I wanted to keep this incredible woman.

And I did.

Scratching my cheek lightly with her nails, she let out a long breath and then gave me a shaky smile. Using my thighs, she pushed herself to her feet. "Do you think the arcade is still open?"

I shook my head. "Don't know, don't care. I just want you to take me back to your place."

The arcade had been for a night filled with promise. This was reality.

Chapter Fourteen

Sierra

I got the door shut and the lights turned on and then I was pressed against the wall, Jamie's mouth descending on mine.

Yes. This. I wanted this. I could channel everything I'd seen, everything I felt, into this. Into her. Divert it from the bond I could feel trying to build. I hitched my leg over her hip, pulling her closer.

Her tongue licked at my lips. She paused and then licked again as if seeking something out. I flicked my tongue against hers and then I tasted it. Salt. From my tears. Tears I'd cried for her.

I moaned into her mouth, remembering how gently she'd wiped them away as if they were precious. *She* was precious. But that's not what I wanted to think about now.

I gripped the back of her neck, bringing her tighter against me. I didn't want anything between our bodies, not even air. We could breathe each other's breaths.

Jamie seemed to be in complete agreement going by the groan filling my mouth and the force of her hips slamming into me.

Using her lower half to keep me against the wall,

she slid her hands under my shirt. Her fingers brushed against my belly and I shivered.

Suddenly she tore her mouth away and pulled back.

"No," I groaned, reaching for her. "Come back."

"Your room. I want to take off all your clothes."

"It's okay, Ashley isn't here."

"That's what you said last time." Her hands curved around my shirt. "Once I have you naked, no interruptions. Not this time."

Well, when she said it that way. I snatched her hand and led her to my room. I opened the door and didn't stop until I was flat on the bed, arms and legs splayed out, ready for her.

She slowed at the doorway, stopping just inside. She looked at me the same way she had that blank piece of paper, as if she were fantasizing about what she'd create. Except now she wore it staring at me, as if I was somehow the fantasy.

I'd never been the recipient of something like that. I wanted to grab her and wrap my arms around her as tight as they would go. At the same time I wanted to push her away. Tell her she couldn't be going and doing things like that. Kissing. Fundraiser. Dates. Sex. No more. That's what we were to each other.

She stalked to the bed and braced herself on it. Her lips landed on mine, going in for more.

I broke the kiss. Yes, this felt good, great, but I knew what would feel even better. It was time to take this past kissing. Jamie was hurting and I knew what could make her feel better. Orgasms. Orgasms were great healers.

At the same time as I toed off my shoes, I unbuttoned my shirt. I slid it off so fast I was surprised I didn't get cotton burn.

Anticipating her reaction, I glanced at her.

Jamie's eyes were narrowed and blazing as I'd hoped, but it wasn't my practically see-through bra that held her attention. She was focused on the chipmunk on my side.

Her gaze slid up my ribs to my *empowered* tattoo. As if its very existence offended her, her nostrils flared, her lips pinching tight. The harsh expression remained until her attention returned to the chipmunk she'd given me.

"Show me the others."

I unzipped my pants and pushed them down. Her gaze bypassed my matching lace underwear and went straight to my hip and the flamingo there.

Stepping closer, she framed my tattoo with her hands. Goose bumps exploded over my skin. Possessiveness gave her touch extra weight. She stroked them as if they'd been on loan and now she was reclaiming them and me with them as hers.

Her hand skimmed over my hip and then across my belly to the opposite one. She outlined the tiger sitting on it. "God, I love seeing my art on you."

"I like when you put it there." My voice was more rasp than words.

Her finger paused and she looked at me, a question in her brown eyes. "You get turned on when I work on you?"

I tipped my hips closer. "I'm aroused every time I'm around you. The worst and best are when I can feel your breath against my skin. I wait for it, long for it, and then don't dare move. I worry you'll be able to smell how turned on I am or worse I'll leave a wet spot on your chair."

"You wouldn't be the first actually." She gave a small shrug. "Some people have a pain kink and really get into it."

I hooked my finger in her belt loop. "But my kink isn't the tattoos. It's you."

Her nostrils flared. "How am I ever supposed to be able to work on you again? It was hard enough to be professional with you filling up my seat so perfectly and wanting to play connect the dots with your freckles. Now I have no chance."

"That could be a problem because I'm not done getting tattoos yet." I ran my hands down my body, smoothing them over my breasts, circling my hardened nipples before sliding over my underwear and then down to my inner thigh on my right leg.

She watched my hand like it was the X marking the spot on a treasure map.

"My next one is going to be the demon slayer. It's larger, more detailed." I stuck my index finger in my mouth and sucked on it. When I had it nice and wet, I pulled it free and circled the area on my thigh, leaving a glistening trail. "Right here. That means you'll have to spend a lot of time between my legs. Have to be so careful not to brush against my wet pussy."

Jamie's eyes met mine and they looked like rich soil, which to me was one of the most beautiful things, what with all that went on in its depths. But right now I didn't need to go searching for anything, her desire blazed right on the surface. I had no doubt that we were once again riding the same wavelength. This time it was welcome, so very welcome as we pictured the scene of erotic tattooing.

She reached out and placed her hand over mine. Her wrist brushed against the damp fabric of my underwear and this time it was me sucking in a breath, loud and sharp.

"Like that?"

"Yes, just like that." I tilted my hips, seeking more contact.

"Hm, you're right that could create some problems. It'll be hard not to touch you." She gave me a firmer pass this time.

Oh sweet Jesus. Her clothes brushed against my sensitive skin.

Then she flashed me a wicked smile and slowly, so slowly lowered herself to the floor in front of the bed.

I spread my legs, making room for her.

It didn't matter that I wasn't looking into her eyes, I could feel her gaze on my skin. She knelt close. Her breath. I could feel her breath through the lace of my underwear. I quaked with anticipation.

Her hand landed on my thigh and I jumped.

"Here?" she asked, her voice distant and professional, exactly as if she had asked me a question while she was giving me a tattoo.

I could feel each individual finger on my skin, not nitrile gloves, but skin. Here, right now, I was free to arch into her touch, to gasp, and shiver.

"Yes," I moaned.

She leaned closer, her shoulders spreading my legs even further. "I'll be so close."

My hips jerked, my breath stuttering.

"Hours. I'll spend hours here." Her fingers flexed into the flesh of my thigh. "Breathing you in." She inhaled deeply and held it before slowly releasing it right onto the damp lace. "Mm."

I shifted restlessly on the bed, my muscles twitching. "Then what?"

"When I was done with the tattoo and it was all safe and protected, I'd spread your legs wide on my chair."

She cupped both of my thighs and pushed my legs further apart until my muscles burned deliciously.

"Then what would happen?"

"Your legs nice and spread for me, I'd roll my chair as close as I could get and then I'd reward you for being so good and holding still and letting me work."

Her fingers trailed over my leg in a soft touch that stole my words. Words. I needed to find them in the lustful haze taking over my brain so I could do my part in this role we were acting out.

"How?" I asked, more moan than word. "How would you reward me?"

"Maybe I should show you."

"Yeesss. Show me," I cried. "Please, show me."

She bent and placed a kiss right on my pussy. Her tongue pressed against the lace.

I curled my toes into my comforter. "Take them off. Please."

She slowly drew my underwear down my legs while I lifted my hips as high as they could go, trying to make it easier, faster.

She tossed my thong over her shoulder and then lowered her head close. The sight of her brown hair surrounded by my thighs had a new flash of heat spreading through my body.

Her lips opened. I could hear her breaths, the movement of her tongue, her swallow. I panted.

Then she was there, against me, in me. I clutched the blanket, trying to keep my hips from shooting off the bed. I didn't want to distract her from her task—which seemed to be discovering every bit of me with her tongue.

I gripped the back of her head. The shaved section of her hair rough on my fingers while her tongue was

soft as it licked into me. The contradiction brought me
nearer to the edge. I'd already been close, so close from
her presence, her words, the pictures they'd put in my
mind.

"Mm-hmm." I curled my fingers against her scalp.
"Oh my god. So good."

My muscles tensed and I could feel it on the periph-
ery. What I sought. The sooner I came, the sooner it'd
be my turn to touch and taste her. I pulled her head
closer to me, arching my hips.

Jamie eased back. She looked up at me across my
body. Those eyes. Those beautiful eyes. She traced my
pussy with her finger, her thumb rubbing my clit.

"God, you're gorgeous. So fucking gorgeous," she
said as her finger slowly sank into me, pushing and
stroking. All the while she watched me, gauging my
reactions. She twisted again, flexing her finger in me.

I slid my hand down the mattress and covered her
wrist, squeezing. "I don't have penetrative orgasms."

Tension gathered in her body, her fingers stilling.

"It's okay." I smiled at her. "That feels good and I
don't mind, not at all, but I won't be able to get off that
way."

"Oh, okay." Jamie's cheeks went from a low flush
to a deep red. She pulled her fingers free, and leaned
back, no part of us touching anymore.

I twisted my body, rolls be damned, until I could cup
her hot cheek. "You don't have to stop. I just wanted
you to know my body doesn't work that way." I ran my
fingers from her shoulder down to her hand. I brought
it to my clit. "I like your hands on me."

I waited, hoping I hadn't just ruined this moment
now that it was finally happening. A fierce, determined
expression stole over her face and I felt it in her touch

and down to my bones. Oh, yes. Unlike some other hookups, this wasn't going to present a problem for her. She was up for the challenge.

Desire thrummed in my blood, pulsing through my veins. I hadn't been lying, her touch felt incredible. Amazing.

Jamie found a firm, steady rhythm that had my hips jerking. Her breath against me was my only warning before her tongue was licking me again.

My climax bore down on me. My muscles tensed and I pushed my head into the mattress, closing my eyes, waiting, almost there, needed it, so bad.

Jamie pulled back.

No. I moaned and groaned, keeping my eyes squeezed tight. So close. I was almost there. Wouldn't take much. I needed her to give it to me.

"You like this? Want more of it?"

I thrashed on the bed in response to her cocky tone. If she'd kept her thumb on my clit I probably could have come from her voice and my moving.

She knew the answer. Had to know it from all the sounds making their way out of my throat. Still she waited. "Yes. Fuck, yes. More please. Almost there."

She chuckled, the diabolical edge to it caused goose bumps to roll out over my arms. Then her tongue was back, licking deep.

I shook, my muscles clenched, pulling so tight it felt like something would snap. And then I found it. It was there. I cried out, trembling as I came.

Jamie

Sierra threw her head back, her hips launching off the bed. I looked up at her face, taking in every detail as

I continued to lick at her and fill my mouth with her taste as she came.

There'd been a horrifying moment when I feared I wouldn't be able to do this for her. Unnecessary fear since I was swallowing the evidence of just how much I'd done it for her.

God she was beautiful. Beautiful when she laughed and teased, beautiful when she cried for me, beautiful when she found her pleasure.

Her legs eased away from the sides of my head, sliding down over the edge of the bed.

Unable to resist, I leaned forward and placed a kiss on the large freckle on her thigh. I kept kissing a chain of freckles all the way up her leg.

"Mm." The sound she made was more content rumble than word. "It's my turn to touch you." She knocked her knee against my shoulder. "You should come up here so I can do it."

"I should, huh?"

"Mm-hmm."

I climbed up the bed, making sure to skim along as much of her naked skin as I could. It hadn't escaped my notice what a thing she had for me rubbing up against her. The button of my shirt passed over the tip of her nipple poking through the lace of her bra.

"Oh," she moaned. "Do that again."

I did. Over and over.

As good as this felt, I wanted it naked. Nipple to nipple. I leaned back and shucked off my shirts. I kneeled before her in my bra.

"Oh, yes." She sprang up to her knees, her hands outstretched. Her fingers trailed around my neck until I wore a necklace of lingering impressions. The only kind of jewelry I'd be interested in wearing. She rose higher on her knees and then moved to my side and around my back.

God, I wanted to throw her down to the mattress. To open my legs wide and demand that she let me climax. There was an equal part of me that was willing to let her explore and caress my body for as long as she showed interest.

She paused at my upper shoulder blade. "It's beautiful," she said. Her finger traced the outline of the elephant I had inked there.

MJ had done it when I'd first started at Thorn & Thistle. I'd had hopes that I'd found the type of family I'd always envisioned, one where everybody contributed and had your back and I'd gotten the tattoo to commemorate it. It'd taken a while but we had that at the shop now.

When I did Sierra's elephant, who would she be thinking of? I curled my toes into the comforter, trying to fight off the hope that it would be me.

Her fingers moved on from my tattoo to the clasp of my bra which she deftly unhooked and then slid down my arms. My nipples pebbled even further in the surprisingly humid air in her room. Anticipation speared me as I waited, exposed, while she made her way to my front.

"Oh," she breathed out, leaning back and taking me in.

I pulled my shoulders back. I didn't have a hate relationship with my breasts. Never really had. I could do without them when I was running or when I'd played soccer, but I liked them fine, especially when they gave my partner pleasure. But I had a mirror. Gravity was taking a toll.

Insecurity didn't have a chance against the appreciation in Sierra's gaze. This beautiful, vibrant, caring woman was licking her lips as she stared at me without my shirt.

She nodded toward my lower half. "Take those off. I want to see all of you." She ran her tongue around her lips, pink and swollen from our kisses. "I want to taste all of you."

I stood and got to work, taking my pants off. My underwear quickly made it to the pile of clothes on her bedroom floor.

She lay down on her side, a beautiful presentation of curves and freckles and temptation. She crooked her finger at me.

The time for playing and exploring was over. I couldn't wait any longer, my body desperate for her touch.

I crawled on the bed. She came up over me and I willingly went on my back. She kissed the side of my neck and then licked her way up to my ear. "I want to feel your legs wrapped around me." Her hand squeezed my calf. "Tight."

When I'd started playing soccer my calf muscles had enlarged. I'd had to stop because my parents didn't have the money for all the fees and it required too much time for practice and games, but my muscles had stayed pretty firm.

I'd never thought of my calves as something someone would find attractive about me, but Sierra did love to prove me wrong.

She made her way down my body. God, had her energy been something I'd initially viewed as a negative? She was everywhere. Kissing. Sucking. Flicking her tongue against me.

She stopped at my hip bones, mouthing first one side and then the other.

"Remember I want to feel those legs around me. Squeeze me."

Her tongue pressed against my core and she gave one long swipe, gathering the proof of how aroused she'd made me. Then she focused on my clit, attacking it in the best of ways.

Oh, god. I was drowning. It was all sensations. I couldn't think. I couldn't—

She tapped my calves.

I lifted my head from her lemon scented pillow. And what a sight to greet me. Her face buried against me as she continued to eat me out, her glittering eyes staring up at me. She smacked my calf again. Harder this time.

My legs. She wanted to feel my legs around her. I lifted them and put them on her shoulders, pressing against the side of her head. Now all I could see was the top of her bright red hair between my legs. The sketch this would make. It'd be one to frame. Though there was no way my fingers could hold a pencil, all I could manage now was to clench and unclench them in her comforter.

I'd never done this. Never lain back and had someone take the lead in bed. I'd always been expected to be the top in my relationships with women. It'd been a role I was comfortable with. My first priority was making sure my partner was satisfied, and there was satisfaction for me in pleasing them.

It wasn't like I'd been with pillow princesses. They'd given back. But this was different.

There was no denying that Sierra was in the driver's seat right now and I was a passenger. It was freeing to let go of that control and let someone else have it for a moment.

Sierra sucked my clit into her mouth, and my hips

jerked off the bed. Moans left me one after another until there was no space between them, no room for me to breathe because Sierra just kept licking me. I squeezed my legs tight, tighter. My release gathered more strength.

Then her finger was there, pushing inside me. My body was distracted by this new sensation, holding my orgasm off as I adjusted.

Adjusted to the fact that there was a part of Sierra inside me.

"Oh shit yeah, like that. Deeper. Harder."

I felt her smile against me. She worked her finger, pushing and pulling in a fast rhythm that matched her licks. She eased a second finger inside.

A drop of sweat slid down my forehead as my body clenched. Almost there. So close. Just needed— Sierra sucked my clit into her mouth again. I let go, the orgasm taking control and seizing my muscles.

Sierra didn't slow. She kept going and going and so did my orgasm, my body lurching, my brain blessedly shutting down and just accepting the relief she was giving me.

Sierra's touch gentled. Her fingers slid out and rested against my pussy lips.

I lowered my legs, my muscles protesting the move, my mind protesting it even more for breaking that connection with her.

Sierra wiped her mouth on the inside of my thigh and then crawled over me to lie next to me, her leg draped over my hip.

I grabbed her hand and kissed her fingers, smelling myself on her. I brought her middle finger to my mouth and sucked softly. She hitched her leg higher on me until I could feel her wetness against my skin.

I let out a breath, releasing more than oxygen from my lungs. I let go of this night. Let go of what brought us here.

I tugged her even closer to me and kissed the top of her head. "I cannot believe I held off on that."

"So stubborn." She cupped my pussy, drawing a final shudder from me. "Good thing it was worth it."

A fissure of alarm tried to work its way in, warning that now that she'd gotten what she wanted, my use for her might be over. I pushed it aside. Instead I'd remember the way she'd kissed every inch of my body, even the boring parts.

Sierra tucked tighter into me, placing her head on my shoulder. She rubbed it back and forth, as if trying to get the perfect fit.

I savored the moment until I started to nod off. It was late and it'd been a long day. "Hey, you awake?" I asked, a yawn trying to mix in with my words.

"Mm-hmm." She made a contented sound, her body completely relaxed against mine.

I jostled my shoulder that she was using as a pillow.

"Uh." She blinked open her eyes and stared up at me blearily. She reached out and gently ran her finger over my eyelashes. "Soft." Her eyes opened further and her rumpled expression disappeared. She scrambled back, throwing herself to the other side of the mattress. "Oh, sorry. Didn't mean to do that."

"I don't mind. I was enjoying it. I'm about to fall asleep myself, but I don't want to if I'm not invited."

"Invited?"

I couldn't tell if it was because of her tiredness that she wasn't catching my drift, or if the concept of someone spending the night was that foreign to her. Either way it gave me a clue to how this was probably gonna go down. "Yeah. I'm wondering if I should gather up my clothes or if I can stay."

Her eyes went wide. Had she paled? Her freckles were really standing out. "That's what you want? To stay?"

Did I want to stay here in her peaceful room with her naked body against me, keeping me warm after another tiring bout with my parents? "Yeah. A lot."

There was probably some rule that I wasn't supposed to admit that. I wasn't interested in playing games. I spent so much time smoothing and sorting things out, I didn't want to have to do it regarding myself. The best way to ensure that was to be straightforward.

Her eyes held the wariness I'd come to expect when it came to us taking any kind of step together. "Do you think it's a good idea?"

"For me, yes. I don't know for you. Only you can answer that." This was obviously a big thing, and I wouldn't want her to go ahead with it because she was feeling sorry for me thanks to what she'd seen earlier. I wanted it to be something she wanted. It stung, an ache below the skin, that she didn't.

"I don't want to push," I said, sliding to the edge of the bed.

"Wait." Sierra held up her hand. "Let me just—"

"Sierra—"

"Shh. Thinking."

I more than shushed, I froze, barely daring to breathe as I awaited her answer.

Her gaze went from my face down to my shoulder that was still warm from where she'd been pressed against me. She swallowed loud enough for me to hear. "Yeah, I think it's fine this once. Stay."

Damn, but this woman had the power to send me floating. She'd chosen this. Me.

I crawled back to where I'd been. She inched closer and placed her head on my shoulder. She'd left the light on which wouldn't present a problem for me, I often fell asleep on the couch with the lights on. Right now I was grateful for it because it gave me the opportunity to look at her.

With her head tucked into me as it was it left her neck visible. Her bare neck. Beautiful, creamy skin. I wanted my ink there.

In that location she wouldn't be able to see it unless she looked in the mirror. All of her other tattoos had been purposefully placed so she could easily see them because they were there for her. This would be for me.

The intensity of that desire frightened me.

Whoa. Time to get a grip. I was fantasizing about marking a woman that I couldn't promise any time to. A woman who'd been spooked with me staying the night. A mere seven hours.

But she'd said yes.

God, let everything else in my life stay on track so I could make it more than one night.

Chapter Fifteen

Jamie

I rummaged through Sierra's cupboards, trying to find what I would need. It'd been hard to leave her in the bed. For someone who hadn't been keen on sharing her bed at first, that'd all changed once she'd fallen asleep. She'd become as clingy as one of the vines on her plants.

Cuddling with Sierra could become a favorite pastime.

Once again I was going for a real heart-stopping one.

Now I was on a mission to show her there were other benefits to having an older lover stay over other than a snuggle buddy.

I'd just cracked some eggs into a large mixing bowl when arms came around my waist and a body pressed against my back. I knew those curves, had spent all night learning them.

"Morning," I said, turning my head toward her.

"Mm, morning." She pressed a kiss to the side of my face, her mouth minty fresh. "What are you doing?"

"I was going for breakfast."

"Mm-hmm." She nipped my neck and then pulled back. Like me she'd put on some of her sweats. We were both rocking buns high on our heads. "I've always liked the sound of breakfast."

"'The sound of.' You don't normally have it?"

"Not when it's between that and more sleep. I grab some Pop-Tarts and a kombucha."

I shuddered. "Yes, I saw those in there." I poured some milk into the bowl. "Do I need to be making enough for three?"

Sierra leaned against the counter next to me, her hip a nice distraction. "Nope. Ashley'll already be on her way to classes. Even if she were here, you don't have to cook for her." She kissed my cheek. "But it's nice of you."

She seemed overly impressed for something as simple as cooking enough for her roommate. It confirmed what I'd already suspected—that people in her past had not put in much effort with her. I couldn't imagine it. She deserved so much, effort being the least of it.

She clapped her hands together. "What can I do to help?"

"Nothing. This is something I'm doing for you."

"And now I'm up and we can do it together. Think how much more fun that'll be."

Looking at her dazzling smile, I had to agree. Things were better when she was around. I mentally adjusted my plan to cook for her into a combined effort. The outcome was better than my original. "How about you grate some cheese if you have it and any vegetables you like in your scramble?"

"On it."

Once she was back next to me, I watched as she chopped vegetables in a way that suggested she had some experience.

"You like cooking?" I asked.

"'Like' might be taking it a bit far. We tolerate each other."

"What?" It tickled me the way she answered what I would think would be a straightforward question with such flair. "Explain that one to me."

"I don't like cooking, but I like the results. I've got to eat."

I turned on the burner. "I can see that. I only cook because it's healthier and less expensive."

She tossed the bell peppers into the bowl. "Did you start when you had your daughter?"

"No, I was younger. Probably too young but my parents couldn't always be trusted to make sure my brother and I were fed. On the weekends I took over."

She reached out and squeezed my hip. "I can see why you don't like it much."

That was another nice thing to having Sierra know my long-held family secrets. To her it wasn't so abnormal and in turn she didn't make me feel odd or defensive talking about it. It just was.

I knocked my elbow into hers, careful to wait until she wasn't chopping. "What about you? When did your 'tolerant' relationship start?"

"I was young too, but it wasn't coz I had to. My uncle doesn't cook. Never has. Never will. He lives off takeout. When I first started living with him I would cook meals to show him how thankful I was for him taking me in."

I wiped my hands on a dishtowel and then squeezed the back of her neck. "I'm sure he loved it."

"He says he did." She flashed me a smile, the very tip of her tongue impishly between her teeth. "I don't know how it could have compared to the restaurants he was used to, but he would eat everything."

"Because when it's made with love, it's the best food." I made my way back over to my side of the counter. "Hey, we should take a class together. This has been fun. We could make cooking something we actually like."

She didn't say anything for a long moment. Long enough for her to dice a quarter of a tomato. "We could do that. We already eat together and cooking kind of goes with that."

I shot her a quick look, trying to wrap my head around another one of her mind-twister answers. "It sure does. We would eat what we cook." Stepping back and making use of the dishtowel again, I pulled out my phone. "Wow. Apparently I'm not the only one with this brilliant idea. There's all kinds of options. They even have couples classes."

Sierra chopped harder, tomato juice squirting. "Oh?"

My stomach sank as I stared at the schedules. "Most of them are on the weekends." I worked Saturday and had Riley on Sunday.

"Well, you tried."

I guessed I could take a Saturday off, if I planned far enough in advance. It was my busiest day though, and I'd been hoping for something we could do together soon.

Sierra reached up and ran her finger along the side of my eyes. "Your lines are showing," she said, winking.

I much preferred the touch to my eyelashes last night.

"It's not that big of a deal." Humming, she cleaned her knife.

I stuffed my phone back into my pocket and stared at her expression. She didn't look resentful of that fact, nor even disappointed that this wasn't going to happen.

None of the disappointment that was trying to grab hold of me.

"It was just an idea," I said, picking the whisk back up. I'd have to think of something else that'd work better. For now I needed to get back to our original conversation, not ready to let it go, wanting to learn more about her. "Is your uncle the reason that you got into what you do?"

"Yeah. It was only because of him that I didn't stay in foster care. I was there for a few weeks until things got sorted out and it wasn't good for me."

Abandoning the eggs, I wrapped my arm around her shoulders, pulling her in close.

Her shoulder remained tight under my touch. "I wanted to help other kids. I wanted to work in the system and make it better."

"You do. I'm sure of it."

Her face twisted in a grimace. "Maybe. It's harder than I thought. Instead of getting more resources, places are getting less. Everything is spread so thin and that means there's not enough to make people success stories."

"Yet, you're there every day doing what you can. That's pretty amazing." I'd already admired her passion for what she did, but now knowing her painfully deep connection to it and seeing the way she didn't let it deter her—well, admire was too tame for how I felt. It wasn't the energy of youth or life not having beaten her down yet that allowed her doggedness. Life had already delivered the blows. It was her.

I shot another quick glance at her face, to check she wasn't getting upset by the subject, and was faced with another example of her resilience. Her face showed nothing but strength and that passion.

"I don't know about amazing," she said. "But I couldn't live with myself if I didn't do something. I want to make sure kids get the services they need so they don't feel so helpless."

"I'm sure it's not easy. Now or then. Your grandmother already gone and then your mom."

Sierra pulled away and shook her head. "Oh, my grandmother wasn't dead then. She just didn't want me."

I drew in a deep breath, but caught it before it turned into a gasp. I couldn't conceive of that. Not wanting Sierra. Wanting her too much had always been the problem for me. "Without knowing her or her circumstances I can say that she was wrong. Very wrong. Now I understand why you had such a hard look on your face when you mentioned her at the food trucks."

"You remember that?"

"Yeah. You remember things that interest you."

Sierra's face softened and she bumped her hip into mine. "You interest me too."

I caught the bowl before I fumbled it and poured the eggs into the now sizzling pan.

Staying close, Sierra put her head on my arm, watching while the eggs cooked in the skillet. Never would I have believed I'd get to experience the peace of a lazy morning just learning about each other with the woman who'd sat in my tattoo chair and practically had to be held down so she didn't bounce her way out of it.

Her arm came around my waist, her fingers caressing my side in a provocative slide. "Do you have time to enjoy more than breakfast?"

Straightening, I couldn't help a huff of laughter at the very different directions our thoughts had gone in. So maybe she wasn't as content with a slower pace. "Nice thing about working at a tattoo shop is we open late."

Breakfast ready, we went to the small dining set. Sitting across from me, her knee pressed against mine, Sierra took her first bite. Her eyes slid closed and she let out a low moan.

Now there was a sound designed to make me wet. Not only because it was almost an exact replica to the one she made when I licked her clit, but because now I associated it with her pleasure at something I'd done for her.

Feeling settled and content, I put a forkful of eggs in my mouth.

"I couldn't help noticing that you like penetrative sex."

I inhaled my eggs down the wrong pipe. Hacking, my eyes watering, I set my fork down.

Sierra's lips twitched, laughter lighting her eyes as she watched me attempt breathing and swallowing at the same time.

I would not squirm. I was thirty-seven years old. I was a mother. I could and would talk about sex.

Once I was safely breathing again, Sierra said, "So about that penetrative sex. You like it?"

"Uh, yeah, I guess I do."

"I'm totally open to using toys. Just because they don't do anything for me, doesn't mean I don't want to see you get off any way you like."

My cheeks would never get back to their original color. Especially with her sitting here looking so damn young and innocent in her sweats and freckles, talking about sex toys.

"I got off just fine. But thanks for offering."

"I want it to be more than fine. I want fireworks and if we need to use toys to make it happen, I'm all for it."

I reached out and grabbed her hand, rubbing my

thumb over her lime green nail polish. "It was more than fine and you know it."

"Facts." She cocked her head while she studied me. "So how uncomfortable are you? Okay to keep talking about this or should I stop?"

I waved her on. I took another bite to prove to both of us that I could handle it.

"Is it only toys or sometimes do you like something more?"

It took a few chews to figure out what she might be asking. Even then I wasn't one hundred percent sure. So I would get clarification, like an adult. "Are you asking me if I like dick, as in, attached to a man?"

She smiled around her fork and nodded.

"No. At least not anymore."

She poked her toe into my shin. "Don't stop there. Tell me more."

The one and only thing in my life that had any chance of shocking her didn't even earn a gasp, an extra puff of air, anything.

"When I was a teenager I was looking for a quick way to feel good and sex was how I did it. I knew I was attracted to women and probably a lesbian, but guys were happy to experiment and get some action and it was easy—exactly what I was looking for. I was still able to get pleasure out of the act and that's all I needed at the time."

No shock or disgust at my admission. Sierra nodded and smiled at me across the table. So different than past reactions. Especially Nicki. I'd been her first female relationship and she'd gone all in, done with men. Any time a dildo was mentioned she would become uncomfortable. To her, anything penis related had become something not to be enjoyed.

"We aren't that far off on that front," Sierra said.

"You knew you were into women but found it too much effort because you were just trying to blow off some steam?"

"No. I went out with and had sex with boys even though I was pretty sure I was queer."

I pushed my plate aside and hooked my ankles around the chair legs and leaned forward. "Yeah?"

"Yeah. My uncle is gay and I was worried I was making myself gay so he'd love me more because we had that in common." She shrugged. "So I tested it. I mean, what are the chances that there'd be multiple queer members in the same family. But I am." She looked me over and then licked her lips. "I most definitely am."

"I caught on to that last night."

"Oh, good. I'd hate to think I was giving you mixed signals."

"No, your signals were just right."

Her foot slid up mine and then she worked her way under the bottom edge of the sweatpants, her toes wiggling against me. "I'm trying to give you more signals."

"I'm getting them." Yes, arousal burned in me and I knew we'd be making a return trip to her bedroom, but right now I felt closer to her, more intimate than last night when we were falling asleep naked, and I wanted to enjoy the sensation for just a little longer.

Sierra

Balancing my Thermos in one hand and a box of granola bars in the other, I used my foot to nudge open the door to the group room at Haven Bridge. Well, not just group. The room also acted as one of the places we used to meet with families. Large stuffed chairs and a table with a lamp made up the decor. No desks or office chairs. It was all about trying to give a homey feel. I didn't know how successful it was, considering I didn't think anyone could forget this was not their home, but I loved that the center tried regardless.

I ripped the top off the box of granola bars and spread them on the mini fridge that had some bottles of water the kids could grab. Some people might think that chocolate or chips would be the better option for a group of teens and preteens, but I purposefully bought granola bars. They were more expensive than basic junk food, and when you didn't have money they were hard to come by. I still remember the jealousy at school of watching other kids eat them from their lunches. When I'd occasionally score one off someone they tasted like everything I'd ever been denied.

Hearing approaching footsteps, I turned and booked it for the green overstuffed chair on the left side of the room. We didn't have many rules in group, but first one who arrived got dibs on seating. The green chair was by far the most comfortable.

Trey was the first to walk in followed quickly by Roger. Roger had been a client of the center and in our boys' housing since he'd started high school and at this point would probably age out with us. I nodded at the others who slowly drifted in. Last came a girl who looked to be early teens. I checked my phone. Silvia. A newcomer who'd surprised her caseworker, Rachel, by wanting to attend. Silvia took a seat on the far end of the couch and pulled her knees up to her chest, looking like she wanted to disappear into the cushions.

"All right, we ready?" At their nods, I continued. "Anyone want to get started?"

As could always be counted on, Roger raised his hand.

"Go for it." I settled back, ready to pipe in if someone asked me anything directly or break things up if the talks got too heated. My goal here was to stay out of the way and hope they got what this group was intended for—companionship, help, relating with others in similar situations. People participated if they wanted to. None of that bullshit about calling on people or asking questions and putting anyone on the spot. This was supposed to be a safe place.

For the next thirty minutes they discussed everything from what they liked about therapy to the crappy food at the center.

When conversation had wound down, I looked around. "Anyone else?"

"Yeah," Silvia piped up from her spot in the cushions. "What's the point?"

I bit my lip. It was hard to keep my mouth closed, not to rush to assure her there was one, but first I wanted to see if someone else—

"Because this is only now," Roger said. "Hit eighteen and you're free. Then you're an adult and you do what you want. You have the control of your future." I could hear how close Roger's freedom was in his voice.

His words obviously didn't bring Silvia the same comfort as they did him. Her eyes were so bleak and barren, like the word "future" had lost all meaning to her.

I remembered that feeling well. And I'd only had to experience it for a few short weeks.

When my first caseworker had started plotting my permanency plan, I'd had no interest in the future. I'd been ten and sure I didn't have one. I'd just lost my mom. The one person who knew me. Loved me. I'd only wanted to be left alone. The only meeting that had been able to spark anything in me was when I'd been told my uncle had been approved for long-term placement. Unfortunately, the chances of Silvia getting any such meetings were nil.

When no one else spoke, I leaned forward in my chair. "Okay, here's the part I know you've all been waiting for. Time for me to whip out my words of wisdom and change your lives forever."

I nodded at the very generous chuckle coming my way and waved off the groans. I turned serious—as serious as what I was going to say deserved. "I know right now it feels like you have very little control in your life. But there's one thing you can always count on and that's yourself. So you take care of yourself and look out for yourself how you need to. Think on that."

Trey rolled his eyes. Roger nodded. Some others rushed out of the room, probably not even listening to what I'd said, chalking me up as another person who didn't understand what they were going through. But that was okay. Maybe someone would hear it, could use it.

After grabbing the trash we'd left behind, I headed back to my desk. I turned my phone back on, checking my notifications.

Ashley: Emergency night out. Bad grade on paper. Prof. HATES me.

Sierra: :(I'm in

It was only six. Plenty of time to catch up on some files and then go home and put some shine on.

My phone buzzed again. This time Jamie's name was on the screen. I forced myself to slowly pick it up instead of the snatch and grab I wanted to.

Jamie: Hey. Hope you had a good day. I was wondering if you're free tonight.

Thank god Ashley's text had come first. It'd keep me from being stupid and inviting Jamie over again.

I'd spent so much time working to get her to my place and into my bed, only to discover, hey, that might not have been the brightest idea. Now when I went into the kitchen, I pictured her there cooking, smiling, bumping me with her hip, wanting to take a class together. And that was just the kitchen. There was the bathroom where we'd shared a just-brushed kiss. And by far the worst was my bed. I'd never gotten a better night's sleep than the night she spent with me. Each night since had been pure crap.

Sierra: Sorry got plans.

Jamie: Oh, okay. Maybe some other time soon.

Ugh, I could almost see her disappointment in that text, the same disappointment I was trying to fight off. My leg bounced under my desk.

Oh hell, there'd be other people there. Jamie was the most dangerous when we were one on one.

Sierra: You can come if you want.

Jamie

Standing in the back alley behind the shop before my next client arrived, I stared down at Sierra's text.

I should have known she wouldn't be free. I might not have a social life, but the same wasn't true for her.

My only thoughts were that I'd had some free time and I'd wanted to spend it with her.

Did I want to spend it with her friends too?

I had to at some point if I wanted to keep this going. Which I very much did. Things were going good. Yeah, there was some getting used to our age difference, and our different schedules, but it hadn't been the deal breaker I'd feared so far. Maybe it'd be the same with her friends. Ashley'd been all right.

Jamie: Count me in.

Sierra: Yaas.

Sierra: Oh shit. Forgot. Going to a bar. That cool with u?

Not exactly a surprise considering the pictures I'd seen on her Instagram. You couldn't expect a twenty-five-year-old and her friends not to want to drink and hang out in a bar. It wasn't like I'd never been to one or even couldn't go in. I'd gone plenty of times when Nicki wanted to meet up with friends and have drinks. I just preferred to avoid them.

Jamie: Yeah, that's fine.

She responded with a smiley face and the name of the bar they were meeting at.

The bar I discovered three hours later was nothing like I was expecting. First there were no strobe lights that I would have to worry about triggering some weird headache. There weren't people pressing against each other, yelling for service. Instead a few people waited patiently as the bartenders filled orders. There was even dim lighting that gave it a kind of a nice, relaxing ambience.

I didn't usually care how I dressed so long as it was comfortable. I'd been known to go into shows at the theater in cargos and a button-down because I wasn't there to see other people or impress them. Tonight I was very aware that my clothes were neither fashionable nor sexy.

Gaze scanning the room, I stopped at the sight of Sierra on the other side, waving.

I skirted the bar, avoiding the low tables with sitting areas scattered around the interior.

Sierra met me, smiling. Her clothes were more on par with what the other patrons wore. Black, tight pants and a low-cut blue blouse with a shine the lights picked up on.

"Hey," she said, leaning up to kiss me.

I couldn't stop the flinch at the slight taste of alcohol on her lips. "Hi."

"Come on, I'll introduce you to everyone." She turned and started walking, but not before grabbing my wrist to pull me with her. That touch went a long way to keep me from dwelling on the first dissatisfying kiss I'd ever had with her.

There were six women seated on a low-slung couch done in black leather. I recognized Ashley, who stood when we reached them.

"Hey, welcome." She pulled me into a hug.

"Thanks for letting me crash this."

"Totally. It's overdue. They've been wanting to meet you."

That didn't sound ominous or anything. But I'd take it because it meant Sierra had brought me up to her friends. And since she'd kissed me in full view, she'd announced I was more than her tattoo artist or helping her with the fundraiser.

After being introduced to the other women, I slid onto the couch and Sierra took the space on the end next to me. This wasn't bad. All of the women had glasses in front of them, but I hadn't heard one slurred word or a laugh that was unnaturally loud. They all seemed aware and in control. I slid deeper onto the couch.

"Let me get you something to drink," Sierra said.

My gaze snapped to her.

She winked. "Don't worry, I got you, boo."

Boo. It was hard, but I didn't make a face, knowing that's exactly what she wanted by using that ridiculous word.

Laughing, she twirled and made her way through the larger crowd than I would have expected after ten on a weeknight. Sierra's body bounced with that walk that never failed to capture me.

"Can I ask you a question?"

I turned to the woman on my left. I couldn't remember her name, but I did know she had a friendly smile and I hadn't caught one side-eye look, which had me predisposed to like her.

I angled myself toward her. "Sure."

"It's about tattooing." She made a face. "I understand if you don't want to answer. You're not on the clock. Work is the last thing I want to talk about, or even think about, until my next shift."

As long as she didn't ask me what year I'd graduated, she could ask me whatever else she wanted. "It's fine. I love tattooing and am happy to talk about it. Hit me."

"Well, I've been thinking of getting another one. But it's the rib." She leaned forward and stared at me intently. "Honestly, how bad is it?"

Ah, the million-dollar question. As in, I'd have a million dollars if I charged people a dollar who asked me about the pain. "It varies for everyone. But yeah, it's up there for most people. The few times I've had someone pass out on me, it's been a rib piece."

Her expression fell. "Does it matter where or how much fat a person has?"

"Well, it—"

Suddenly she pulled up her shirt on the side, holding it to the edge of her bra and showing me all the skin in between. "I was thinking right here." She touched the side of the ribs, smack dab in the middle of her right side.

Holy shit. My head jerked up and I looked straight into Sierra's eyes.

Her gaze slid past me to her friend with her shirt still up, waiting for me to inspect the area, then back to me. Her eyebrows rose. "For someone who was against hookups, you're making some moves."

"I... She... It's not..."

"Yeah, yeah, don't strain yourself," she said, laughing. Shaking her head, she regarded her friend. "Oh my god, Crystal. Are you on about the rib tattoo again? No matter how many people you ask, the answer is the same. Yes, they hurt."

Crystal dropped her shirt and let out a gusty sigh that lifted her bangs off her forehead. "Okay."

Sierra handed me a glass of clear liquid with bubbles. "Club soda," she whispered in my ear.

I knocked my glass against hers that looked to have exactly the same thing, but after that kiss, I knew it didn't. "Thank you."

Now that everything was nicely covered and I didn't have to worry about Sierra thinking I was hitting on her friend or something, I chuckled at the woman. "How'd you handle your other ones?"

"They hurt."

From her face I was guessing they more than hurt. Not enough to keep her from getting another one, because she had multiples. But yeah, I was betting being her artist wasn't exactly fun either.

"You might want to rethink your placement."

She sighed. "I was afraid you were going to say that. They just look so cool."

"It's all about the tattoo, not the placement."

She laughed. "It makes sense you would say that. Do you have a card?"

I nodded and pulled one out of my wallet. That had all of her friends requesting ones.

Talk moved on to jobs and I listened. I was always interested in what other people did for a living and the things they bitched about. For the most part it seemed to be pretty much the same. Co-workers. Workload. Not being appreciated. In Ashley's case, a professor who hated her. I could have swapped out these women for the girls of Thorn & Thistle and the conversation would boil down to the same life concerns. Keeping money in the bank account. Managing time. Trying to get sleep.

"How about you, Sierra?" a brunette on the opposite side of the couch asked. "Have you heard anything more about the cuts?"

I jerked my head in Sierra's direction, scooting forward on the couch so I could see her better.

She kept her attention on the friend who'd asked. "No. They're starting to move some duties over to volunteers. They tried that with my groups until I said I'd do them on my own time. But I don't see how that'll be enough. To really save money they're going to have to cut staff."

Holy shit. Sierra was facing job cuts? "You didn't tell me that the center was having trouble."

Her eyes widened. "Um, no. Sammantha and I talk about work."

Uh-huh. I waited but no more came. "You can talk to me."

"Oh." Her tongue came out and did a quick swipe over her lips, but I couldn't even properly enjoy it, still struck that she hadn't shared this. "Yeah, I know."

She knew, but chose not to? Except instead of her usual sounding sure and confident, she looked like I'd put her in the interrogation chair and she wasn't sure her alibi was as airtight as she thought.

When she'd said she wasn't used to relationships, she hadn't been kidding. I could introduce her to one of the benefits of a relationship I missed the most. Talking everything out. Making sure you were on the same page. "I mean it. I'm happy to listen any time you want to talk. About anything."

Her gaze searched mine and she gave a single nod. "Okay."

Breaking off the side conversation she had going on with the person next to her, Ashley leaned forward. "So tell us about you, Jamie. What do you like to do for fun?"

Fun. Well, shit. For most people this probably wasn't a trick question. "Um, I used to play soccer."

"Were you good?" Sierra asked, her hair sliding over her shoulder as she turned to look at me.

"I made varsity my sophomore year." An embarrassing amount of pride infused my voice.

"Oh," one of her friends exclaimed, leaning forward.

"We have some good college teams here. And the adult leagues too. My ex used to play. Maybe we'll have to come watch you when they start up again."

There was no way I was going to explain that when I said sophomore I meant high school. I hadn't done adult league because they were so time consuming, and with Riley and my parents and job—yeah, not happening.

"I like to go to Thorns games," I blurted. I nudged Sierra with my elbow. "Do you ever go?"

"No, but I know they're a good team."

"Better than good. Two time champions." My voice was boastful, like my rooting for them had somehow played a part in those championships. "Did you play?"

"No. I mean, I did when I had to in P.E., but never because I wanted to. I just remember it being a lot of running and I was not going to be hitting that ball with my head."

I laughed. "Headers don't hurt."

"Uh-huh." Her gaze went pointedly to my top lip.

I rubbed my finger over the little scar. "That was a freak accident. Honest, it doesn't hurt."

"That's what they said about volleyball and my arms would be red and sting for hours."

Laughing all over again, I reached down and rubbed her forearm as if I could take away the hurt from years ago. "How is it you can get tattooed like a champ, but not handle a little sting?"

"Because at least then I have something lasting to show for the pain."

"We should go to a game. I'll get us tickets in the Riveters section. You'll love being with that loud bunch."

"Ohh. Yeah, that sounds like fun. We could all go together."

I turned to face her friends who were all looking

excited at the idea. I'd actually meant Sierra and me.
Depending on how things were going, maybe Riley
too. But yeah, most people had more friends than their
ex-wife and co-workers. I forced a smile. "Yeah, that'd
be great."

Sammantha—the friend Sierra talked to about work—
slapped her thighs. "Are we ready to hit the next one?"

I glanced at Sierra. "Next one?"

"Yeah. We do a crawl over the next couple blocks.
There's some nice bars."

Was I actually going to do this? A bar crawl?

Yes, I was. And not only because I'd seen the women
drinking and knew now that I didn't need to make sure
they'd be okay. I wanted to do this. To experience it. Sierra was inviting me to enjoy a night out unencumbered.
Around her, I could almost believe I was.

I followed after Sierra as we hit the next one. This
bar's music was louder and the seating arrangements
didn't have the lounge feel, but it was still nice.

Not so for the third. It was dark and the floor was
sticky. But the drinks were cheap and that seemed to
be all the girls cared about. With each drink they had,
their laughter got louder and longer. Occasional shouts
as they tried to talk over one another. But even though
I looked for it, no signs of anger or control slipping.
We were still in good-natured fun territory. At least it
seemed fun for them.

Sierra plopped down next to me, giving me a wide
smile. She'd been making the rounds with her friends,
spending the same amount of time with them as she
talked and then moved to the next one. Guess it was
my turn again.

I leaned into Sierra, not catching a hint of lemon.

It'd been overpowered by the gin and tonics she'd been consuming. "So how long do these things usually last?"

Her smile dimmed as she stared at me and I hated that I was the cause of it. "Oh. Yeah. You're probably tired. And this can't be much fun for you." She shot a quick look at her friends and then leaned in closer until our noses almost touched. In a voice I was guessing she thought was a whisper she asked, "Are you feeling very uncomfortable?"

There was no point in lying. "I've reached my limit." And I didn't think I was the only one.

"Okay." She patted my thigh and then stood. "So we're going to call it a night."

"Good idea. Me too." Crystal pulled out her phone. "Who wants to share a Lyft?"

Her friends were being responsible and not driving. That should untwist my stomach. I wasn't sure anyone had actually driven in the first place. Except me, because I didn't know the bar crawl preparations.

Sierra turned toward me. "Do you want me to get a ride or…"

"I'll take you."

"I knew there was a reason I invited you along," she said, bumping her shoulder against mine.

"Glad, I can be good for something." To be responsible. That was me. I could be counted on. I chomped on an ice cube from my latest club soda to give my jaw something to do.

"Ready?" Sierra asked.

"Yeah." Two bars ago. Four drinks ago.

Out in the fresh air and walking down the street back to the original bar, I tried to just enjoy holding hands with Sierra. Not possible when I couldn't stop myself from watching for any signs of unsteadiness or stumbling. My stomach refused to settle even when I didn't find any.

The car ride back to her apartment was conversation-free, instead the interior filled with Sierra singing along to the radio. At least I knew that wasn't a result of the alcohol. She'd done that every time we'd ridden together. Tonight, though, I didn't feel like joining in.

I pulled up to the curb at her place, instead of parking in a guest spot.

Stopping mid-chorus, she whipped toward me. "You're not coming up? It's okay. It's worth it for your arms. We'll just have to wait a week afterward."

This time, her answers that didn't quite make sense weren't cute. I didn't want to have to puzzle out what she was saying and how much of it was because of the alcohol.

"Nah, not tonight. I'm going to head home. I need to pick up Riley in the morning." I would not think about how few hours it was until that would happen.

"Oh." Her mouth turned down and she leaned closer to me, walking her fingers up the buttons of my shirt. "Is there any way I can change your mind?"

The smell of alcohol on her breath soured my stomach even further. I leaned back until my head clunked against my window. "Not tonight. I've had enough."

Chapter Sixteen

Sierra

I walked into my uncle's house and jerked to a stop.
Uncle Drew sat on the living room couch, laptop balanced on his knees. According to him, the living room
was not for actually living. It was his business card. If
he'd had any other kids this was where they would have
plotted their rebellions by jumping on the couches or
eating over the rug. I still avoided it as much as I could.

"Hey, Sunshine," he said, glancing up at me.

His smile eased the knot in my stomach. His on-point
hair and ensemble of jeans, button-down shirt, and vest
untangled it all together.

Whatever he'd called me over here for wouldn't be
like last time. No death announcements.

He gestured to the cushion next to him. "Sit. Tell me
what's going on. You haven't stopped by for a while."

I gingerly sat on the cushion of the light gray sofa.
"Sorry about that. I've been busy with the fundraiser...
and some other things."

"Yeah. And how's the fundraiser going?"

"Good. Really good. Jamie, my tattoo artist, did the
most amazing design for it. I'm going to get it right
here the first night."

He smiled and then patted my thigh where I'd pointed. "I'm so proud of you for doing this."

It didn't matter that I was an adult, those words from him got me pumped and made me all the more determined to live up to them.

"Now let's get back to those other things." He pointed his finger at me, his eyes narrowing. "Don't think I missed that."

"I met someone. Someone real nice. And we're seeing each other when we can."

My uncle gave a knowing laugh. "Ahh. One of those 'it's complicated' things."

"Yes. Very."

"Will I like her?"

I paused, considering. Was Jamie someone he would seek out in everyday life? Probably not. Uncle Drew was drawn to flair, but he would appreciate her work ethic and her unconditional love for her daughter. "You'd like the way she treats me and how good she makes me feel."

Such a mundane word for all that went through me when I was around her. Yes, good. And calmed. And balanced. And terrified.

"That's all that really matters." I could hear in his voice that he was prepared to like her.

And now I regretted bringing Jamie up.

Next he'd be asking to meet her.

He was determined he would eventually be meeting a "someone special," no matter what I said. This was the closest I'd come for there to be someone for him to meet. But nope, not happening, and not only because her texts since Wednesday night had a definite frost to them. Introducing someone to your family, to your one family member, meant you were planning for them to become more entangled in your life. She was entangled enough.

I might not want it to go further, but I didn't like where things were now with this chill between us. I'd messed up that night. I'd gotten buzzed and put her in a situation where she was uncomfortable. My apology text wasn't going to cut it. I needed more, needed to show her that I respected her, and hopefully we could get back to trying to find times to hookup. Friendly texts were nice. I missed them. My day just wasn't the same without her proper periods and question marks. I'd even found myself adding them to my texts.

Wanting to divert attention from Jamie, both Drew's and mine, I said, "Now don't we need to find someone for you?"

"From your lips to God's ears," he said, glancing up at the ceiling.

Uh-huh. Him and religion had a complicated relationship and had decided it was best if they split.

He flopped back against the cushions. Since the couch had been bought with aesthetics and not comfort in mind, he sprang right back up. "Maybe I can meet him on my upcoming trip."

"Yeah, where am I going to be jealous of now?" It wasn't unusual for him to take off to places for design inspiration or go and consult for the occasional out of state client.

"Bennet."

My foot stopped bouncing, my fingers stopped tracing my purse strap. The only thing still going was my now racing heart. "What?"

"Yeah, that's about how I reacted." All humor fled his face, leaving nothing but starkness. "I got another interesting phone call."

"About?"

"It seems I was named in my mother's living trust. The only one." Even with time to digest, he looked shook. "I guess in her mind me, a fag, inheriting her stuff, trumps anything going to the bloodline of the sister who stole her man. I'm doing everything I can to settle the estate from here, but some things like putting the house up for sale and closing her accounts will be easier to do in person."

Bennet. My worst days were spent there. The day my mother died. Her funeral. My grandmother telling me she wouldn't take me, that I'd taken enough from her.

Most of my best days were there too. Days I'd spent with my mother. Days we'd laughed and played. Days she'd pick me up from school so excited to see me.

God, how terrible would it be for my uncle? Did he even have memories of good days to try and combat all the bad?

"When are you going?"

"Next week. I've got to finish up some client projects, but then I'll fly back. I want to get things finalized there."

I scooted closer and wrapped my arm around him. It hadn't escaped me that he had to call it "there." And he'd be going back there alone.

I rubbed my hand on my right thigh where my protective demon slayer would be going. "I'll come with you."

He smiled and squeezed my knee. "You don't have to do that."

Didn't I? It felt like something I did need to do. For him. Maybe for me.

He had given me a home, but more he'd given me stability and love. He probably would have given me more if I would have accepted it.

"I want to. Let me know when you have a better time frame and I'll get some time off of work."

Oh god, work. I'd be asking for it at the worst time. I did not want to put more pressure on my co-workers, and I sure as hell didn't want them to discover that they got along fine while I was gone and would be okay without me. And the fundraiser. It was coming up.

I didn't have a choice. I needed to do this for him. I needed to show him what we could be to each other.

He inclined his head and gave a big sigh. "You don't have to, but I thank you. I don't know what it's going to be like to go back in that house. To see her things."

Neither did I.

We would find out together.

Chapter Seventeen

Jamie

When the knock came, half of me wanted to vault over the top of the sofa to get to the door, and the other half didn't want to open it at all. Tonight Sierra was coming over for a gaming night. Her idea. It would be the first time I'd seen her since the bar crawl. Would there be that spark of adventure and newness when I saw her, or would I see someone I thought of as another responsibility?

I knew she'd done nothing wrong, that she had every right to go out with her friends and drink. She hadn't asked me to look after her. It still didn't change that I'd felt I'd had to that night.

I opened the door, got one look at Sierra and burst out laughing.

"Sweet Jesus. What are you wearing?" I asked when I could finally catch my breath.

"Oh this?" She brought her hands up to her face, careful not to touch the eye black she had swiped across her upper cheeks. "You said you were competitive. Well, I'm ready." She lifted her lips in a snarl and flexed her arms in front of her. An awkward thing, well, more awkward, thanks to the grocery bags hanging from her wrists.

I busted up again.

"Hey now, none of that. I'm ready for some serious gaming." She breezed past me. "I brought snacks."

Shutting the door, I followed behind her. Question answered—the spark was still there.

She heaved the bags onto my counter, grunting. "This one is for you. It's got trail mix and some licorice. This one," she said, pulling the second bag close to her. "This one is mine." Out came chocolate bars, potato chips, and then a tub of French onion dip.

"It looks like you came prepared." I reached up into my cupboard and pulled out some bowls for our snacks.

"I think I'm going to like this gaming stuff."

"Maybe you should wait until you actually try it."

She walked past me, bumping me with her hip. Hard. "Don't be trying to get into my head with your negativity. It won't work."

She bypassed the couch and the controllers I already had all set up, and instead she went to the wall behind the TV where I had a collage of pictures hung up. When I'd put them up Riley had complained that she didn't have any siblings to share the honor—that being my term, hers had been misery—of being in every single picture and therefore the focus of the entire wall.

Sierra stepped closer to the picture of Riley, Nicki, and me from last year at the aquarium, with all of us posed in front of an otter and holding a life preserver.

"It's nice that you and Nicki have stayed so close."

"Yeah. If possible I think you should stay on good terms for the kids, but in our case it's no hardship. She's my best friend."

Sierra turned from the picture and looked back at

me. I blinked, thrown for a second again by the stripes on her face. "How did you two get together, if you don't mind my asking."

"Of course not." I was kinda keyed up that she was showing some interest when she hadn't before. "She was a friend of a co-worker at the insurance agency I worked at and needed a room cheap. I had one so I offered it up. She'd just had Riley and had gotten out of a bad situation with her ex who wasn't stepping up, so they came to me."

"It sounds like it was meant to be."

"Yeah. I got to be with Riley from practically the beginning." I couldn't stop my soft smile. "You should have seen her. All cheeks. She was the cutest thing I'd ever seen."

Sierra looked back at the wall, zeroing in on one of Riley when she'd just started walking. "She was."

I went to stand next to her, taking a deep breath and inhaling the fresh scent of lemon and nothing more. "So anyway Nicki and I grew close as she started a new life, and I helped out as much as I could. It slowly progressed. I couldn't even tell you the exact moment I knew that it was no longer a friendship, but that we were in a relationship."

She laughed and brushed her shoulder into mine. "'Harold, they're lesbians.' Except this time you were living it."

"Yeah, pretty much."

"You must have been born with that caretaker gene, huh?"

Had I? I didn't know. Didn't think I ever would. I'd kind of been forced into it so young, but maybe it came naturally. Now it was the only thing I knew. "I'm not the only one, Ms. Social Worker."

She cocked her head and turned so that she faced me. "Huh. I don't really think of that as my role. I'm not taking care of them, so much as helping them get what they are entitled to so that they can live and succeed."

"That's a good way to look at what you do. A selfless way." I could not say the same for the reasons I helped people. There was definitely something in it for me.

"I guess. I want everyone to hit eighteen and step out with the anthem of Destiny's Child 'Survivor' as their background music, ready to take on the world."

"Is that what you did?"

She lifted her chin and stared me directly in the eyes. "I do it every damn day."

I was struck by the determination and strength in her gaze.

Sierra released a breath and then lifted a finger, shaking it at me. "There you go again with your mind tricks. Won't work. Remember, I'm a survivor. Now let's get to playing."

Snatching up a pack of licorice and a candy bar, she made her way to the couch where I had everything set up. She picked up the controller, flipping it over and then back to the front, looking at the buttons. After setting it down, she took a bite of licorice and then pointed to the screen with the rest of the piece. "Who's the mammal with attitude?"

"That is Sonic and he's a hedgehog."

"And we're going to play him?"

"Yes."

"Okay, show me what the buttons do on this bad boy."

Oh, this was going to be too easy.

I demonstrated what everything did, as requested.

While I was getting into the finer points of the D-pad she kissed the underside of my chin.

The controller slid to the floor with a thud. "Now who's doing mind games?"

She shrugged. "I couldn't resist. Besides I've got this."

"Ah, cocky youth."

Dropping the remaining bit of her licorice onto the table, she sat up. "That's it. Turn it on. I'm ready. I'll show you what sharp eye and hand coordination can do."

"Oh, really?" With quite a bit of satisfaction I hit the button for two player and the screen split in half.

"Wait. Which one am I?"

"Tails. The one on the bottom screen. Show me what that eye-hand coordination can do," I said, my grin so wide it made talking difficult.

"You just watch."

I hit the button and we were off. Or I was.

"It's not going. Oh, there it goes. Faster. Faster." She swung her arm to the right, nearly knocking me in the nose as she got Tails going in that direction.

When I deemed it safe, I leaned toward her, not even having to look at the screen at this point. "The objective is to go fast and beat the other person. Me," I told her helpfully. "Oh and those rings you keep passing, you're supposed to be getting them."

"Jump," she cried out. "Jump now." She launched off the couch, moving the controller.

I hadn't thought to have my phone next to me, but I really needed a video of this. I hit pause.

"Hey. Why'd you do that? I was just starting to get somewhere."

"No. You really weren't." I nodded toward her hands. "What are you doing there?"

"I'm playing."

"Quite vigorously. You know you just have to press the buttons. None of this other stuff." I motioned to her whole body.

She looked down at her hands. "It's habit. With the Wii my uncle got me one Christmas, you had to move the whole white thing to make it go."

I bit my lip and shrugged. "Okay, your way works too. And hey, it's entertaining for me."

"I'm not trying to entertain you. I'm trying to kick your ass."

"Well, then." I hit the button and our screens went live again.

It took her a good three seconds to realize she was looking at the wrong half of the screen and get Tails moving.

Twenty minutes later, she flopped back on the cushions. "Holy crap that's hard. Who knew gaming was cardio."

"It's not usually." I put my arm around her shoulders and kissed the side of her damp head.

"I have to say I'm disappointed. You were supposed to be a scary, fierce gamer. All you've done is laugh."

"My apologies for being too distracted."

"Uh-huh. Well, while I take a breather, you go ahead. Now remember I want yelling and at least one throw of the controller."

Had I actually managed to wear her out before me? I could do a gaming session all afternoon. I exited out of our game and switched to one player mode.

Her hand on my thigh stopped me from hitting play.

"Before you do I want to say one thing."

I turned to look at her, alerted by the seriousness of her tone.

"I want to apologize for the other night. You were uncomfortable and I'm sorry. I'm sorry, knowing your past, that I didn't remain more aware and check in with you. I should have stopped before it got to the point that you felt like you had to leave."

My fingers on the controller, which usually felt like an extension of my hand, felt awkward. "I brought myself into it. I agreed to go and could have left. I can't expect someone your age not to—"

"Stop, please. Don't give me an out. Or blame it on my age. I'm a responsible adult and I should have known better. I promise that it won't happen again. You would never have done that to me. I think of you as…" She stopped, for once her words not spilling forth.

Fingers tightening on the hard plastic, I waited to hear what she thought of me.

"Safe. You make me feel safe and I want to do the same for you."

Safe. That was a good word. How I wanted people to feel around me. Safe. Went with reliable. Helpful.

Did I feel safe with Sierra? Did I believe that any affection, any feelings I gave her would be returned, that she wouldn't find me too boring, or want someone her own age? No.

But I was getting there. Even more so after this talk.

"You're forgiven and I'm glad I make you feel safe."

She nodded and then she gave me a crooked grin. "So now that I've just gone and assured you that I'm a responsible adult, I have something else to tell you."

"Okay."

"I'm going back to my hometown."

"And where is that?"

"Bennet, Missouri. My uncle needs to clear up some of my grandmother's estate stuff, and I don't want him to go back there alone."

I pulled back enough that I could see her face. "Is this the grandma you told me about? The one that…"

"Didn't want me," she finished. "Yeah. She died in May."

I rubbed my hand down her arm. When she'd told me on the night at the food trucks that her grandmother was dead, I hadn't known it'd just happened.

"So you're going there to settle things?"

Her fingers traced my outer pant leg seam. "Well, I'm going to be with my uncle."

But she'd be at her grandmother's. I didn't like the thought of her being anywhere near someone who'd been so cruel to her, dead or not. "What day? For how long? Maybe I can reschedule some appointments or…"

Shit. There was no way I'd be able to pull it off. Not with Riley. Not with work. Not with my parents. I couldn't trust that they wouldn't do something.

All my adult life, and even before that too often, I'd been helping my parents, keeping an eye on them, trying to keep them on track. I'd almost worn it as a badge of honor, showing that I was capable of doing that and living a full life. It was a sign of my responsibility.

Never had I resented it like I did now.

"Not necessary," Sierra said. "I really am going for him. She doesn't have any power over me." She gave me a smile that could only be called fond. "Besides, it's better you stay here. Something might come up with the fundraiser. I'm sorry that I'm leaving you with it though."

At least I'd be useful for something. "I'm happy to."

"Thank you." She leaned her head onto my shoulder and I slowly wrapped my arm around her, careful not to drag her closer. I'd keep it just like this. She was always affectionate, touching, patting, but this was the first time she seemed to seek me out for comfort.

"It really is my pleasure," I said, placing a whisper of a kiss against her red hair.

Her head popped back up, making me wish I'd kept my damn mouth shut. "Speaking of pleasure. I'd like to look after your pleasure."

I groaned. "So corny."

"It's only corny if it doesn't work. But it's working isn't it? You're thinking about it."

I couldn't even hold out for two seconds. Give me that sexy look and say the word pleasure and there was only one place my mind was going. "Yes, damn you."

She jumped up from the couch—pretty damn fast for someone who had just complained she'd had a hard workout—and helped pull me to my feet. "Hey, do you have any toys in your bedroom?"

No doubt about what kind of toy she was talking about. I brushed my cheek against my shoulder and cleared my throat. "It's been a while. I don't even know where I have them. Maybe some other time."

"Mm-hmm. I'll hold you to that. But for now I'll make you feel good without them."

I didn't doubt that. And I'd be doing the same for her. Thanks to our schedules, tonight would be her send-off before she went to Missouri. Since I couldn't go there with her, I had to remind her just what would be waiting for her when she came back.

Chapter Eighteen

Sierra

"You ready?" Uncle Drew asked, his fingers squeezing mine tight.

We stood outside my grandmother's house. It looked smaller than I remembered. More ordinary. A normal suburban home with normal-looking neighboring houses. It'd all seemed so large and intimidating when I'd been a girl.

"Are you?"

"I don't know. But since we've come all this way, I guess we better go in."

I nodded and still holding hands we started toward the front door.

He inserted the key he'd picked up at the lawyer's office and then pushed the door open.

We stood on the faded welcome mat without going in, as if allowing any trapped souls to escape before we entered.

Stepping over the threshold, we went in together. The air was stale and I didn't know how much of it had to do with it being left empty and how much with the woman who had lived here.

I reached out and trailed my fingers on the entry-

way wall. My mom had grown up here. I didn't have
any memories of her in this place. Oh, I had memories
of this place—of the digs my grandmother would give
about how my mom had done so much with her life
before she had me—but thankfully none of her in this
house. When I thought of my mom, I didn't think of
here. I thought about our apartment. Or the park close
to her work. Only bad memories were housed here, and
my mother was never a bad memory.

Uncle Drew stared around him without the pain I'd
expected. If anything, he looked disappointed.

"It looks the same," he said. He went further down
the hall lined with pictures.

I slowed to study the photos. I vaguely recognized
one of my grandmother's friends and I assumed her
kids. I stepped further down the row and sucked in a
breath. My mom. God, she looked so young and beautiful. Her eyes light and bright and missing the tiredness I always remembered. The corner of the picture
was marked with the year 1993. She would have been
fifteen. In a few short years she'd be having me.

Neither Uncle Drew nor I made an appearance on
the wall.

He hadn't slowed, going straight to the living room.
"Exactly the same," he repeated.

I stood next to him and stared out at the living room.
I couldn't be sure that it was the exact sofa, but yes, I
knew what he meant. It was all the same, right down
to the oppressive feeling.

The last time I'd been in here, I'd been hiding out from
the reception taking place in the kitchen and dining room
after my mother's funeral. I'd sat in here and listened,
wondering how anybody could be laughing.

Now, I understood better. For some people loss and laughter and life were all mixed together.

I kept a close eye on Uncle Drew. Was he too thinking of the last time he was in this house? When his mother had told him that she never wanted to see or hear from him again because of who he was attracted to? Had it happened in this very room?

"This helps," my uncle said, doing a slow walk around the perimeter of the room.

His voice sounded lighter without the sharpness of his tension. I could see it physically with the way he moved, as if he'd ditched some extra baggage.

"You don't see her everywhere you look?" I asked.

"Yes and no." He went over to the side table and picked up a girl with a hook and sheep figurine next to the lamp. "She had this before I was born." Arms held out, he turned in a circle. "See? It's all the same. She was the same. She was still the woman who kicked my ass out and there was nothing that would have made me welcome."

I stepped up to him and hugged him from behind. "She missed out. You're amazing."

"Aw, thanks, Sunshine." He squeezed the arm I had wrapped around him. "This is going to be okay."

I squished him really hard before I stepped back. It would be okay. He'd be okay. We'd make sure of it.

"It looks much smaller than I remember," I said. "And brighter. I always thought of it as this dark, scary place."

Uncle Drew laughed and turned to face me. "No, that was just the woman who lived here."

"She really was." I reached out and traced the shape of a white porcelain horse figurine. So cold. "I'm glad she didn't want me. I would've missed out on being raised by the kindest, most creative, caring man in the world."

He stepped up to me and cupped my cheek. "I hate the thought of what would have happened to you if she sank her ugly claws in you." He sniffed, tears tracking down his cheeks. "But mostly I hate the thought because then you wouldn't have come to me. You've given my life so much purpose."

I wrapped him in a hug, squeezing him tight. After a long moment, I pushed away and gave him a watery smile. "You're only saying that because you like my chicken tacos."

He grabbed me by the shoulders, shaking his head vigorously. "No. It's you. I love you. I will always love you. I've never loved anything like I love you."

I swallowed and flung myself at him for another hug. "I love you too. Thank you. Thank you for taking such good care of me."

We cried together. We'd always been close. We supported each other, but I can't say we ever really comforted each other. Yes, a hug or a pat. But that wasn't what we did. Except now, here, I could feel that we would.

He pulled away, wiping at his face with the back of his hand. "Jesus. Wasn't expecting this today." He gave me a wobbly smile. "I don't think I've ever seen you cry. Weren't you supposed to do that nonstop as a teenager and while I watched helplessly?"

I wiped my cheek with the neck of my shirt. "We didn't have a normal teenager and guardian relationship."

Face falling, he stepped back. "We didn't, did we? What else besides not letting you get rid of your hormonal angst did I mess up on?"

"No, no. You didn't mess up. I was very happy. I wouldn't have wanted it any other way." I could see in his eyes that he was getting ready to rehash all our years together, trying to guess what other things he might have missed as a bachelor, unprepared to raise a kid. "Honest. I wouldn't have let myself accept any more, too scared it'd be taken away."

"God," he said with a little sob. "That makes it worse. I should have known."

"I promise from now on, I'll tell you if there's anything I feel like I need or am not getting."

He sent me a warning look, completely ruined by his tears. "You better."

"I will. Starting now." I handed him a tissue that vaguely smelled florally. "I feel like I need to get out of here. If it's all right with you, I'd like to go visit with someone."

"Yeah, go," he said with an understanding smile, handing me the keys to the rental car.

I stepped back outside and blinked against the bright light. That's right, it was still daylight. A sunny, beautiful morning.

The last time I'd been in this city I hadn't been close to old enough to drive, but I still found my way. Everything about it was implanted in my brain.

I made my way down the fifth section, walking on the carefully tended grass until I reached the fourteenth grave marker. "Hey, Momma."

Jamie

Forty minutes until my next appointment. Time enough to finish ordering supplies, do a little shopping, and have dinner with Riley when she got to Thorn & Thistle.

I typed in "three" for the boxes of toilet paper and then set my tablet aside. At least I didn't have far to go for my next task. I strolled up the main aisle of the shop, pleased that my eardrums weren't waving the white flag. No yelling. Cursing, but in conversation, not at each other. It was so much quieter than a year ago. Well, as quiet as it could get. It was still a tattoo shop.

I stopped outside of Vivian's station, my timing spot on because she was between clients as well.

"Hey," she said, looking up from a sketch she was working on.

"Hey, so I was wondering if I could take that off your hands." I nodded to the sad, pathetic creature on her counter that had once been a plant.

"Oh." She turned to look at it, almost seeming surprised to see it there. "Yeah, a client gave that to me. I guess I've kind of neglected it."

That might not be the best thing for someone who was a certified caregiver for her dad, but hey, I was happy to get rid of the evidence for her. She didn't have time to take care of plants. "Kind of."

"It probably should just be thrown away."

"I know someone who can save it. Or at least try." Sierra might say she didn't have the caregiver gene in her, but I didn't believe it. Even if I didn't count her job, there was the way she cared for her plants, and for Jordan…and the way she'd taken care of me on gaming night.

"Go for it," Vivian said, waving me over to it.

I took the plant back to my station. That done I headed to the front to wait for Riley. While waiting, I checked my phone. No messages. Not one from Sierra since she'd texted to let me know her plane landed. I was sure she was busy. Instead of being comforted by that thought, it just made it worse, leaving me wondering how I could be helping, making things easier for her. Instead I was procuring a dead plant as a welcome back gift.

The door opened and Nicki walked in, Riley trailing after her. I took in my daughter's bent head and rounded shoulders. My gaze shot to Nicki who shook her head and gave a little shrug.

"Hey, Jelly Bean, ready to hang out?"

"I guess." She shrugged, her gaze not lifting from the concrete floors of the shop. Yeah, they had a cool glazed effect but she'd seen it plenty of times before.

"I've got dinner set up in the back."

She nodded, went three steps, before seeming to remember that we had taught her manners. "Bye, Mom. See you later."

"I'll be back in a little bit." Nicki kissed my cheek. "Thanks for watching her on such short notice."

"You know I don't mind." I tilted my head toward the break room that Riley just walked into. "What's up?"

Nicki shrugged. "I'm hoping you can get it out of her. Every time I've asked, she's shut down."

"I'm on it."

"Let me know what you discover," she said before turning and rushing out of the shop.

In the break room I found Riley sitting at the round table I'd set our dinners on. Prepared meat, cheese, and crackers packs wouldn't be getting me mom of the year awards any time, but it'd work. I assembled my crackers, ham, and cheese as if it was a complex puzzle while waiting for Riley to work up the courage to tell me whatever was going on.

"Momma J."

"What's up, Jelly Bean?"

"I've got something to tell you."

"All right."

Riley bit her lip and looked at me from under her lashes, a replica of Nicki when she did that. "I'm afraid you'll get mad."

"I might. That doesn't mean I love you any less."

She chewed her lip, studying me before scooting her chair closer to the table. "Grandma came to see me."

My cracker crumbled in my fingers. "Where?"

"At school."

I had to work, work hard, to keep my face blank. "Grandma Pat came to your school? While it was in?"

"Uh-huh."

"What did she want?"

Riley shrugged, tucking her cheek into her shoulder.

With every second that passed my chest constricted. Tighter and tighter. So fucking tight.

I was supposed to be her safe place. In this I would happily take the name boring. I wanted to be so boring and dependable that my daughter always came to me. But she looked uncertain. Of me.

"She, um, said it was an emergency and had them get me out of class so I could talk to her in the office." She untucked her head enough to look at me. "I thought something had happened to you or Mom."

In her blue eyes I could see the remembered fear. Fear my mother had caused.

Deep breath. Keep it together. My girl needed me. "I bet that was scary."

"Uh-huh."

I reached under the table and squeezed her knee. I wanted to promise her that nothing would happen to Nicki or me, but of course I couldn't promise that. And

I did not give my daughter false promises. Ever. I knew all too well what those were like.

"I'm sorry you had to go through that. Do you want to tell me what she wanted?"

"She just came to talk and ask me for stuff."

"Stuff?" I asked, but I knew. I already knew.

"For some money. She said they were going to lose their jobs and were scared. She wanted me to say I needed money for a school project and then give it to her." Her eyes filled with accusation. "She said you weren't helping them anymore."

A piece of my heart hardened, right there in my chest. "That was not okay of her. Not going to your school and not asking you to lie for her."

"I don't want them to get kicked out of their house. They need help."

"And you won't" went unspoken, but it was there, lingering between us.

Rage raced through my veins, wanting to explode from my very pores, obliterating that cool, calm layer that had always shielded me.

So much I'd read about alcoholism said it was the alcohol in control. It was the alcohol that had my mother going to the school on a weekday, and seeking out Riley. It was damn hard to reconcile that some liquid was responsible instead of the person who birthed you and was supposed to care about you.

She'd made my daughter look at me with doubt, to question if I was good.

Never would she have that opportunity again. I was done giving her access to my life, to my time, to my daughter.

I grabbed Riley's hands and held them in mine, tighter than I'd probably ever touched her. But she had to know. I had to make sure she knew. "I have been helping her." For far too long. "I couldn't give her any more money. I don't have any more to give." No more money. No more energy. No more fucks.

The panic relaxed its hold on me enough that I could loosen my grip. But I knew that part of my heart would never soften.

"I wouldn't ever purposefully hurt Grandma or Grandpa." Not like they did me. "I love them."

I loved them and it wasn't returned. It couldn't be, not if they were willing to bring Riley into this, the single most important thing to me.

I'd always suspected, but to know. My parents didn't love me. They loved what I did for them, but not me.

Riley pulled her hands free, but that was as far as she went.

"I don't want her to be mad at you." She made a face. "I hate when you're mad at me. Or disappointed in me. Ugh, that's the worst."

Even through the pain trying to asphyxiate me, Riley could make me smile.

I made my way around the table and knelt in front of her, pressing our foreheads together, looking into her eyes. "This isn't something you have to worry about."

"My birthday's next month. I mean, I know we're not super close or anything, but she's always been there, and I don't want you guys fighting."

Riley might not carry any of my genes, but she was definitely all my kid. Of course I couldn't tell her not to worry and expect it to fly.

As a kid I'd been told so many times that I didn't need to worry, that it was the adults' job to worry. That didn't matter if the adults weren't doing what needed to be done.

"I promise that whether she's there or not, if we work it out or not, it has nothing to do with you." I ran my hand down her ponytail. "You're the best thing that ever happened to me, you know that?"

"Yeah. Yeah. No getting emo." She pulled away and then went back to her food.

At least she looked to be feeling better after unburdening. I stared at my own food and knew there was no way I could eat it. I felt shaky, like I'd narrowly caught something irreplaceable before it shattered on the floor.

Vivian stuck her head into the break room. "Hey, Riley, I was wondering if I could get your help on some designs."

Riley shoved her last bite of food in her mouth and jumped up. "Yup."

Vivian looked at me. "Your next client's here."

"Thanks. Could you tell them I'll be a few minutes?"

"Sure thing."

I crammed the remains of our dinner in the fridge and then headed out to the back alley. My breath came in short pants as I pulled out my phone and hit Nicki's name. It rang two times before she picked up.

"Hey, everything okay?"

"No."

There was a moment's pause and then, "Let me get to somewhere quieter." I could hear voices and laughter in the background. And the distinctive clink of glasses. "Okay, what is it?"

"I talked to Riley, found out what's wrong."

"And?"

"My mom pulled her out of school to ask her for money. Told her that I wasn't being good to them."

"That bitch. Oh, that's it. I'm going to let her know

for damn sure she is not allowed to go anywhere near my daughter. Ever. You just watch."

I closed my eyes and leaned against the side of the building, the cold concrete doing nothing to cool my anger. "Actually I'd like to handle it."

"Jamie, she's got to know this isn't okay. No excuses. I don't care what's going on in her life. I don't want her around Riley."

"I know. Neither do I."

There was silence on the other end.

"I mean it. I'm done."

Another long pause on her end. "You really mean it?"

"Yes. I'm done helping them, enabling them."

"Well, good. It's about damn time."

It was.

Always I prided myself on fixing other people's lives. It was damn time I fixed mine.

I got off the phone and then just breathed. I needed to get in there, to get to my client. If anything could soothe me it would be the art. It's what I'd turned to when I wanted to get away from the stress of my parents. When I no longer had soccer or friends to console me it'd been the art.

This time I wasn't sure it'd be enough. This time I longed for a redhead.

Chapter Nineteen

Sierra

I dropped to my knees in the still wet grass in the cemetery. I traced the letters of my mom's name and the dates inscribed on the plaque. When I reached the part of beloved mother, I stroked the word over and over.

"You were," I whispered. "*Are* so beloved. I haven't forgotten. I'll never forget."

Keeping my hands on the plaque, I closed my eyes. I'd made it. I was back.

I squeezed my eyes tighter, trying to quiet my breathing, my mind, the nature around me. I didn't want to miss it. Miss her. Seconds passed. Minutes. The dampness soaked through my pants as I waited. Nothing moved, not even the wind, a bird, anything that I could convince myself was a sign.

Nothing.

She wasn't here.

I didn't feel any closer to her than when I was home in Oregon.

I wiped the tears from my face. I'd hoped. God, I'd hoped she'd be here, waiting for me. I wanted that sign that she saw me, that she wasn't completely gone.

That's all I wanted. One more time of being loved

like that. Of feeling so secure and safe and accepted. There was nothing like it. Of knowing that someone loves you, everything about you. That they understood you and accepted you. There was a security in that. You took it with you throughout the day, that love.

And it could suddenly be taken away from you. Gone. Left with none of it. All because they crashed into a tree. That one split instant meant my mom had been taken from me, and I was left to the mercy of a grandmother who wanted nothing to do with me. She'd thought I'd been nothing but a mistake since my mom had me. I had been alone and scared.

I'd tried to make sure that never happened again. That I didn't count on one person for more than one thing. They could be taken but if they were I wouldn't lose everything. Even then you could only count on yourself. That's where the security was. Knowing no matter what happened you could do it on your own.

But it was never quite the same.

As I'd experienced today. Crying against Uncle Drew, promising to lean on him more, accept more, there was a security in that I couldn't duplicate.

An image of Jamie's face flashed in my mind, but I pushed it out.

I took in my mom's grave marker, the surrounding area. I wouldn't be coming back. There was no point.

Out of my purse, I took the plant clipping I'd brought with me. I dug a small hole in the grass with my fingers. When it was deep enough, I gently placed the clipping in and then patted the dirt around it.

"Here, Momma. I brought you this. I want to leave something with you."

Just as I knew she wasn't there watching me, that in fact I was talking to the air, I knew she wouldn't be seeing the dracaena. Within a few days it'd be sucked up in a lawnmower or die from the transplanting shock. It still felt right to leave it here.

When I stood I didn't feel lighter. I'd always known it probably wouldn't happen. That I wouldn't feel anything. That she really was gone. But it hadn't stopped me from hoping—even secretly imagining—that flying back to see her would mean I could feel her here.

So that was that. I would never feel the safety and peace I'd felt from her again.

From her.

I could have it again. Maybe. From someone else.

Someone who could be taken from me.

Was it better to go on as I had? My life wasn't bad. I had friends. I had my clients. My uncle. Did I have to have more? A few months ago the answer would have been no.

But now... Now there was Jamie's face in my mind again.

This time I didn't push it away.

I'd fought this connection between us. Fought so hard to stop it from growing. But I could feel it. No matter how much time we spent apart. The distances I put between our lives.

What if I stopped fighting? What if I let it happen?

Things might change on my end, but she hadn't said they had on hers. She still had her parents and Riley and her job that she needed to focus on.

Was it worth it to try?

I made my way to the rental and then pulled out my phone. It was early there, what with Oregon being two hours behind. Jamie was an early riser, as I unfortunately had firsthand knowledge of, but this was early even for her. If I sent a text, it might wake her up be-

cause she always had her phone close by in case someone needed her.

I needed her. I needed to do this.

Sierra: I miss you. I can't wait to see you when I get
back. Maybe we could do a movie while cuddling on
the couch?

Jamie

I stared down at my phone, smiling. Smiling. Sierra had
me smiling on the morning after one of the worst days
in my life. I'd wanted a text and boy had she delivered.
She missed me. She wanted a movie and cuddling. Cuddling. Beyond that first night, she hadn't even stayed
long enough for a good snuggle after sex. Sex that always occurred at my place. God, how I'd needed that
text, especially as I now sat outside my mother's work.

If my mom wanted to cross lines and bring her secrets
out in the open, well then here I was.

I watched the insurance agents blearily march their
way into the office, knowing I'd timed it wrong. My
mom wouldn't add a cushion to her commute in case
there was an accident or unexpected lane closures.

Two minutes to the top of the hour, my mother's
Toyota pulled into the lot.

Time for this to end. Hand steady, I opened my door
and stepped out. I was strung so tight it felt like the
slightest brush, a light gust of wind, could snap me.
Most people would take one look at me and turn right
back around. Not my mom. She'd brazen it out.

"Jamie, what are you doing here?" she asked while
getting out. Her smile was firmly in place.

At least my reason for smiling today was a beautiful

woman who injected my life with the very spark my mother had spent her life trying to put out. My mom's only reason for smiling was to try and hide her truth.

Too late.

I stepped forward, going to her. I didn't want her near anything of mine, not even my car. With each step I took, I should be leaving a trail of frost. "No games. You know exactly why I'm here."

Her eyes—clear, I couldn't help noticing, just like I couldn't stop myself from checking her breath: also clear—were staring at me with false innocence. "I'm not trying to play games. I'm trying to get into work. Exactly what you told me I needed to make sure to do. I don't want to be late."

Ah yes, her job. The one I'd secured for her before I'd left to do tattooing full time. I'd wanted her to go with a larger company that paid better benefits and had more opportunities for advancement. The more stability in her life the better.

"Don't worry. This won't take long. It's really simple." I stepped up to her until the tips of my Chucks brushed her flats. "Stay away from Riley. Never go near her again. I've already contacted her school. You're no longer allowed on the grounds."

My mom swallowed, looking around the parking lot before lifting her chin.

"What? You don't want your co-workers to know you lied to your granddaughter and then tried to bum some money off of her?"

"Is that what she told you? This is just a misunderstanding."

The ice inside me, protecting me, protecting her from the rage, thickened. "Do. Not. Call my daughter a liar."

She shook her head, her gaze barely grazing mine.

In shame? Was she finally feeling it for some of her actions? I wasn't sure she was capable anymore.

"That's not what I was doing, I was—"

"No," I cut her off. "It doesn't matter. Whatever you have to say, what excuse you come up with, it doesn't matter."

What a waste. All the time, effort, resources I'd spent on them. All for nothing. I'd wasted so much of my life. With absolutely nothing to show for it. "First Ryan, now me. That's your only family you're alienating. For what? At most you could have got a couple of hundred dollars."

"I know. I just—"

"No. No just. That's your granddaughter."

My mother flushed, a frustrated look flashing.

I stepped back, away from the woman who'd birthed me. How could she not feel the same love in her veins that I did when I looked at Riley? How could that need to protect not be stronger than anything else?

I turned away from her.

This time I did not doubt my resolve. I might not have had the strength to put an end to this for myself, but I did for my daughter.

Chapter Twenty

Sierra

I plopped into the seat in front of my least favorite desk. The one in the office in the back without a window. Oh, well. Stopping and picking up Mickey D's to start the day had been worth it. That jet lag was for real. And whoa, I think I should've gone with the larger coffee. I'd only been gone a few days but there were files and more files waiting for me. I wiggled my fingers over the keyboard and got to it.

As good as it felt to review case notes and set up meetings, my mind wasn't only on the work directly in front of me. I couldn't stop glancing at the time display on the corner of my monitor. Nine forty-five. Nine forty-nine. Nine fifty-two.

Finally it read ten. Wendy would be arriving now.

I pushed my seat back. Speed walking through the halls, I nodded and smiled, but didn't stop to chat. They weren't who I wanted to talk to.

Nope, that would be Wendy. I knocked on her office door, a mix of excitement and trepidation rushing through me, which made for a trippy experience.

Wendy looked up and smiled, in the middle of taking off her coat. "Sierra, come in."

"Thanks. I was hoping to speak with you."

"Of course." She dropped her purse in her desk drawer. "Not too much longer for your fundraiser," she said once I'd taken a seat. "Jordan's certainly excited about it. She's trying not to let on, but it slips when she talks about it. There's some kind of slayer."

"Yes! It's so cool. It's the tattoo we helped design. Jordan even was able to draw part of it."

"Yeah? I'm excited to see how this turns out."

"It's going to be amazing. It's not just me and Jordan who are excited. So are the artists."

One in particular. Jamie, who was using so much of her precious time. Though it helped that Jordan was also involved, which meant Riley didn't mind hanging out while we all worked.

"I have no doubt." She tilted her head, pulling the notepad on her desk closer. "So you wanted to talk to me?"

"Yeah, it's actually about a fundraiser. Another one. I had an idea and I wanted to run it by you."

"A second fundraiser already?" she asked, laughing.

"Yes. I love them. I had no idea. I mean, I kind of always saw them as bumming some money off rich people. But it's so much more. It's trying to solve a problem while creatively highlighting it. I didn't think I had it in me, but I'm finding I do." Or at least a very talented artist was brushing off on me.

"I can see that."

"You have any more you want done, send them my way."

"If only I could. Unfortunately, I need you right where you are. Organizing fundraisers, as nice and important as it is, isn't something we can pay some-one for."

It should be. The government couldn't be expected to focus on such individualized things, as it needed to help as many people as quickly as possible, but that's where we could step in. More specialized. We could make such a difference, have such an impact on our clients' futures. Focus on them not only living their life, but thriving.

"So tell me what your next fundraiser would be." Wendy tapped her pencil against the edge of her desk. The action reminded me of Jamie, who did that when she was thinking.

It was hard to pull my thoughts away from imaging what it would be like if that was a paid position. What it would be like to do that every day. It would bring so much joy.

Nope. Nuh-uh. I needed to focus on what was possible.

I leaned forward in my chair. "Okay, so I was thinking…"

After talking with Wendy I headed back to my dreary desk. I'd just sat back down when my phone chimed.

My heart raced and my stomach went with an all-out flip, jostling the hash browns I'd had.

Jamie: Hi there. I hope you're having a good day. I was wondering if we could get together tonight. I would really like to see you.

God I wanted to see her, throw myself in her arms.

Sierra: It's going good. Busy. Crazy busy. There's a lot of catching up at work I need to do. It's going to be a long one.

Jamie: I understand. I have some artwork for the fund-raiser I'd like to show you.

Sierra: Can't wait to see it. But I'd be there anyways, no artwork needed, just warning you it might be late.

There was a long pause before another response came in.

Jamie: I'll be here. Come whenever you can. Doesn't matter how late.

Sierra: Will do.

I stared down at the screen. I could stop here.

No, I was going to do this. My fingers trembled and I hit the wrong key, but for once thank god for auto-correct as it knew what I meant.

Sierra: I need a Jamie hug.

Chapter Twenty-One

Sierra

"Sorry, I couldn't make it earlier," I said through my open window as I parked in the back alley of Thorn & Thistle.

Jamie stood next to her own car, her hands shoved into her pockets. She shrugged. "I told you whenever and I meant it."

Getting out of the car, I was greeted by Jamie pushing me back against my door and pressing a kiss to my lips.

My body buzzed. One week. It'd been one week since we touched. My appropriate length of time to go between seeing each other. But god I'd missed this.

No, I'd missed so much more. I'd missed the way she always went to interlace our fingers. I'd missed the way she listened to me like what I had to say was important. I'd missed her foot pressed against mine and feeling centered. But instead of pulling away from those, I leaned toward her.

Jamie's hand curled around the back of my neck, holding me against her. Her mouth opened and I couldn't resist.

I slipped my tongue into her mouth, moaning at how

eagerly I was welcomed. I caught faint traces of peppermint, causing my tongue to tingle. It was new and unexpected, but I missed that homey, sweet taste I'd come to know.

"Hi," she said, squeezing my hip.

"Hi."

"Okay, let's get you that hug. I, uh, probably should have started with that, but I got carried away."

"I don't mind. Not one bit." I stepped into the arms she held outstretched for me. I wrapped my arms around her neck, rested my head on her shoulder, closed my eyes, and just breathed her in.

She enfolded me in her arms, surrounding me in her strength, her support.

God it felt good. Necessary. It'd been so long.

A long while later, she pulled away, smiling down into my face. "Good?"

"One more."

This one lasted even longer than the first, but I was starved for it. For her.

"Okay," I said. "That should hold me. You said you had something to show me."

"I do." She grabbed my hand and interlaced our fingers as she led me to the back of her SUV.

She popped open the back. Between the dome light and the light above the shop, I could easily see the large cardboard box taking up most of her cargo area. In the space next to it was a plant in a pot with foil paper wrapped around it and a bow.

"You have a kalanchoe."

"*You* have one, if you want it."

I gasped and stepped closer. I inspected the droopy leaves and the brown ones that had fallen off, lying on top of the dried-out soil. There was only the slightest bit of green at the stem. It would need so much care. "Yes! I definitely want it."

"I thought you would."

I kissed her cheek. "You know how to spoil a gal."

A pleased smile on her face, Jamie leaned into the back of her car. My gaze dropped to her ass. So high and firm and tight. It'd make a great plate to eat a meal off of. Hello there, idea for our next date.

She stood and turned and held up a large poster board. Thoughts of her ass vanished.

I blinked but it wasn't enough to catch the tears. On the poster were the pictures of the different tattoos the artists had designed.

They'd done this. They'd done this for the kids. All to show them that they mattered and their dreams were important.

"Oh my god. They're beautiful."

"Yeah. They came out pretty great." She looked at me with open affection as I sniffed and tried to shut off the tear faucet. "This is what will go on the front desk in the lobby."

Awed, I leaned closer, trying to see each tattoo.

"Save your eyes. I also had individual displays made." She bent over and when she straightened she had an 11x14 of our slayer.

I vibrated. "I need this on me like now."

"Not too much longer." She smiled at me, her closed lip one, and then shook her head. "We'll see how my self-control holds out."

Feeling more comfortable, less exposed, with the direction the conversation had taken, I backed up and tucked my ass up against her, grinding against her front. "I'll do my best to behave but…"

She groaned and set the poster aside. "Be kind to me. There's going to be press there."

"I know. I'm the one who called them."

Keeping me tucked against her with a hand on my hip, she reached and grabbed the next one off the pile.

"Oh, wow." It was of a skeleton face with dark piercing eyes. The bones of the face didn't quite fit together, like they'd been broken and never healed. "Whose is that?"

Jamie put her chin on my shoulder. "I forget sometimes that you're not in the scene and don't know just by looking at them. It's MJ's."

"It's good. Dark, but good."

"Kind of fitting. You can tell hers by the edging and shading. It just pops. This—" She pointed to the dark abyss of the eyes. "Is why I started working with her. I wanted to stay sharp and keep learning and she's the best."

Yeah, it was nice, great even, but it didn't compare to Jamie's. "I think you are the best."

She snorted. "And you're not biased at all."

"Nope. Not a bit. Now show me the next one."

She set MJ's aside and produced one that was paint splatters with the world reflected in them. "Who do you think did this one?" she asked. She slowly tilted it in different directions, so I could see it from all angles.

Hm. I stared at the tattoo as a whole. There was a mix of styles from the bright paint splotches to the whimsical pieces of the earth inside, giving it an almost bohemian feel. I took that with what I knew of the other artists. "Maya, because of how much is going on."

"Yup. She's made busy her thing."

I gasped before Jamie even had the next poster free

of the box. "Cassie. It's Cassie's. I can feel it." I clutched my chest.

"Yeah. I don't know how she does it. It's not something that can be taught." She stared at it for a few more seconds and then shook her head as if wowed all over, her hair brushing against mine.

I liked that she wasn't jealous of her fellow artists in what I knew could be a cutthroat business, instead ready to celebrate them and their talents.

Jamie revealed the last poster.

"Oh. I would have known it was Vivian's even if it wasn't the only one left. I recognize those swirls and loops." Once I'd seen a client of hers leaving with a beautiful necklace of lace around their neck. The delicate detail had looked so real, I'd wanted to reach out and touch it just to be certain that I wouldn't be able to feel the texture.

"Yup. She's the best at the jewelry pieces."

The one Vivian had designed looked like a pin. I knew there was some fancy name for them. We'd found a ton of them at my grandmother's house. At least Vivian's design was nothing like my grandmother would have worn. In the center of the pin was a bright red heart, looking like it'd been torn from someone's chest, surrounded by a circle of filigree and diamonds at the top and bottom.

I leaned my head back against Jamie's shoulder. "These are amazing. I can't believe you guys are making this happen."

Jamie kissed my temple. "*We* are." She wrapped her arm around my waist and drew me even tighter to her. "I didn't know how much I needed this."

I twisted my head, trying to get a look at her face, having a hard time figuring out her tone. I'd caught both anger and sadness. I studied her jawline, which was my barometer of how she was doing. It was definitely firmer than normal.

She stared out into the darkness of the alley. "It's nice to put my energy toward something where good comes out of it."

"I think you do plenty, but I'm glad you like doing it. Maybe we shouldn't stop with this one."

"Hm, maybe." Jamie placed another kiss to my head and then pulled away to pack everything up. "Did you have a chance to eat?"

"Nope."

"Hop in."

Once I was in and buckled in her very clean car, like freakishly clean, I angled toward her.

"Anywhere special you wanted to go?" she asked.

"Nope. You choose."

"Just the answer I was hoping for."

With those intriguing—and could it be playful?—words, she started driving toward Goose Hollow.

With her alternative rock music playing in the background—a choice, I was sure, because she liked me singing along to her songs, even though I didn't know all the words—I stared at her profile in the passing streetlights and the glow of oncoming headlights. I wanted to look at this face every day.

She parked on a side street and since it was after seven it was free. I got out of the car and went around to meet her at the bumper, my heart beating erratically.

Jamie snagged my hand and my attention. "God it's good to see you."

"You too." And it was. So good. Scary how much. I squeezed her hand. "Which way?"

She shrugged. "Don't really have a plan. I was thinking we could just walk and find somewhere that looks promising."

I smiled and pressed closer into her side and then hooked my arm around her waist. "You mean we don't have to be back in time for the news?"

The lines around her eyes didn't even tighten the slightest bit, and she didn't shoot me a look. I would've thought I'd miss that special glower she gave me, but no, this relaxed smile was better. "Not tonight."

Chapter Twenty-Two

Jamie

Sierra and I peered into a sandwich shop. There were half a dozen iron tables and chairs with ornate scrolls. I glanced at her out of the corner of my eye and found her already doing the same. We shook our heads.

Next we hit an Italian food place. She wrinkled her nose.

"Moving on," I said.

I swung our entwined hands as we walked, unable to stop myself. I was just happy. I'd been happy all day at the thought of seeing her. Then I'd received her text that she wanted to see me, not because of the art I had needed to show her, but because she wanted a hug—a hug of all things—from me. Winning fan favorite for best tattooer couldn't beat those words.

As we turned another corner, neither of us paused at the restaurant with its menu posted behind a glass display and candles flickering inside.

She waited for a car to pass and then we jaywalked to the other side of the street.

"Um, I hope you have a good sense of direction because I have no idea how to get back to where I parked."

Sierra pulled to a stop and since our hands were

connected so did I. Her eyes twinkled up at me, lifting my mood impossibly higher.

"You don't know which way we came from?" she asked.

"Well…" I twisted to look around us. "Originally, that way, I think." I pointed to the left with my free hand. But when I turned the other way that seemed kind of familiar. "Or back there. It's hard to know. We've taken a lot of turns."

"Two." She held up as many fingers. "We've taken two turns and parked that way."

I looked in the direction she indicated. "Huh. That would've been my last guess."

She pumped her fist in the air. "Finally! I've finally found a flaw with you. I mean, it's not much of one— more like a cute quirk—but I'll take it."

"Says the social worker organizing a fundraiser because she saw a need not being met."

Sierra's smile dimmed. "That I left you with. Sorry again about that."

"It really is okay. Though next time something comes up, I wouldn't mind being there with you." *Mind.* Knowing me, I'd be demanding it. I hadn't liked being so far away and not knowing what she might be facing and if she needed help.

"Next time I might insist you come with me." Before I could respond to that ground-shattering statement, she tugged on my hand. "Come on. Let's keep going."

Half a block later her pace picked up. She stared at a small storefront with yellow lights and painted writing all over the windows, advertising everything from tacos to pad thai.

Through the propped open door I could see a long

counter laid out like a sub-making station. Whatever was in the metal bins was steaming.

I put on the brakes. "That looks like food poisoning waiting to happen."

She nodded, her smile bright. "These places are the best. You're either sick for two days and want to die or it's the best food you ever ate."

"Or it's the best food and later you want to die."

She inclined her head toward me. "Point." She gave the questionable restaurant another long look.

Well, tonight had already been on track to be memorable. Why not?

"Let's try it," I said.

"Yeah?"

"Yeah." I pulled her across the street with me, her laughter drowning out the sound of the approaching MAX train.

I stepped in and took an appreciative sniff. It smelled good. I caught hints of garlic and cumin and peppers. At the counter I ordered chicken enchiladas and Sierra went with carnitas tacos.

We took a seat at one of the only five tables—hopefully not a sign that they didn't need more because everyone else knew to stay away.

"Here," she said pulling out her phone and motioning me closer. "I want to get a before picture of us. Hopefully we'll still be looking this good after."

I leaned my head close to hers and waited for the snap.

Her fingers flew over the screen and then she nodded. "There. Posted."

I was going to be making an appearance on her social media accounts. "You should have gotten one with the art in the background so you could tease it."

"No. I wanted one of us."

I pressed my foot against Sierra's.

"So tell me what's going on with you," she said. "I'm out of the loop."

I traced a pirate ship in her freckles while I answered. "A lot. You missed an actually not boring week."

She gave me a look while she extended her arm across the table, so I'd have more room to work with. "Says the woman who gets to spend it doing awesome tattoos on cool people."

I nodded, my lips twitching. The thing with Sierra was when she said cool people she didn't mean just people that were trendy or had some quality that made people stare. Out of my clients this week she'd probably think the seventy-year-old woman I'd given her first tattoo—a hummingbird to honor her mother—was the coolest of the bunch.

"So fill me in. What happened?"

Here it was, what I never wanted to have to confess. That I'd failed to help someone. That I might not be able to fix everything. What reason would someone have to like me, love me? But Sierra had already seen that. She'd seen my parents and she was still here, still sitting across from me, smiling at me.

"My mom went to Riley's school and asked her for money."

"Whoa. That's a big boundary to cross." She made a sympathetic face and ran her finger along the outside of my hand.

"Too big." Vocalizing my mom's actions didn't re-ignite the cold burn of anger like I feared. I'd grown numb to it.

Her brown eyes were serious as she stared across the table at me.

It used to be that if I didn't see those beautiful browns twinkling or paired with her big smile, I was sure I was responsible for bringing her down. Now I knew the smile was not only a sign of happiness, but a shield. And sometimes she let me see a little more.

"How did Riley feel about it?"

My chest felt too small to hold the rush of emotions. That she even thought to ask about my daughter. Oh, this woman, she was more than getting under my skin, she was burrowing into my heart.

"Not good at first. She blamed me." I told her what my mother had done and what Riley had said, and more, I told her how it'd made me feel.

I was wrong. The anger wasn't so much going away, but going deeper, further into me.

"Did you talk to your mom?"

"Oh, yeah. Went about as you'd expect. It was all a misunderstanding, of course. I really got through to her. I've received two texts since then. One asking me for the name of their insurance agent and the other wishing Nicki a happy birthday. Her birthday's not for another two months."

And damned if my stomach hadn't clenched when I'd read that text, seen further proof that things were escalating with them.

"How did you respond?"

"I didn't." And I wouldn't. Not until I knew exactly how to go about it.

She slid her feet around mine, trapping them in between. Our knees pressed together. "Is that what you want to do? Keep ignoring them?"

I wiped my hand over my face. "I don't know. I don't know what to do next. I could really use your help figuring it out." I'd asked for help and the world didn't shatter. I didn't shatter.

Sierra's hand clutched mine and she sat up straighter. "Of course, I'll help. Where are you at now? How are you feeling?"

"I don't want them in my life. I don't want to keep living like I have. But I don't know whether to ignore them completely. Do I tell them goodbye? Leave the door open if they get help? Not contact them at all?"

"You could always tell them where you're at. Explain how you're feeling and what you want—for them to get help. Give them one last chance. Then lay out the consequences if they don't."

"An intervention."

She shrugged. "It's an option."

I nodded. "Yeah, I like that. Their choice and then I'm done."

Squeezing my hand, she gave me a small smile that seemed like it was just for me. Opposed to her bright, light-up-the-room ones, this one shined only on me. "As someone that just had some closure, I recommend it."

"I'm going to do it." I pulled out my phone. Sierra's eyes widened, obviously not expecting me to do it here and now, but I had a plan, there was no reason to wait.

"Hey, Mom," I said when she answered.

"Jamie, I thought—"

"I wanted to come by and talk to you and Dad. Will you be home on Friday night?" My last customer of the night was a regular who would understand. I'd come in on a day off if I had to. I needed to get this done. Closure, like Sierra said.

"Yes, we should be."

"I'll see you then." I hit end, having nothing more to say until then.

I glanced up at Sierra. "All right, it's set."

"I'm proud of you."

My chest tightened. Never. Never would I have expected those words from someone when I was asking for help, admitting my weaknesses. And it wasn't just the words. It was the look in her eyes, the admiration I could so plainly see.

"Did you want me there? I've never led an intervention, but if you think my being there would help, I'm willing."

"Thanks for offering, but I need the separation on this one. This has a good chance of getting nasty and things will be said I don't want my girlfriend to hear."

Her palm went damp against mine.

Ah, yes. Girlfriend. I'd used the word.

Girlfriend was a scary thing for her, but she wasn't alone. Girlfriend meant I had a place in her life. It would mean I would have to fit into her life and hope she liked what she saw.

Before I always had a role, was needed for something. That was not the case with Sierra.

She swallowed loud enough for me to be able to hear across the table, but after a fraught second, she caressed my pinkie with her thumb. "Whatever you or they said wouldn't affect what I thought of you."

And just what did she think of me?

She pulled her hand away, but it was okay because she used it to cup my cheek, lightly scratching with her pink polished nails. "But I understand."

If only I could be certain we could forge a bond that benefitted both of us.

The food was a start. Like she'd predicted, it was the best meal ever. Both the enchiladas and the company.

Once we were finished, Sierra led us back to my car with no problem.

Seat belt on, I looked to her. "Where to next? I have all night."

She laid her head back on the headrest and seemed to think it over.

"Anywhere you want," I said. "We could go meet up with your friends if you want."

No more parents. No more talk of the fundraiser. Just something for us tonight, doing it together. I could meet with her friends again. This time I was determined it would end better.

She turned to look at me. "Home. Either yours or mine. I'm ready for that movie and a cuddle."

"I mean it, whatever you want to do."

"That's what I want."

This incredible woman who was being offered the chance to pick anywhere or anything of her choosing was choosing me. Where the only entertainment was me. There had to be a point where I started believing her that this was, that *I* was, what she wanted.

That time was now.

Sierra

I rushed into the room at Haven Bridge, but I was late and everyone was already seated. "Dang it."

Trey snickered from the comfy green chair.

This is what I got for getting caught up in looking at websites of other nonprofits. Now I was stuck with the middle couch cushion unless I wanted to kick it on the floor. Not happening. I had total respect for our janitorial staff, but a lot of times it felt like they were fighting a losing battle.

I sat on the torture device everyone had so kindly left for me and tossed a handful of fruit snack packs onto the table.

"All right, are we ready?" Everyone nodded except for Silvia who stayed huddled against the arm of the couch on my left side. "Anyone have anything they want to talk about?"

After waiting a few seconds for a response, Roger leaned forward. "I do."

"Go for it."

I sat back and listened to what started as Roger complaining about someone stealing his socks. It turned into a debate about whether it'd be better to live in a studio apartment dump or a nice place and have a roommate.

"It'll always be the studio," argued Roger. "With a roommate you'd always have to watch your back."

That got a lot of nods.

When no one else responded, I leaned forward. "Okay if I say something?" I asked. At their nods I slid forward. "I mean, I agree that the only person you can control is yourself, but I don't necessarily think every single roommate is going to be someone you have to guard against. Plus there's locks, and cameras if needed. But there's a chance you could have more than a roommate. You could have a friend, a confidant, someone to have your back."

Roger stared at me like my lips had started spouting straight-up bullshit.

I got it. I'd always agreed with him on some level. Until Jamie. In Jamie I'd been reminded how good it felt to have someone filling multiple roles in my life. There was a richness and depth in that. Not only was I getting closer with Jamie but Ashley and Uncle Drew. With everyone in my life. It was becoming a mass of layers.

"Anything else?" I asked. At their silence I continued, "Okay, well, this week I'd love for you to think of what gives you strength."

"Money," Trey said, probably not joking.

"Gotta have a job for that," one of the other kids flung out.

"That's why I'm going to work in software so I can bring in major bank," Trey said, already trying the haughty rich man look on with his nose in the air.

"Do you even know how to code?"

"I'll learn."

"I'm going to do something I actually like," Roger said. He gave Trey a look. "And know."

Next to me, Silvia sat forward. "Music gives me strength," she said. Her voice was music in itself, a sad song of loss and sorrow and pain.

At least we got streaming music sites at the center. She could still have access to some music. That was something.

But was it enough? We didn't have anything more to give her.

As they left, the kids weren't the only ones who needed to dwell on their futures and what made them happy.

Chapter Twenty-Three

Jamie

Outside my parents' house, I rested against the bumper of my car, staring up at the night sky. Just on time came the obnoxious rumble of an overpriced toy.

"Hey," Ryan said, coming to lean against the bumper with me.

"Thanks for being here. I know you said you were done."

He shrugged. "I am done. I'm not here for them, I'm here for you."

"Thanks," I wheezed. I pushed up from my car and hugged him. I squeezed him tight, leaning into him.

Pulling back, he gave me a worried look.

Okay, so yeah, our hugs usually consisted of me smacking his back, or squeezing his shoulders, trying to give him strength. But this time, I was the one who needed it.

We walked up to the house, our steps not impeded by tall grass or trash bags or lawn ornaments. Had my dad finally done it or had one of the neighbors gotten sick of looking at it?

Going to knock, I froze at the sight of the lit doorbell button. I kept my finger suspended over that little yellow glow before pushing it. I hadn't heard that chime in years. Unlike then I wasn't wary of what would be outside the door, I was wary of who was behind it.

It was only a few seconds before the door opened and my mom was there with a wide smile. "Hi, come on in. I'm so glad you're both here."

This was the weeknight mother of my childhood. She smiled and seemed perfectly normal and allowed me to believe things weren't that bad. I knew better now. That smile wasn't to be trusted. My mom wasn't to be trusted.

I stepped inside, not saying a word. Everything that I needed to say was written on a piece of paper.

A fake florally smell filled the house, but underneath I still detected a staleness as if whatever had been sprayed to hide it wasn't quite up to the job. Was it the same with the clean-looking house? If I opened a closet door would it be filled with bags of trash?

I didn't care enough to go looking.

"We're glad you're here. We have some news to tell you."

I nodded and headed to the living room. My brother shot me a warning glance as if to say not to believe whatever they were going to say. He didn't need to worry on that front. Not anymore.

The room was quiet and for the first time in a long time, the TV was off. My father stood as we entered the room. He was dressed in clean jeans and a green polo, not just a dingy undershirt.

"Hey, honey." He hugged me, the movement awkward since I kept my arms at my sides. "I'm glad to see you."

When I didn't give him a response, he turned to Ryan. "Son, I'm glad you're here." Seeming to read my brother's body language, he didn't go in for a hug, instead offering a smile.

Turning away, I went and took my customary seat by the fireplace. Ryan opted for his usual of standing and facing our parents like a human bullshit detector primed to go off. Everything I'd read said to be open and not defensive with them, down to our posture, but this was Ryan. I couldn't remember the last time he'd sat with us.

Scooting to the edge of the sofa, my mom smiled. "So as you can see your father and I are doing much better." Her gaze went from me to my brother and back to me where it stayed. "Everything is going to be all right. We even called about meetings."

For one brief second my heart soared. They were— Reality slammed into me. Every word needed to be examined for any possible escape routes.

"You've quit drinking and are going to meetings?" I asked.

"No. But now we know where they are if we let things get too far again."

The crash of my hopes didn't even hurt. They hadn't gotten very high. I didn't know that they even could anymore. Not after being dashed so many times.

"We hardly do it anymore," my mom rushed to add. "Only to relax on the weekends. You'll see. We've changed a lot. We—" She shot a quick look at my dad who nodded at her. "We see now that it got too out of hand and it can't happen again."

I'd been waiting for this acknowledgment, these very words, for so long. Through school when I had to quit soccer to be available for Ryan. When they missed Riley's first birthday party because it happened to fall on a weekend. When I had to set up automatic bill pay because they kept forgetting to pay them. Now that it was happening it wasn't enough.

The yard. The doorbell. The "seeing the light." Not enough. Their actions were thin. Could revert back at any time. There wasn't even a promise to maintain it.

The silence got heavier in the room as we stared at each other. My mom buckled first, not able to withstand the weight of close scrutiny. She clasped her hands together in her lap, her fingers twirling restlessly like a pile of snakes writhing around each other.

"So what was it you wanted to talk to us about?"

My jaw clenched tight. A shooting pain radiated all the way up to my temple, forcing me to relax it.

A talk. To her this was just a talk.

"I want to read something to you. I want you to listen, really listen. It's not so much about you, but me."

"Well, that sounds serious." She leaned forward, suddenly the attentive mother. "Go ahead, honey. Whatever you need."

It was hard not to imagine what it would be like if this were real. If I had a parent who wanted to listen to me with no other motive than being interested in me and my life.

I might not have a parent who was interested. But I did have Sierra. I'd experienced some of that with her.

"After she's done, I've got something too," Ryan said.

I pulled out my paper and stared down at my truth. My hands didn't tremble and I knew when I spoke my voice would be steady. I'd let my emotions out when I wrote it.

"First I'd like to say that I love you guys, probably always will. This is about my life and what it's been like because of your drinking. It wasn't all bad and terrible. I have some great memories. Like the time you took us to the arcade and let Ryan and me play all afternoon. I remember bowling. And my favorite when we'd have movie night and get pizza from that place on the corner before it closed down. I liked doing yard work with you, Dad, and planting the flowers at the end of spring with you, Mom."

I checked in to see if they were listening, if this was having any effect at all. My parents looked at each other and shared a smile. Smiling because they too were remembering good memories or because they thought this little con was going to work?

"I wish there were more memories like that," I continued. "Unfortunately, they aren't the first things I think of about my childhood. No, I think about waking up on the weekends and while other kids were going to the living room to turn on cartoons and eat their cereal, I was checking to make sure you were still breathing. I think about searching the house for spare change and walking Ryan to Taco Bell and getting a burrito to share because that's all the money I'd found. I remember worrying if we'd have enough to pay the electricity and you coming home with bottles from the liquor store."

I folded my piece of paper back up. I didn't need it for this last part. "I don't want any more memories of you and alcohol."

Their smiles were gone now. I could feel the defensiveness rolling in. Any window we had to try and get through to them was shutting. I nodded at Ryan.

My mother opened her mouth, but one look from my brother silenced her.

"I don't have those memories that Jamie was talking about. I don't remember bowling or pizza nights. I do remember Taco Bell. I remember the times she gave me her half because I was still hungry. I didn't know then that meant she went without. I remember me and Jamie going outside to play and throw a ball around. I knew it was early on the weekends. I didn't know it was because she was trying to protect me from having to see you guys sleeping it off in the living room."

He turned his head and looked right at me. The stoic face that I'd become so familiar with as he'd grown into his teens and then adulthood faded and I saw the young boy I'd helped pack his bag for his first sleepover.

"Most of all I remember knowing that I was loved. Because of Jamie. She looked out for me. You guys were my parents in name, but Jamie was in action. That's what I remember."

My chest squeezed tight. I blinked tears back because I didn't want to miss even a second of him looking at me with such open love.

He inclined his head to me in the smallest of nods and then looked back at our parents. "I'd like to have a mother and father, to have that relationship we should have. It's not too late."

Oh, my sweet Ryan. He still had it too. The longing of a child for stable, loving parents no matter how many times they'd proven they weren't capable of being that.

My mother held out her hands, her cheeks pale in a way that couldn't be faked. "But we're better. We're not going to get like that again. Everything will be fine. It'll go back to the way it was."

The way it was. Me trying to catch them if they went into another downward spiral and keep them from harming themselves or someone else. Me swooping in if something arose. Me giving and giving and them taking and taking.

"I don't believe you," I said.

I looked first at my mother and then my dad. I let myself really see them, as they were now. The ruddiness of their cheeks and noses, the puffiness of their skin. How dull my mother's hair looked.

"It's time for me to take back my life. I won't be coming back here unless you're sober. I hope you can find the will to do it, if not for me, or Ryan, or Riley, then for yourselves."

My mother jumped to her feet. "You can't just kick us out of our granddaughter's life."

"I'm not. Your actions did."

I went and stood by Ryan.

Turning toward me, he said, "I'm good."

I nodded and together we turned and walked out of the room.

I wasn't alone.

Well hell. I just might break down crying after all.

They didn't call after us, didn't come rushing up to us with pleas and promises on their lips.

And I accepted it.

At the curb I turned to my brother and wrapped him in a hug. This time we leaned on each other equally for a long time.

"Thank you for coming tonight."

"Thank you for taking care of me all those years."

"Any time."

"Back at you, sis. Any time."

"Yeah?" I stared at him, his face having remained open to me. It made me hopeful that we could get back to the closeness we'd had as kids. I wanted that. I missed him so damn much. "Do you want to go get something to eat?"

"I can't tonight, but soon, okay? Call me."

I nodded, hoping he meant it.

I got in my car and thought of my future. I wanted to have a partnership with someone. No, not someone: Sierra. I wanted a partnership with Sierra. It was time that I got it.

Chapter Twenty-Four

Sierra

At the sound of footsteps approaching, I flung open the door.

Jamie blinked and then came into my outstretched arms.

Holding her tight, I stayed alert for signs of tears, my knees braced to support her weight if she collapsed into me. She stayed upright, her grip firm. She leaned down and pressed her nose against my neck, inhaling deeply.

Had I been wrong and her parents were receptive?

Stepping back, I searched her face. It took a moment to see past the "keep calm I've got this" expression. But there, in the tightness around her jaw, the way it thinned her lips, I found my answer. "I'm sorry."

She cupped my face. Using her thumb, she traced the outline of my lips and then pulled them up into a smile. "I'm not."

"No?"

Jamie was a realist, something I appreciated and respected about her, but I knew there was a part of her, a part that I wanted to stand guard over and protect, that still had hope. I was sure that part had been hoping for a different outcome.

"No." She pressed a quick kiss on my lips and then moved to below my eye where I had a darker cluster of freckles. "The only thing I'm sorry about is wasting so many years. Taking care of them had become some sick kind of achievement for me. I took pride in it. That's not love, it's some screwed-up codependency. It needed to end."

She did seem lighter. Relieving yourself of the two alcoholics you've been caring for from your shoulders would lighten anyone.

She reached for my hands, squeezing our fingers together. "I've got to let them live their life and I need to live mine. I haven't been doing so good on that last part and I'm going to change that."

Her eyes bored into mine. That innocent, hopeful part of her was looking at me. Like I was the source of the hope.

My pulse took off. It was here. This went beyond dating, beyond a relationship. We'd traveled into support and necessity territory. We'd become attached. It didn't matter how much time passed between seeing each other, it didn't matter if we went on dates. It'd been about feelings and what we found in each other.

I'd let the silence go too long. Even though our hands were still entwined, I could feel her pulling back, protecting herself.

She didn't need to. Not now.

I squeezed her hands. "I am so proud of you."

Her lips curved, but oh, it was her eyes, that shined so bright. "Thank you. Maybe it's still coming, but I don't feel guilty. It's all relief."

"I hope it stays that way, but if not, I'll be here to remind you that you did everything you could and you deserve a life."

"You will, huh?" Jamie stepped back, her gaze traveling over me, taking in my leggings and baggy shirt. "I'd like that."

I searched her eyes, trying to figure out what exactly she needed from me. More talking? Venting? Sharing? Physical touch? That seemed way too easy. But then didn't Jamie make everything easier?

"So, I, um, brought something."

Clued in by the blush starting to spread over her cheeks, I stepped closer, cupping the heat. "What kind of something?"

"The kind that needs to be seen in your bedroom."

"Ohh. My favorite kind." I grabbed her hand and started in the direction of my room.

Once we were inside and the door was firmly shut and locked, Jamie slid her ever-present backpack from her shoulder. She crouched on the floor. My gaze dropped to her ass, staying there until she turned and I got a look at what she held in her hands.

A dildo lay across her palm.

"I thought you might, um, want to use this on me. Only—"

"Oh, yeah." I grabbed it out of her hand. "Look how pretty, all purple and glittery. And there's a switch and it lights up. It has LEDs."

"Yeah, I'm not sure how I feel about lights going inside me."

"Oh, they're going inside you. Deep, deep inside." I winked. "So are you ready to try this baby out?"

Laughing, Jamie toed her shoes off. "What you lack in romance, you make up for in enthusiasm."

I turned and caged her between myself and the nightstand. "Do you want someone who tries to please you with movies and walks on the beach or by fucking you with a dildo and making you orgasm out of your mind?"

Jamie widened her stance and pulled me closer with a hand on each hip. "That one," she said, kissing me. "That one sounds good."

"That's what I thought. Now hurry up and get naked so we can make that happen."

Jamie grinned. Oh what a beautiful sight, especially on such an emotional night for her. It was that twist of her lips that held my attention even as she shed her shirt and then her pants.

I stepped back and likewise got naked. Yes, this experience was for her, but this incredible woman liked me naked.

Once I was completely bare, I crawled on the bed, sliding over her until we were face to face. "Now just lay back and I'll take care of everything."

An odd expression crossed her face. The desire was still there, along with the endearing hint of embarrassment, but something else softer, like wonder.

"I know," she said. "I know you will."

This was for her, to give her something she seemed uncomfortable asking for.

But I needed it too. To give it to her.

Ready, beyond ready, for my mission, I placed one chaste kiss on her lips. Another went right above them on her soccer injury scar.

From there I hit the hollow of her throat that never failed to produce a shiver.

I slowly moved my way down her body, kissing every inch of exposed skin. I cataloged each reaction, from the tiniest sighs, to the way she bit her lip when I licked her nipples. I'd never before needed to worry about memorizing every response to be able to use that knowledge in the future to drive someone wild.

By the time I reached her belly button, she was moaning, her body twisting on the sheets.

Oh, she did make the best noises.

"Sierra," she panted. "Sierra, please."

I glanced up the length of her body as I mouthed at her hip bone. "Mm?"

Her hips lifted off the bed, pressing into my face. "Please, I'm dying."

"But I'm not done yet. There's so much more I want to explore."

She groaned and slammed her hips back down to the mattress. "Ugh."

I gave her hip a soothing pat and then got back to my very important work. Operation Leave-Not-One-Part-Of-Her-Untouched was going very well.

Spreading her legs to make room for myself, I smiled at the way her body tensed and froze, obviously anticipating my next destination.

Nah. If I touched her pussy it'd be over for both of us.

I worked my way down her legs, delighting at how sensitive she was behind her knees. Next I got distracted at the non-erogenous zone for her, but very much so for me, of her calves and thighs. I caressed and massaged them, pushing my thumbs into the hard, large muscles.

"Sierra," she said, pounding her fists on the mattress.

Her eyes glittered. She looked close already.

She wasn't the only one.

I only had to be near her to be aroused and getting to touch her, kiss her, breathe her in—well, I was right there with her.

Leaning up on my knees, I gently threaded my finger

through her brown, trimmed hair and then down to her pussy lips.

"Look at how wet you are. You're excited for this." I slid my fingers through the wetness gathered there.

"I'm excited by you," she said, her hips rocking into my hand before settling again.

I brought my fingers to my nose and inhaled deeply. "Yeah, you are." Holding her gaze, I sucked the tip of my fingers.

Her eyes latched on as I licked every bit of her essence away.

She gasped and bucked.

I reached for the dildo. She was trusting me with this. To make it good for her. I wouldn't let her down.

Jamie

I lay back on the bed, literally and figuratively wide open for Sierra.

She rose on her knees, the gleam of fire in her eyes snatching my breath. That fire was from looking at me, from being here with me.

Tonight I just wanted to experience this with her. To take what she wanted to give.

I could be gracious like that. We were talking about orgasms here.

Her finger went from slowly sliding up and down the entrance of my pussy to slipping inside me. God, that touch felt like it went so much deeper than the length of her finger, like she was going to my core.

She rocked her finger back and forth, a smooth, even rhythm. I let my legs fall all the way open and any lingering uncomfortableness fled. This was Sierra. There was no shame for my desires, no judgment. I released the moan in my throat, letting her know how much I enjoyed this and if that didn't get it across, my humping her hand sure would.

Slowly, torturously so, she withdrew her finger, rubbing against my sensitive flesh.

She leaned up and grinned down at me. "Ready?"

I ground my heels into the bed. "Yes." God yes.

"Me too." She reached to her side and I knew she was grabbing the dildo but I didn't look away from her eyes. I stared into those brown depths as the toy rubbed against my entrance, cold after her fingers, but very welcome.

She slid it inside me.

"Oh, that's pretty," she said.

I propped myself on my elbows and looked down. She hadn't turned on any weird lights. It was just me she was looking at. Wet for her. From her touch. From everything about her.

She rocked the dildo inside me and I flopped back on the bed. I groaned, loving the feeling of fullness but more loving knowing her hand controlled it.

I was more connected right now, with her, with a piece of silicone in me, than I ever had been when I'd had a flesh and blood penis in me.

Harder. She pushed it harder. Her grin my warning, she slowly slid it out of me only to slam it back in. She kept at that same rhythm—slow, so damn slow where I felt it sliding over my nerves, and then pushing it in with force.

"Mm. Yes, like that." I was being loud and demanding and I didn't care.

And she let me.

Her flushed cheeks and large pupils reassured me it was turning her on too. There was no hurt there that I liked this inanimate object, no jealousy that I was getting too much pleasure from it.

"Faster, please. Faster."

Sierra rose up higher and met my pleas with another deep thrust. She drove it in and out of me. Her breasts shook with each action, her face fierce in concentration, the perfect match to what she was doing to my body.

So fast. So far. So deep. My hips lifted off the bed, trying to catch more of it.

"You're so wet, I can hear it. It's running out of you and almost reaching my hand. Let me feel it."

My muscles tightened, pushing up into her. The promise of ecstasy lay just out of reach. I wanted it.

"Almost…so close…need…"

Sierra leaned up, her hips brushed against my inner thighs. I could feel her around me, everywhere.

Complete, I let go.

The pleasure crashed over me. It wiped out all thoughts of the past, what had happened tonight, leaving only now.

Awareness slowly crept in and I blinked, liking the sensation of coming back to myself surrounded by greenery. Sierra lay between my legs, her cheek resting on my stomach. I reached down and ran my fingers through the thick strands of her hair.

"Thank you," I said. My voice sounded ragged and I wondered how loud I had gotten at the end. I was too wrung out to get all uptight because of what her roommate might have heard.

She kissed my stomach. "It was my pleasure."

I continued to caress her. Energy was coming back to me, enough that I wanted to keep touching her, to make sure I gave her the pleasure she gave me.

"Come here," I said, trying to drag her closer, over

me. She helped me out by climbing up me until we were face to face and I could kiss her. Our tongues lazily slid against each other and then I rolled so she was beneath me.

She smiled and wrapped her legs around my waist, squeezing tight. I slid my fingers to her wet opening. Wet from what she had done to me. Overwhelmed by a rush of gratitude and affection, I pressed a kiss to her neck and rubbed her clit.

She grabbed my wrist. "Not tonight. Tonight was for you."

"But—"

"Please."

My pulse that had started to slow, spiked right back up. But I had to do this for her. I needed to—

Shut up. I needed to shut up and just enjoy this. I deserved this night.

I deserved more than this night. I deserved to live my life without trying to earn people's respect, affection— even their love—by doing things for them.

I slowly eased my fingers from her.

Sighing, she tucked her head into my neck and threw her leg over my hip. "Mm."

I think this was my favorite position of them all.

"Are you tired?" Sierra's voice didn't break the peace but added to it.

I didn't even take offense at the words. "After that?"

"Oh, good." She flopped onto her back, the bed bouncing. "I wanted to talk something over with you."

She wanted to talk to me. No hiding. No putting up boundaries. She was sharing.

I'd earned this trust.

Slowly.

Sierra had shown me what could happen if a relationship that started not with one partner in a crisis that needed to be solved, but because two people were attracted to each other. It wasn't all deep emotions and an immediate sense of responsibility. With Sierra it'd been a natural progression of getting to know her and liking her more.

And it felt stronger, deeper than any I'd ever experienced before.

"I'd love to hear it."

Chapter Twenty-Five

Sierra

I looked away from Jamie's expectant expression and instead to my plants hanging from the ceiling on the far wall. Was I really going to do this? My speed racer heart said I was. I wasn't going to Sammantha, my usual go-to for all things work related. I was turning to Jamie. She was going to take up another role in my life, one I was willingly giving her. It was her face that popped into my head when I knew I wanted to talk it out, not Sammantha's.

"It's about work."

The pillow rustled as she turned and tightened her arm around me. "Did you hear something about the cuts?"

"No. Right now they're just trying to eliminate as many nonessential things as possible and see if that'll make up the difference to keep all of us on."

Her hand slid up and down my shoulder in a movement as careful as her next words. "With our governor and legislature there's unlikely to be any spending cuts for services on the state level. It just might be enough."

"Yeah, thing is I'm not sure it'll be enough for me anymore. I've loved planning the fundraiser. Loved everything about it. Besides just working with you, I mean. I love that we're giving the kids something to be passionate about. It's made me passionate. I want to do more of it."

"Yeah? That's awesome. I bet you can come up with all kinds of ideas. God knows there's a million things they probably could use that they're not getting. Sports equipment. Electronics. New clothes they pick out."

I flipped to my side, facing her. "But I want even more than that. More than just fundraisers. I want to help kids discover and embrace that side of their lives. Their passions, their interests. All of it. More than just making it through, but finding something to inspire."

Silence met my words.

I swallowed and let out my breath, my fingers stroking my sheets.

"There are people that do that," I said. "Program directors. They don't focus strictly on the necessities. They organize activities, they encourage kids to learn and explore. I didn't pay much attention to that side of things when I was getting my degree, because I didn't think that's where my interests were. But I did some research. I think that's something I could do."

I stared at Jamie, my blood bouncing in my veins, like I'd been shaken and was waiting for someone to pop me open so we could celebrate.

Jamie's hand paused and it was a long moment before she said anything. "Is there a lot of demand for a position like that?"

I deflated back into the pillow. "I saw a few positions."

"Huh. A program director. From what you said about the duties it includes, I'd be worried about job security. It seems like if an organization was having financial problems, that would be the first to go. You're already having to live with that stress, I hate the thought of you experiencing even more of it."

"Yeah." I sighed.

Why had I been expecting more? More excitement. More encouragement. She'd done the same when I'd first suggested the fundraiser for art supplies. But so many other things had changed since then. Why would I have thought this would too? Like then, she made good points. All reasons not to make this change. But what about happiness? My happiness. What if I'd found my version of tattooing. My art. The thing I'm not only supposed to do but also fulfills me.

"That's something I have to think about," I said.

Jamie kissed the side of my forehead, no doubt responding to the flatness of my voice. "You could still volunteer. We could. You know how much I love doing it."

Volunteering wouldn't be the same. But she was right. There would be even less security as a program director. I liked my job. I went home feeling satisfied. Would I still when more and more of my group time was taken over by non-staff? When I'd be assigned more cases and their paperwork?

Her gaze met mine, her look tentative but hopeful. "Maybe it's something we could include Riley in. Might be really good for her."

Riley. My heart quickened but in manageable terrain. We'd reached that point. This part-time relationship had crossed over into full time and with that came Riley. "Yeah, that could be fun."

Her lips curved in a smile and her foot ran across my calf under the blanket. "I think so too. I'd like that a lot."

"Mm-hmm." I liked seeing Jamie excited by something. It didn't come often enough. But right now I just couldn't share her enthusiasm.

Because she hadn't shared mine. We weren't on the same wavelength here.

She kissed my shoulder. "I didn't mean to be a wet blanket on your idea. I just wanted to make sure you were looking at all sides. I know how it can be, getting wrapped up in something when you're—"

I jerked my head up and glared at her across the pillow. "If you say something about my age right now, I will hurt you."

She shook her head, her lip twitching. "Not your age. Was going to say 'eager.' I know how hard it can be to look at all the angles when you're eager. That's all I was trying to do—help you see all of the angles, so you didn't make a mistake."

"Was tattooing, was going after what made you excited, a mistake?"

"No. I love what I do, but it took me nine years. I had to save up money and know that I could take the time to build up a clientele and hone my skills before I started to see a return."

"Right." Nine years. I couldn't imagine waiting that long. At this point even one more day seemed too long. The thought of what else I could do, could be, had hounded me since I'd left Wendy's office. Each second there was this bubble of excitement and fear poking at me, urging me. Was I supposed to just go around keyed up for nine years?

Did I have much choice? My savings was less of a cushion and more like a threadbare patch. I didn't spend wildly. I liked clothes, but my closet was small so it kept me from getting too many. No, it was that I was a social worker at a nonprofit and Portland was expensive.

These were all good points. Points I would need to

think about, weigh, maybe break out the old pros and cons list.

If only she could have brought them up without making it feel like she was indulgently pointing out the mistakes of someone young and fanciful who didn't know better.

Jamie kissed along the rim of my ear. "I can hear your brain spinning. I take it I gave you something to think about."

I snorted. Those were almost the exact words I used when ending group. "You sure have."

She'd given me something to think about and more than just the change of direction in my job.

I'd thought after talking to her I'd feel better. Calmed. Centered. Because I'd be talking with someone who supported me, who understood. This wasn't it. I should've just called Sammantha. Next time I would.

Relief should be chasing away the disappointment. Everything would go back to before. Nothing had changed between us. Yeah, no, the disappointment was still there and it was growing. Wrapped in Jamie's arms—the place I'd come to love above all others—I felt a hole where I'd made a place for her to fill. And she'd left it empty.

Jamie

I stared at the cash in my client's hand and wondered how rude it'd be to just pluck it from between her fingers. I'd done the tatt, gone over aftercare, and now it was time for her to pay up. I usually didn't mind some post-appointment chitchat, but I'd already spent extra time reworking the design when she'd gone from wanting it on her left shoulder to her calf. I was going to be late for meeting Riley and Nicki at my apartment if this client didn't leave right now.

"Well, thanks," she said. "It wasn't nearly as painful as I thought it'd be."

"Good." I smiled, took the cash without even checking the tip and headed back to my station to clean up.

I'd just rubbed down my chair when footsteps came down the main rise at a fast clip, veered off for a few seconds, and then came back. I didn't stop what I was doing while I waited for Maya to quit getting distracted and actually make it all the way down to see me.

"Hey," she said, coming into my station.

"What's up?" I asked, not stopping.

"So I'm working on my application and have a question."

Wad of paper towels suspended over my tray, I paused long enough to look at Maya. She was applying to be on a televised tattoo competition. Something she'd been talking about since the moment I met her. At the time, I hadn't even been able to picture such an impossibility, with all the coordinating it might take. Now I could admit to being a bit envious that she would get to go to a different city, and maybe even experience a reality TV show.

"What kind of question?"

She made a face and thrust out papers to me. "I'm pretty sure I messed up the last section and I don't want to fuck it up. Can you look it over? Help me out?"

Well shit. She had to go and need this now, when I was running late. But how could I say no? She was coming to me. Exactly what I wanted. Exactly what I needed if I was going to keep earning her respect.

No. I didn't do that anymore. I didn't earn people's goodwill by doing things for them.

She was going to have to like me, respect me, whether I did things for her or not.

"I'm sorry, I can't."

"No?" Maya's eyes bulged.

I locked my knees. "Nope. Sorry. I'm running late. Maybe someone else can help."

"Yeah." She sighed. "Fine. Have a good night. Say hi to Sierra for me." She made a kissing face, complete with obnoxious kissing noises as she left.

Nothing had changed. I hadn't lost her respect.

Holy hell, it worked. Mind whirling, I finished cleaning and then booked it out of there.

Thanking the parking gods that a spot was available not too far from my place—not always a given with my late hours—I rushed up the stairs.

Nicki and Riley waited outside my door.

"Hey guys, hope you haven't been waiting long."

"Nope. We practically just got here."

"Good." I opened the door and motioned for them to go inside.

Nicki gave my cheek a quick kiss as she breezed past. On her way to the couch, her pace slowed and she looked around like a bloodhound that had caught a new scent.

Her gaze went to the African violet on my counter and then to the other plants strewn around my apartment in hopes Sierra would feel more at home when she came over. I'd also changed to fleece sheets since Sierra was keen on all things fuzzy, but my ex-wife would not be seeing those.

Nicki shot me a speculative look over her shoulder as she made her way to the opposite end of the couch from Riley, leaving the middle open for me.

I sat, taking the hand Nicki outstretched to me, and then angled myself toward Riley.

Riley narrowed her eyes and looked from Nicki to me. "What's going on?"

"So we want to talk to you about something," I started. "It's about your grandparents."

Riley held her hands up and leaned back. "She hasn't come to see me or anything. I haven't talked to her. Either of them."

"Okay, well, that's good." Always nice to know your parents hadn't been harassing your daughter. "Hopefully it'll remain that way. I won't be seeing them either." I rubbed my hand over my mouth and stared into my daughter's eyes, trying to see what she thought of that, desperately hoping not to see the accusation that had gutted me when she'd accused me of not taking care of them.

"Why?"

Nicki's hand squeezed mine tighter.

It was nice, but I couldn't help but wish that my empty left hand was being squeezed by a freckled one.

"Grandma Pat and Grandpa Joe need help. And they refuse to get it. They're alcoholics. You know what that is, right?"

Riley rolled her eyes. "Yeah, they drink too much."

"That's right."

The couch cushions dipped as Nicki leaned forward. "Momma J isn't going to be seeing them until they get help, which might be a long time, if ever. When you're an alcoholic you do things that hurt others and Momma J can't be hurt anymore, so she needs to step back."

Riley nodded. "Yeah, I figured there was something wrong with them."

"You did?" I shouldn't be surprised. Riley was an

observant kid. But I'd taken such pains to hide that side of my parents' life from her.

"Yeah. They sound different on the phone sometimes. And they'd promise things and when I saw them it was like they didn't remember."

I winced. "Yeah, that's the alcohol. They're not always aware of everything, including when they hurt people."

Riley nodded and shot Nicki a look over my shoulder.

"How are you feeling about this, sweetie?" Nicki asked.

God help me, I was wanting her to say not great. Nothing major, just a little upset that I could help her through. I was pretty sure I was going through Ms. Fix-It withdrawals. There was an adrenaline rush in being looked at to jump in and help someone.

"Fine," she said. "It's not like I saw them much anyway. And I don't want them hurting you, Momma J."

My chest filled with so much love for this incredible being.

It felt good to have this in the open. To not have to worry about hiding it from her in the future. I wanted everything out in the open.

Which left one thing. Her reaction had the power to alter what I envisioned for my future. Our future.

"All right," Nicki said slapping her palms against her thighs, obviously intending to get up.

"Actually there's one more thing I would like to talk to you about." I stood and moved to sit on the edge of the wood coffee table so that I faced them. "Both of you."

Nicki's eyebrow rose and then her gaze went to the violet. She gave a small, encouraging smile, obviously having guessed what this was about.

"What?" Riley asked.

"I wanted to talk to you about Sierra, the woman who—"

"I know who she is." Riley sat up straighter. She twisted to look at the door. "Are her and Jordan coming over to work on something? Because that's totally cool. They can do it while I'm here."

"No. They're not coming."

Riley deflated back into the cushions. "Oh."

Now if only I could get her excited at the prospect of Sierra coming over if it didn't involve Jordan.

We'd start slow and keep it rare. I knew it'd take time for Riley to get used to the idea. I didn't want her to feel like she was being pushed out of my life and being replaced with someone new.

Nicki had dates and Riley had met a few, but this could be different since she already spent less time with me.

"So I brought up Sierra because I wanted to know what you thought of her."

Riley shrugged. "She's fine."

Not exactly the "she completes us" I'd been magically hoping for, but better than "I think she's a serial killer."

"I'm asking because I really like her." I was so far past like. What I was thinking was another four letter word that started with L.

Riley's baby blues just stared up at me.

Ugh, when had my daughter become so uncommunicative. When I wanted her to speak, that's when.

"Like really like her."

She groaned and covered her face. "Oh my god. It's obvious you're crushing on her. You've got no chill."

"And how do you feel about that?"

"It's cool, I guess." She dropped her hands to give

me a warning look. "Just don't go embarrassing yourself and being all slobbery."

I was pretty sure I did that on a daily basis. The great
thing was Sierra didn't seem to mind.

"Thank you for being so open to this. You're always
my number one. I want you to come to me if you have
any problems with this."

"Momma J," she whined. "I know all of that. It's
cool. She's nice. Now are we done?"

"Yes."

Riley jumped to her feet and hightailed it to her room.

Nicki stood and kissed me on the cheek. Before she
pulled away, she cupped it. "I'm happy for you."

That had gone well. The new things occupying my
time might not give me the boost that I got from helping
people, but it was forcing me to sort out my life. To figure out what was important. It wasn't an age difference.
It was how a person treated me. How we connected and
interacted. What we got and needed from each other.

My parents were older than Sierra and had never
cared for me like she did. Nicki was older than Sierra,
but my ex-wife had hurt me by needing me only for
what I could give her.

Sierra did not need that. Heck, considering her reaction to my advice about her career, she didn't want
much more than my support. She wasn't looking for me
to fix anything for her.

It would take some adjustment, but I could do that.
I could learn and she could be my teacher.

My life was coming together.

Chapter Twenty-Six

Sierra

Why hadn't I done gymnastics, ballet, or something that could get me off the ground so my body could do what my heart was? It was happening. Tonight was the night. The fundraiser.

I moved in a slow circle, soaking in Thorn & Thistle.

"It looks amazing," Jamie said next to me.

The way she stared around us with pride and obvious delight almost snatched some of my joy. How could she see all that we'd accomplished, feel the satisfaction from it, and not understand why I wanted to do this for a living?

No, she understood. I'm sure she did. She was being practical. It was just taking me longer than I'd like to get over losing what I thought would be shared excitement. I was seeing the other side of that steadfastness I so adored. Couldn't have one without the other.

"What? There's something you'd want to change?" Jamie asked.

"Hm?" Oh, the shop. She'd been talking about that. "Nope. It looks amazing."

I swept my gaze over her. "It's not the only thing."

She wore black slacks and a bright red shirt and over

it she had a black velvet vest with metal chains connecting the buttons. So much to touch. Which I was sure was why she'd worn it. She knew I liked to caress things, especially if they were on her.

But not now. Now I was going to bask in the results of the first fundraiser I'd planned.

The shop had closed to regular clients at five, giving us time to deck the shop out with red, black, and white balloons. There were drinks, snacks, and cupcakes decorated with the designs of the tattoos. The artists had already started up a bet over whose cupcakes would be all eaten first.

Everyone had dressed up, treating it like a special occasion. They all looked so sharp that Cassie had demanded they get a group photo to update the shop's social media with.

Everything and everyone looked great. We were ready.

"I have been looking forward to this for forever," Jamie said, her arm coming around my waist.

"I know. I can't believe it's finally here. I betcha even MJ is impressed with us."

"I don't know if I'd go that far." Jamie leaned closer to me, her mouth brushing the tip of my ear as she spoke. "I actually meant that I finally get to ink you. I've been thinking about laying that demon slayer on you since the day we created her."

"I thought you wanted me to behave. You know, because of the press and all."

She groaned, the sound against my skin causing goose bumps. "At least give me a kiss while you're in the chair."

"We'll see." I gave her one now. At least that still felt right.

"Oh my god, do you never stop?"

I turned to Jordan, who stared at us in disgust. "You ready?"

Instead of answering, her frown morphed into a harsh glare.

"What are you doing?" I asked.

"I'm practicing my 'it's for charity' face."

"Oh."

"What do you think?"

"Hm." I leaned back so I could appreciate it in all its glory. "If it were me I'd go more Puss in Boots, less dragon."

"Yeah, I was gonna go with that, but then I thought mean mugging would fit in better here."

"You're not wrong there," Jamie said.

"All right, I'm opening the doors," MJ called out. "Everyone get your asses out here."

Oh god. This was it. I grabbed Jamie's hand and pushed closer to the door.

MJ turned and grinned at us before she flipped the lock and flung open the door. She stepped into the doorway and addressed the crowd like she was the star attraction at a sold-out show. "You all looking for some exclusive tattoos from Thorn & Thistle?"

When the crowd cheered MJ swept her arm out. "Then get in here and let's raise some money for people who need it by getting some awesome fucking ink."

People streamed into the shop. Most of them were regulars and walked up to their artists, already knowing them. I smiled and waved as I caught sight of Ashley, Crystal and Sammantha. The rest of my crew was coming later.

"It's time," Jamie said, hooking her fingers in the pockets of my skirt—because yes, I'd found the most awesome store online that had dresses and skirts with pockets. She started pulling me toward her station, her smile a near perfect copy of the one she gave when she was leading me to the bedroom.

How in the heck were we going to manage this with witnesses?

"Sierra, girl. This is amazing."

I whirled around and smiled at Wendy who was making her way to us. "Hi."

"Look at what you did." She hugged me. Her face was the most animated I'd ever seen it. "This is truly great."

"It's all thanks to the amazing women of Thorn & Thistle. Especially this one." I glanced over at Jamie. "Wendy, I'd like to introduce you to my girlfriend, Jamie. She's an artist here and the one who helped me organize this."

Jamie's breath hitched and it took a moment for her to shake out of whatever place my words had taken her to and hold her hand out.

"It's nice to meet you," Wendy said, shaking her hand. "Thank you so much for making this happen with Sierra. We are all so excited and grateful."

"It was a team effort, but I'm glad you're pleased with the results."

"Oh, very." Wendy looked around us again. The noise in the shop was louder now that a tattoo gu— nope, I was with an artist now so I had to call it by its right name—now that a tattoo machine started up.

"It's so much bigger than what I even imagined." My boss smiled. "I can see why you're so anxious to do another one."

"Yeah." I tried to make eye contact and subtly shake my head at Wendy. Jamie already knew I was looking to do more fundraisers, but she didn't know what my plan was for the next one.

Wendy missed my attempts, turning to face Jamie fully.

"It's nice that Sierra found another work horse like she is. For this next one, you're going to be even more instrumental."

Jamie continued to smile, but the look she shot me was a big question mark. "I am?"

"Oh, yes. What did she say? 'I never knew having an artist around would be so useful.' She's going to be able to do a lot with you."

"Useful," Jamie repeated. She turned toward me. Gone was the woman who looked at me like she knew every inch of me, adored every inch. Instead she stared at me like I was a stranger. No, an enemy.

"It seems you've failed to fill me in on some things."

Jamie

Not her. Not Sierra too. Please, not Sierra.

"What fundraiser? You need me to work on something else for you?"

A sigh escaped her, a small, nothing sound. "I was going to tell you. It's just… Everything's been wild getting this one ready. And I thought it could wait."

Never would I have imagined it necessary to analyze her words like I did my parents', looking for hidden meaning, for evasive answers. Yet, here I was. Her answer had told me absolutely nothing. "But is what she said true?"

"Yes. You know I—"

I put my hand up, desperate to stop her. So much for not needing anything from me. So much for being enough just as I am.

I hadn't thought I had any hopes left that could be crushed. I'd been wrong. With her I'd had hopes. So many of them.

"Jamie." Her eyes pleaded with me.

To what? Not understand? Not realize the truth?

"It's not—"

"Why did you let me believe that you weren't looking for anything from me, that I was enough, if it was all bullshit?"

Her face drained of all color. Her freckles—those freckles I spent so much time tracing—stood out. "Because it's not." She stepped closer to me. "It's not bullshit. You are enough."

God, I wished I could block my nostrils from taking in any more of her lemon scent. I didn't need it fucking with my head. I couldn't imagine smelling a lemon and not thinking of her. Or seeing freckles, or red hair, or a sad little plant. There was so much. So fucking much because she'd invaded my life, until it felt like she was part of it. Part of me.

I couldn't fathom living without her.

And I didn't need to live without her. Having to earn people's love, to do things for them to be worthy of it— that was nothing new. I allowed that with her.

No.

Anger hit me. Real, true anger. No cold, no ice. Anger.

I had changed. I was proud of the direction I was taking my life. I was done being used. I said no. She'd helped do that. Sierra. It had been because of her. Because she'd made me believe I was worth it.

And now she wanted me to revert back.

I wasn't going back. Not even for her.

"You made me think things could be different."

She shook her head. I glanced away from the fiery

strands. "You've got this wrong. You're disappointed. I get it. We're discovering we're not perfect for each other every second but for—"

"No. No more." I couldn't hear her explanations. I wasn't strong enough. If there was anyone who could tempt me to abandon this new me, it was Sierra. My anger flared hotter. "Just stop! I don't want to hear any more."

Sierra's expression hardened. She shot a quick glance over her shoulder and then closed the distance between us. "This isn't the place. And this isn't about us."

"There is no us."

A loud gasp echoed in the shop. Echoed because there were no other sounds. No machines going. No talking. No laughing.

The dizzying rush of adrenaline receded. Stiffening, I followed her gaze.

Everyone stared at us. My co-workers, who I had always harped at to act professional. My co-workers, who now wore shocked expressions. Clients stared at me. Guests. And Jesus, the reporters. The reporters invited to showcase the fundraiser, not my meltdown. They all stared at me.

I turned back at Sierra. None of this would be happening if I hadn't let myself believe. If I hadn't gotten so wrapped up in her.

"I'm done. The Jamie help desk is closed for good."

Chapter Twenty-Seven

Sierra

I stared at the computer screen in front of me and could not find the energy to move my hand on the mouse. Doing this, going through these motions, didn't feel right. Being here didn't feel right anymore.

Nowhere did. Not my apartment. Not here in one of the many offices I had to use. Not answering concerned texts from friends. The only place that did feel right was wherever Jamie was. And I wasn't wanted there.

She'd thrust me out of her life. All of this time, I'd protected against losing someone. If only I'd known that wasn't what I needed to fear. No, it was being cast out. The results were terribly similar—a gaping hole where companionship and security had once been.

Someone tapped on the outside of the door and I jerked. Wendy stood there, two cups of coffee in her hands.

"I am so sorry, Sierra." She plopped down on the metal chair wedged between the side of the desk and the wall, sliding one of the coffees toward me. "I had no idea she didn't know."

I shook my head. "It's okay. Not your fault."

"I feel terrible."

No more so than me. I was experiencing exactly what I'd never wanted to again, and all without being given the chance to explain.

"It's okay." I offered a wan smile. "If it wasn't that then it would have been something. We obviously weren't on as firm a ground as I thought." Not even close.

Wendy's grip on her cup relaxed in obvious relief. "If it's any consolation, the fundraiser was amazing. Our website has never seen so much traffic and Jordan has already been fielding calls from people with questions about how they can help."

I knew at some point that news would make me happy, but right now the sensations were so tangled with Jamie. It was impossible to feel any joy about that night.

She squeezed my shoulder. "Breakups are hard. Sometimes the best thing you can do is throw yourself into work and try to get over them."

Get over her. Pretend we'd never been more than client and tattoo artist. That wouldn't make everything better. Even if I could pluck every memory of Jamie from my mind, I wouldn't be the same person.

Grabbing her coffee, she stood. "I'll leave you to it."

"Wait." I turned to face her, away from the desk, away from the computer that was probably filling with new names of people in need that I would never meet.

"Hm?"

I stared at Wendy, my heart finally doing something more than beat dully in my chest. Now wasn't the time to make these decisions. Not when I was scared and hurting and everything seemed bad. Yet, it felt right. It felt right in a way nothing else did in my life. I needed to follow that feeling. "I'm… I'm giving my notice. I love Haven Bridge and you and the other staff, but I don't think it's the right fit for me anymore."

I was going to take the risk, not on other people and letting them in, but on myself.

No matter what happened I'd make it through.

Jamie

When I'd called this meeting, I should have expected delays. Of course if I'd called it at dawn like I really wanted to, no one would have shown up. My co-workers were not early risers. Or at least most of them. They also weren't usually quiet, but they were now. Another drop of sweat slid down my back to add to my growing collection.

The back door swung open and Vivian rushed inside. "Sorry," she said, taking a seat next to Maya. "Dad would not take his medicine this morning. Anyways, um…"

I stepped forward and met the gaze of each of my Thorn & Thistle family. "I'm sorry. So sorry. You guys worked so hard to make the event happen. Last night was meant to showcase the shop and instead I made it a spectacle."

I crossed my arms behind my back and lifted my chin, ready to take whatever they doled out. I deserved it.

Silence. Complete silence met my apology. Instead of the angry yells I'd been expecting, I saw worry in their gazes. Somehow that was just as loud in the large room.

Had they already read the write-ups? Not only had I experienced my heartbreak in real time, I got to read about it. The consensus was that I'd "…brought the drama, reminiscent of what we used to expect from

Thorn & Thistle." Texts from reporters this morning, who asked for follow-up interviews, had made for a historic first. Normally they wanted MJ for flair or Cassie for solid information. I had turned my phone off completely.

I turned to MJ directly. One look at her expression showed how little there'd been of the flattering press she'd been promised. Arms crossed over her chest, she leaned against the wall, her dark gaze piercing me.

"I'm sorry. It won't happen again."

Never. I would never be so broken in front of people again. No one but Sierra had that kind of power to hurt me.

"You about done?" MJ asked.

I nodded.

"Great." MJ clapped her hands together. "Then get out there and clean that shit up. I want it fucking sparkling before we open."

Well, hell. That's what I should have been doing this morning instead of pacing my apartment. It would have been a hell of a lot more productive. As part of my apology, the girls could have come to a clean shop, and I could erase all proof of what had transpired.

Except I'd never be able to forget the look on Sierra's face after I told her there was no us. The devastation. She'd looked so young and alone. The hurt coursing through my body had been visible in her too.

Nope. No more thinking about her. Maybe cleaning would work where pacing had failed. I whirled toward the doorway to find it blocked by Cassie. She gave me a gentle smile and my arm an even gentler squeeze before making her way to the main floor of the shop.

Vivian followed her, nodding as she passed. "I didn't know you could get that raw. It was very inspiring."

Up next, Gina clapped my shoulder. "It always seems much worse when it's happening to you. It was a long night and by the end most people probably forgot."

Not according to my new social media follower counts, but it was nice of her to say so. "Thank you."

Maya stood in the wings, obviously waiting for her chance in this line of support, except I was sure hers wouldn't be as kind. Now was her chance to pay me back for all of the times I'd lectured her on her behavior in the shop.

"You hanging in there?" she asked.

I rocked back. The emotion that had just been beneath the surface all night rushed to my eyes. "Best I can."

"Anything I can do for you?"

"No." There was nothing anyone could do. This was something I had to get through. To get over.

I didn't see how. This pain was worse than when Nicki had asked for a divorce. At least then it'd made some sense. I'd become no more use for her. She'd no longer needed me to take charge of her life. Mixed in with the hurt and the anger had been a relief that I wouldn't have to try so hard to please her and keep her entertained.

There was no relief with Sierra.

How did you get over someone that flipped your entire life upside down and for the better?

I glanced at MJ, but she stayed across the room, her gaze as hard as ever. I inclined my head and then made my way out to the shop.

I sucked in a sharp breath, starting at the remnants of what should have been a magical night. Crumbs covered the black tablecloth Sierra had put down on the food table. Had that only been yesterday? The balloons were still taped up, but they sagged. A visual representation of how I felt—emptied out, but still moving.

While the girls argued about what should be thrown away and what party supplies could be reused, I headed to get a broom. The floor might be the best place for me to focus right now, less for me to see and be reminded of.

Passing my station, I jerked to a stop. It was still set up, everything in position to ink Sierra. Chest hollow and aching, I stepped in, trailing my finger over the transfer I'd had ready to put on her. I'd pictured a night of us smiling and laughing while she sat in my chair. A night so different than the day she'd come in quiet and subdued, worried about her work. Last night was supposed to have been a circle of sorts with a happy Sierra in my chair. I curled my hand, the transfer crushing in my fist.

I went to turn away and my gaze snagged on an envelope set on the counter of my station. A jolt hit my system, flickering it back to life. I recognized that writing.

Hands trembling, I picked up the card. On the front was a picture of an elephant, no words. Inside was filled with Sierra's beautiful cursive.

Jamie,
Thank you so much for this. I'm so excited for tonight!!! I'm so glad we did this together and I got to know you. You've inspired me and wowed me. For my next project I want to do a fundraiser to send kids to soccer camp in your honor.

P.S. I was hoping we could do this together. Let's make it something fun. Riley can judge the results.
Love, Sierra

At the bottom of the card she'd attempted to draw a chibi elephant.

And oh, god. She'd gifted me with a couples cooking class. She'd managed to find one that worked with my schedule. She'd made the time for us to do this together.

I rubbed my thumb over and over the word love.

A fundraiser. She wanted my involvement in a fundraiser to honor me. She'd wanted to do it *for* me and for kids who needed more in their lives.

I staggered back two steps and sank into my chair.

I jumped when a hand landed on my shoulder then curled around it, staying there in a silent touch of support.

Tilting my head back, I stared up at MJ. "I fucked up," I said.

"Yup. About time. Been waiting for it." She squeezed my shoulder. "Now what are you going to do to fix it?"

Chapter Twenty-Eight

Sierra

I stared at the large stainless steel door handle in front of me. It shouldn't be this hard to open a door. All I had to do was pull. But by doing so, it would mean making it real, final. And that's why I finally did it.

I stepped into the large kitchen. Instead of being met with savory spices and cooking food, it smelled of cleaning products. Worse than the unappetizing chemicals was the sight of the other five cooking stations all occupied with happy pairs. Yup, I'd gone with a couples class. Back when I'd been part of a couple. I breathed through the pain.

My friends had begged to come with me, but this was something I needed to do on my own. I needed to feel this lost sensation. Again. But unlike last time I would not be sectioning off my life. I'd heal with Uncle Drew, Ashley, my other friends. I'd lean on each of them, not as an attempt to keep one person from meaning too much in my life, but because that was too much of an expectation to be put on anyone.

No one could be my mother. No one could replace what I'd lost. No one person could make me feel strong, and loved, and invincible, and secure. At this point I

wasn't sure my own mother could. She'd reached myth-
ical status in my mind. If she'd lived, we would have
argued, had fights, and I would have seen sides to her
that weren't perfect.

Just as I'd seen Jamie's. She wasn't perfect. But she'd
come pretty damn close to being perfect for me.

God, being without her was hell. Having her dis-
miss me had been hell. And I just had to keep on walking through this hell until I could get to the other side.
Maybe then my mind could be filled with the wonderful memories of the time I'd spent with her.

The door behind me opened and I turned automatically. My breath seized. Jamie. Jamie was here. My
gaze latched onto her and wouldn't leave. She wore her
favorite jeans, the ones with the frayed knees and the
zipper that didn't go quite all the way to the top and of
course an overshirt, blue today, but it was her face that
I tracked. She looked like she'd been getting as much
sleep as I had—none. I'd become used to her body, her
arm wrapped around me. Now I couldn't fall or stay
asleep without it.

She was likewise cataloging me, for sure, seeing bags
under my eyes that I'd tried to cover with makeup, and
knowing my style wasn't suddenly windblown chic, but
that I just hadn't bothered to brush my hair.

"Hi," she said, stopping a few feet away and lifting
her hand in an awkward greeting.

"I didn't think I'd see you again." Not as my girlfriend, not even as my tattoo artist. It'd be torture to
sit in that seat and be relegated back to only a client.

Jamie winced and pulled a hand free from her pockets to rub the back of her head.

God, I loved the sound of that. Missed it. My fingers
curled, longing to reach out and do it for her.

"I found the card you left."

Oh, yes. The card. Written when everything had seemed so perfect. I cleared my throat. "Ah. So then you know about the new fundraiser."

"I do. Sierra—"

I held up my hand. "Uh-uh. You didn't let me speak that night. Didn't give me the benefit of the doubt."

"I know. I'm so—"

"Sorry. I bet. Well, don't worry. I still want to do it."

She cocked her head, her gaze questioning and... hopeful? Certainly not holding the hurt and anger when she'd looked at me last.

"The fundraiser," I clarified.

Eyes widened, she rocked back. "You do? But why? I don't deserve that. I dumped you. I shit on the good thing you were trying to do."

Yes. Yes, she had. "I'm doing it for the kids that want to play soccer and be part of a team. I don't want them to have to give up something they love. Maybe they can learn their worth and won't be so doubting of it."

"No. Don't give me an out." I had spoken almost those exact words when she'd tried to give me an out about not taking proper care of her on the bar crawl.

"I'm an adult and supposed to be rational," she said. "Supposed to think before I act and weigh everything that is happening and come to logical conclusions. I have a lot I could still learn from you about how to treat people. How to trust people. I'm sorry. You'll never know how sorry."

I couldn't breathe right. The air wouldn't go in my lungs. They were too busy squeezing. Distantly I was aware that we were doing this in front of people, that they could see us, hear us, but I couldn't look away from Jamie and the pain I saw.

"Thank you for thinking of me. For remembering how soccer was taken from me and how much it meant. The fundraiser is a wonderful thing. Selfless. I turned it into something ugly."

I shook my head, light breaking through the dark that had descended these last days. "I wouldn't go that far. Selfless is pushing it. Some things have been going on since I last saw you."

There was no accusation, no stiffening. The soft, wondering expression she blessed me with didn't change. "Maybe you'd be willing to tell me about them." Her gaze shifted past me, as if she'd just tuned in to our surroundings. "After class, if you have the time."

"Oh, I have it."

"And if you want me to stay."

"Oh, I do."

Jamie held her hand out. That beautiful hand that was able to create such amazing pieces, that could clasp my skin and make me feel that everything was right in the world.

I took it.

God, I'd missed this. My anchor. The touch of her skin against mine.

I flung myself into her arms. "I have all the time in the world for you. I'll prove it."

"You don't have to," Jamie breathed into my hair, holding me close. "I know. I know."

I might be able to survive without her, but I didn't want to. It was so much better with her.

I pulled away, staring into her face. Gone was the tired, drawn woman who had entered the class. Her pink cheeks set off her shining eyes splendidly.

"Every word I wrote in that card is true," I said. "Every single one." Holding on to her shoulders, taking strength, I drew a deep breath. "I love you. I don't want to live even one more day without you in it. These last two days have been pure hell."

Her body trembled against mine, her arms squeezing impossibly tighter. "And I love you. I love who I can be when I'm with you. Who I want to be. You make it all possible."

The edge of the counter dug uncomfortably into my hip, but I didn't care. I didn't care about anything but being back where I belonged—in her arms.

"No more fighting. It's my least favorite thing about a relationship with you."

She let out a husky laugh and then leaned down to kiss me.

When we parted it was to the sound of applause.

We were the focus of the four other couples and oh, look at that. At some point the instructor had come in and was also smiling at us.

I waved. "Sorry about that. Um, that's not what you paid for."

I was almost afraid to check in with Jamie and see how she was faring at being in the spotlight of the class. It'd been the final straw for her at the fundraiser. When I looked, she radiated nothing but happiness and satisfaction.

The instructor smiled at everyone. "Well, after that rousing example of how cooking can bring everyone together, shall we begin?"

I grabbed Jamie's hand and led her to our place in front of the counter. "Yes."

Epilogue

Jamie

I inhaled deeply. Ah. There was nothing like a stadium. The food. The other fans. The outdoors. The only thing missing was the smell of perfectly tended grass, lost in the scents of food and perfume. But it was a small price to be here and getting ready to see my team play some soccer.

Sierra put her drink in the holder and then bent down and grabbed a tot with her tongue.

I watched riveted. Today I could without any fear that Riley would butt in with her "ew"ing. Hers would have only been the start. Then Nicki would join in. Followed by Ryan who would be dressed in a suit, because my brother did not know how to do casual. Sierra's uncle had made it to a few games. And we'd convinced Jordan to come exactly once. They were good games, surrounded by family, but this—this was perfection.

Sierra had surprised me with a trip to Seattle to watch our team in an away game. It was our first trip together, even if it was only a weekend getaway. It was my first time being away period. Away from Riley. Away from my parents. Away from the shop. And just like Sierra had promised, everything was running fine without me. My phone had stayed blessedly silent.

Even when we were at home, my phone was quieter without my parents blowing it up. They hadn't gotten help and I'd stopped taking their calls. If they ever turned around in the future, they could leave a voice mail and I'd call them back. It'd taken me some time to wean myself away from driving down their street and trying to gauge how they were doing by the state of their house. It'd been necessary for my self-care, as Sierra called it.

Sierra twisted in her seat, looking behind us and smiling at the other fans. Since this stadium was only a few hours away we had a good section representing. Facing forward again, she stared at the field below us. "This is pretty far away. You probably need your glasses."

"I can see just fine." Maybe not completely true, but if I put them on now I'd risk getting us escorted out of here. Sierra had a thing for my glasses.

There was a lot about me she liked and I was one lucky woman.

Too bad that luck wasn't with my team. We lost, but considering where we were, the company I was with and the prospect of a hotel room with a hot tub, I couldn't get too down.

"Where to next?" I glanced at Sierra in the passenger seat once we had managed to ditch the stadium traffic. "We could get some dinner. Hit up downtown. Whatever you want."

She leaned forward in that way she did which meant she was excited. "I want to get tattoos."

"When we get back? Yeah, that'd be cool. I need to do the slay—"

"No. Now. I want ones here."

I really hoped she wasn't talking about the highway specifically. "You want me to give you a tattoo?"

"Yes. I want us to get tattoos. A commitment. Me committing to this relationship and you having faith that I won't trade you in for a young CrossFit gal with energy to spare. Here on our first away trip."

"I don't have my equipment," I broke it to her gently. I'd had no reason to believe I'd need it.

Her face fell, but she still looked determined. "Can we buy you one?"

I tried to hide my horror at the thought of not using my machine and my setup and…

"I take that as a no. It has to be here." She poked me in the thigh. "You need to make that happen. Do this for me, please."

"I see how it's going to be." Inside my body was dancing. This felt right. Doing something she wanted, but also knowing that if I failed to, how she felt about me wouldn't change.

I loved the idea of getting ink to make a commitment to each other, but hell no, I didn't like the idea of someone else putting it down on Sierra. That was my job.

"What are you wanting to get?"

"I don't know."

"So artist's choice on placement and design?"

She frowned, thinking it over. "I mean, I've never wanted one on my butt. But yeah, I could live with it."

My gaze automatically dropped to the derriere in question. I could only see the curve of it in the seat. Hm, tempting, but no, I didn't see one there either.

"We'll compromise. We'll get the outlines here that I'll draw up. I'll find someone that'll trace them for us. And we'll finish them up when we get back."

She chewed her bottom lip, obviously not loving the idea, but she nodded. "Okay, compromise is important in relationships so I've heard."

I pushed my seat belt down so I could lean and give her a smacking kiss. "It is."

We went back to the hotel room and after giving her no more than a long kiss, I started my search for a tattoo artist that was both available and would accommodate our requests.

Two and a half hours later, we were being led to separate chairs to get our outlines of the tattoos I'd designed. I'd never be comfortable with someone else inking Sierra and I wasn't too hot for someone I didn't know putting it down on me, but there was something momentous about getting them at the exact same time. We were in this from start to finish together.

I closed my eyes and hardly felt it. There were so many happy endorphins buzzing through me, pain couldn't even register.

Mine done, I headed over to where Sierra was still getting hers. My tattoo had been more complex, but Sierra had started a conversation with the artist about the city and the best restaurants and well, I understood how distracting she could be.

The artist slid his stool back and then took off his gloves. He nodded and winked as he walked past. With only an hour to work with, I'd found damn good artists. Especially since he was giving us privacy for the reveal.

Leaning over I kissed her on the forehead then I held out my hand to help her sit up. I watched for any signs that she was dizzy. Nope, all signs—her bright eyes and smile—pointed to nothing but happy.

"You ready to see it?" I asked her.

"Yes! Oh my god, I can't wait to see what you gave me."

She rushed to the full-length mirror on the opposite wall, stretching her neck to the side to see the tattoo there. Her smile slipped.

"Oh. It's a half-dead plant."

I came up behind her, putting my hands on her shoulder. Her "half-dead plant" was placed on the side of her neck, below her ear. Less than two inches square, it was a potted plant that's leaves were drooping, except for the part of it touched by sun rays.

I met her gaze in the mirror. "It's a plant recovering after some TLC. Would you like to see mine?"

"Yes." She turned and looked at my neck where my tattoo was in the exact same spot as hers.

She stared at the chibi unicorn wearing a fluffy blanket as a cape with the words "you survived now it's time to thrive" surrounding it.

"It's beautiful." She reached out like she was going to touch it, but caught herself in time. "I love it."

"It's yours."

She stepped back, her brow furrowing. "I don't get it."

"This is for you. I can't see my own neck, but you can. Every time you see it, I want you to know it's for you. Just like that plant is for me to see and be reminded. You're my sun's rays."

She gasped, her eyes widening, and it didn't take long for the tears to come.

"Oh my god, I love it. I love you."

"And I love you. So much."

I caught her before she could throw her arms around my neck. Instead wrapping our arms around each other's waists. "I let him do the lettering because you think my writing is so shitty."

"It is." She gave a watery laugh. "Good thing everything else about you is so great."

After we could stop looking at each other's tattoos and giggling and giving happy sighs long enough to get them covered, we paid.

"I have a confession," Sierra whispered.

"Yeah? What?" With her it could be anything from that she didn't really like the dinner even though she said she did, to that she'd be eating Top Ramen because she'd gone overboard on Amazon wish lists again. Either way, I didn't doubt that she would handle it. I didn't look over her shoulder or try to take over. I didn't want to, secure in knowing that's not what she wanted me for.

"Even though I'm the one that pushed for this vacay, I miss work. I'm thinking about the kids."

"I think that's a sign you picked the right job."

Sierra had been hired by a nonprofit long-term shelter for at risk youth. The kids there had been kicked out of their homes, and Sierra helped prepare them for the future. The kids were encouraged to experiment not only in job fields but in extracurricular activities. I was going to be mentoring kids who wanted to try their hand at art.

"I know I did."

Swinging our entwined hands, I led her back to the car. "Our last night," I said, wistfulness in my tone.

"Our last night *here*. That just means we'll have to plan the next one. And the one after that."

There was a freedom in that. In knowing there would be more with her. "I can't wait."

I couldn't wait to do everything with her.

* * * * *

Acknowledgments

Thanks to the Carina Press team, who make this process so exciting and upbeat. Special thanks go to my incredible editor, Carrie Lofty. It is so amazing getting to work with her. I learn so much and look forward to her insight. Also thanks to my agent, Saritza Hernandez. It's wonderful to have someone so experienced and passionate in my corner.

About the Author

Jennie Davids fell in love with romance when she was twelve and snuck her mother's books. For her it wasn't the handsome, dashing heroes that captivated her but the heroines. She is thrilled to be writing what she longed to see then—two heroines falling in love.

She lives in the Pacific Northwest with her rescue animals that somehow never end up as well-behaved as their bios promise. The sound of the rain inspires her as she writes, or maybe it's the gallons of hot chocolate she consumes to stay warm in the damp climate.

When not writing Jennie is reading, watching reality TV, or bemoaning how quickly weeds grow back and keep her from reading.

To learn more about other books by Jennie Davids and stay updated on all the latest news, please visit Jennie's website at www.jenniedavids.com.

Also available from Carina Press and Jennie Davids

A mild-mannered cancer survivor and a badass tattoo artist strike a bargain: Cassie will enact new marketing plans to keep MJ's beloved Thorn & Thistle afloat and MJ will teach Cassie to find her inner bitch.

Read on for an excerpt from
New Ink on Life,
book one of the Thorn & Thistle series.

Chapter One

MJ

One glance at the girl looking around with big eyes and I knew she'd want a butterfly or, worse, a Chinese symbol she'd Googled.

I groaned, not bothering to lower the volume. I didn't give a shit if it wasn't polite. It wasn't polite to expect me to do inferior garbage like that.

Heading to the front of the shop, I stretched my arm behind my back until my shoulder cracked. The girl was studying the designs hung on the wall, all drawn by me and the other employees.

She turned and smiled at me. "Hi. I'm…"

Bending, I snatched a design folder and tossed it on the receptionist's counter. Not that I actually had one of those. Receptionists cost money, money I didn't have. "Here. See if there's anything you like."

While she looked, I propped my elbows on the counter. Close up I could see I'd been wrong. She was a woman not a girl. The pixie haircut and delicate features had tricked me from the distance. Might've got the age wrong, but I wasn't wrong on the type of tattoo.

This pale woman wore a sweater. An honest to god sweater with little pearl buttons.

Ugh. Why couldn't Maya be here? She didn't mind doing the newbies. Hell, she seemed to get a kick out of it. But nope, it was just me. The rest of the staff wouldn't be here for another hour when the shop officially opened. Until then I was here trying to squeeze in some more work. Every dollar and minute counted and I didn't have enough of either.

"See anything you like?"

She set down the binder and went to the wall, tilting her head back. "Everything. I've been an admirer for a long time. Your shading technique is like no other."

I drew my gaze from the blue vein running up her neck to the picture of a lion I'd done. I had to give her some points on taste. That was one I showcased in my bio for magazine articles.

"Something like that is a special commission. It takes a while. Plus, something that big is gonna hurt."

Her lips twisted in a weird kind of smile. "I can handle pain." She turned away from the wall and faced me. "But that's not why I'm here."

"To get a custom piece?"

"To get a tattoo."

I pushed away from the counter. "As much fun as it's been chatting, I don't have time for this shit. I got things I could be doing for clients. You know, paying ones."

"No, please wait. I'm sorry. I'm not explaining this well. I'm here because of Zan."

I did an about face, the name of my mentor guaranteed to get my attention. "What about her?"

"I was her apprentice."

Holy shit. This woman who could barely make eye contact, not only wielded a tattoo gun but had worked with Zan—a fucking trailblazer and one of the best artists ever.

She took my stunned silence as some kind of invitation, stepping closer. "She always talked about you with so much pride."

I jerked my chin at her to cover my flinch. "How long were you with her?"

"Four years."

Well shit. In that time I'd only talked to Zan a few times on the phone and maybe stopped into her shop here in Portland once. That's all I had for the woman who'd made me who I was.

"I'm Cassie Whiteaker by the way."

"MJ Flores." I took the hand she held out, not tempering my grip just because her wrist bones looked like they could bust through her skin. "So what do you want with me?"

"Oh. Um." Her gaze darted around the shop again before grazing me. "When Zan got sick and things started to look bad, I promised her I'd come to you to be my mentor."

"No." I took a giant step back.

Apprenticeships were a time suck. You shared all your skills and knowledge in return for some grunt work. As soon as they were done, they could go and open a shop next to you, take the clients that were yours, not theirs. No thank you. The field was crowded enough.

If I ever did decide to strap myself with an apprentice it wouldn't be this woman, Zan's apprentice or not. I could tell we wouldn't mesh well. She looked like she'd piss herself the first time I smashed something.

"Do you even have any tattoos?" burst from my mouth. Yeah, I believe the words I was looking for were "Get out."

"I do." The woman—Cassie—reached up and unbuttoned the first button of her sweater and then moved on to the next one. There was nothing sexy about her movements and yet I stared at each inch of skin revealed. A light gray T-shirt was underneath, lines of a tattoo peeking out of the scoop collar.

For a short woman with generous hips, I would have expected her to have more on top. She pulled one arm free and it actually took me a few seconds to focus on the tattoo on her forearm, not the pale skin.

Stepping closer, I drew her arm to me. "Better a diamond with a flaw than a pebble without." The lettering was exceptional and there was a small diamond at the top corner of the words that looked so real it practically shined.

Cassie wiggled her other arm from the sweater, revealing a bird flying free from a cage. Not exactly groundbreaking, but the work was impeccable. Dark purple surrounded the cage, fading into black and grays. I reached out and traced the bird that was stark in comparison to the cage it had just sprung from.

"Nice," I conceded and let go of her arm.

Now that her sweater was off and I was this close, I got a good whiff of something sweet. Not like a bouquet of flowers sweet. This was like cinnamon and sugar. It reminded me of the buñuelos my mom used to make.

Not saying anything, she pulled her shirt to the side, exposing a small phoenix on her neck. I bent to get a closer look and inhaled deeply, that sweet fragrance even stronger, like the heat of her body had warmed it and given it additional spice. The lines and color of another tattoo further down snagged my interest. I went to move her shirt to the side, but she stepped back and righted her clothing.

"As you can see I have tattoos."

Well, I'd seen some of them and what I'd seen had

been good. That didn't mean jack shit when it came to actually tattooing. Except Zan, damn it. That meant a hell of a lot. "So you've got your license?"

"Yes." She bent down. When she stood up again she held out a folder.

I grabbed it but didn't open it. Fact remained I didn't want or need an apprentice.

As I continued to stare at her, she wrapped her arms around her stomach, shifting her weight from foot to foot. "This is a really nice shop."

For fuck's sake. If she started on the weather, I really would kick her ass out.

"So you're giving tattoos?"

She shook her head, blond wisps of hair falling over her forehead. "Not to customers. I've given them to other employees at the shop and Zan."

And there went the hope she might not be any good at tattoos. Even though Zan had been a damn pioneer, her skin hadn't been covered. Every single tattoo had a meaning behind it. The day I'd been allowed to add to her collection was one of my proudest. Pressing that needle against Zan's skin had made everything shake all the way to my toes.

"I've never been so honored in my life," Cassie said in a hushed tone expected in church.

I got it. I'd never had so much trust placed in me and I'd wanted to live up to it. Still did today. "Yeah, never had such a fucking rush."

We shared a smile that I quickly flattened on my end. Still didn't need an apprentice.

"Was yours the cat o' nine tails?" she asked.

"Yup."

Her smile widened, showing off straight white teeth that only came from braces. Mine were fairly straight, only my bottom front ones crooked. With four kids to feed that was close enough for my parents.

"I thought that looked like your work."

"Good eye." I pushed her book back toward her. "Still not interested in an apprentice. I've got new hires and the shop to run."

Her face sobered. "Yes. I've heard about your... changes. I think that was one of the reasons Zan made me promise to come to you."

Nice to know my "changes" were making the rounds. Some called them changes. I went with straight up betrayal.

"I could help, take some of the burden off your shoulders. Ordering, front desk help, cleaning."

Usually I had wannabes coming in the door who thought because they were good at art and had watched some show on TV they could become a tattooer. Pissed me the fuck up. Now I had someone begging to be a receptionist or an assistant, not a tattooer. That was either the stupidest pitch or brilliant. It was all the shit I hated doing. Same with my other employees who never failed to bitch when I had them do it.

"I need to finish my apprenticeship and Zan insisted it be you."

Zan. My one fucking weakness.

This woman obviously knew it and was playing it hard.

"Damn it." I flipped open the folder.

Whoa. I whistled at the cherry blossom, its limbs shriveled and the pink petals scattered at the base. A melting stopwatch filled the next page, its numbers sliding from the face. What was supposed to have been a courtesy glance to honor Zan became me poring over every page. How had stuff this dark come out of some-

one looking so sweet? I spent even longer on the pictures of actual tattoos on skin. I studied the line work,
shading and placement.

I glanced up at Cassie who was twisting her hands
in front of her. "You're good. Good enough to be on
your own."

I flipped to the last page. My stomach jackknifed.
I recognized that skin. That wrinkled, rough skin had
guarded one of the softest hearts there was. The skin
also sported a lighthouse that hadn't been there the last
time I'd seen her.

"Well?" I demanded. "Why aren't you?"

"I'm not ready yet. I won't be ready to be a full-time
tattooer until May."

Uh, did this little pixie really not know the way
things worked? Zan couldn't have been that lax. Apprenticeships didn't have a particular end date. When
your mentor thought you were ready, you were ready.
Judging from her portfolio, she was ready.

So why the hell wasn't she tattooing? Maybe she
choked when it was time to work on clients or freaked
them out with her nervousness. There was no way in
hell I'd get ink from someone if their smile had the desperate edge hers did. But it wouldn't take long to teach
her to get it together. Not four months.

In total Zan had spent five years with me. She'd had
a shit load of stuff to work on. The tattooing I'd gotten
down. It was the keeping my lips zipped and not starting shit that had taken so long. But Zan had kept with
it. She'd stuck by me.

Now this Cassie didn't have that. She'd been tossed
out on her own without the best fucking mentor on the
planet. I'd been there, left without the person I revered.
My dad hadn't died, but to him I might as well have.

Shit. I brought my hand up and caught myself before
I put my fingers in my hair. I was using a new gel for
my pompadour. I was going to test every minute of the
fourteen-hour hold it claimed.

"Ten tomorrow. Be here." I pointed my finger at her.
"Not a second late or it's a no. Got it?"

"I'll be here." She'd almost made it to the door before
she came back and grabbed her portfolio, cheeks bright
pink. "You won't regret this."

Cassie

"You're proud of this?"

I dropped my gaze from MJ's brown eyes drilling
into me to my drawing. I'd thought it was good, one of
my best. But if she had to ask, it must mean it wasn't.

"Well?"

And now she was impatient with me. The churn-
ing in my gut intensified. In the three days I'd been at
Thorn & Thistle she'd had two moods with me—impatient and angry. The worst, by far, were the times I'd
caught her looking at me with her lip curled.

"This is the best you can do?" She shook my sketch
in front of my face.

What could I have done to make her like it? Was it
the colors? The line work? If I admitted that yes, that
was my best, how much angrier would she get?

"I... I... I don't think you should do newspaper ads
anymore."

Her expression questioned my sanity. "What?"

Yes—what? Had I thought blurting out my opinion
would impress her? Not working. Definitely not working. A drop of sweat trailed down my back to gather

with the others. Nothing I did impressed her. Not cleaning the bathrooms. Not reorganizing the front desk.

I needed something. Anything. With each hour I
could practically see her regret growing for taking me
on.

I licked my lips and tried to find my voice, which
now, when I wanted it, had gone hiding. "I overheard
you talk about revenue and I don't think you should do
another newspaper ad. It isn't helping."

Slowly, so very slowly, she lowered my sketch. Her
eyes never left me, not even a split-second reprieve from
her severe stare. "Are you listening in to my conversa-
tions now?"

Oh god. What had I done? I was not going to admit
that yes, I listened every opportunity I got. It was all
part of my quest to win her over. Something she said
might give me insight on how to do that.

There were few benefits to being quiet, but one
was how often people forgot I even existed and talked
around me.

"I want to help," I said, hoping we could gloss over
the fact that I'd been eavesdropping, since it was to her
benefit. Beneficial eavesdropping, I'd make it a thing.
"I've asked each new client what's brought them in and
only one person told me the ad. Three days, one person.
The ad was three hundred dollars, but the person's tattoo was only one hundred and twenty. You lost money."

MJ folded her arms over her chest. "Are you a tattooer or a secretary?"

"I don't believe in labels. I'm a lot of things."

Her eyes widened and then her lips started to curve
upward.

I'd done it. I'd gotten her to smile. What a smile it
was. She didn't go all out. But the curving of what I

now realized were surprisingly full lips was enough to soften the edges, to draw my eye to the lines at the side of her mouth instead of the deep grooves in her forehead when she frowned at me.

"Is that right?" She shook her head, her smile disappearing as fast as it'd come. "Three hundred fucking dollars."

Relief pushed out the tension. If she liked that one, I had plenty more. I reached for the little notebook I always kept with me. Before it could even clear my pocket, MJ was lifting my sketch and waving it in my face.

"We were talking about this piece of shit. You were telling me if this was…"

"Hey, I need to talk to you," Jamie, the most senior artist, said, coming to stand by me.

She was already my favorite because she showed me the least hostility. With her perfect timing now, she cemented she'd be getting the best berries from the fruit tray I brought tomorrow.

"What?" MJ snapped.

"We got four more reviews this week."

I took a step back even though MJ's murderous expression wasn't directed at me. If it had I was pretty sure I'd need a defibrillator.

MJ snatched Jamie's phone.

"Don't break it."

"It's not your phone I want to break." MJ glared at the screen. "'Got a tattoo there that looks like my kindergartner's drawing. No wait, he's better.'"

As MJ continued to scroll down and read, I got out my phone and tried to find the site MJ was reading from.

Shop has really gone downhill.

Heard under new management. They suck.

Think all the good artists are gone.

I was so uncomfortable in there I left.

Wow. The one stars had exploded since the last time I'd checked. Once Zan told me that she thought MJ should be my mentor, I'd researched the shop. The truth was that I'd been keeping tabs on MJ's career before that. I'd always been in awe of her talent, while at the same time, it was women like her who had kept me from tattooing. I saw how tough and commanding they were and knew I didn't belong in that club. Until Zan showed me different. From Zan I'd learned that tattoo artists could be anyone. There was room for everyone.

I clicked on the reviews for the two newest team members. They had less experience and their work showed it. But most of the bad reviews, if they listed a specific artist, focused on MJ, Jamie and Vivian, the other senior team member. It made no sense. Their work was unparalleled.

None of these reviewers had left a picture of the tattoos that were supposedly so bad. Nor did any of them have a picture or any identifying information. In fact, for most of them the review of the shop was their only one.

"You guys are being targeted."

Jamie nodded at me before looking back at MJ. "Yeah, we are."

It didn't take a genius to know who was doing the targeting. Months ago MJ's business partner, Heidi, had left the shop, taking half the staff with her. Rumors were there'd been no notice and it'd been far from amicable.

"Fuck them." MJ glared at the screen and then carefully handed Jamie's phone back like she didn't trust herself not to throw it after all. She blew out a breath and tilted her neck from one side to the other until it cracked. "Ugh. Anything else?"

Wait. Else? They needed to focus on this.

I clasped my hands together and swallowed, trying to lubricate my mouth as much as possible. "Ha...have you reported it?"

MJ's head twisted in my direction. Her eyes narrowed in warning. Warning that I was trying her patience? That it was none of my business? That she hadn't given me permission to speak? That look could be used for so many things.

All of them made me want to throw my hands up and promise to never speak again.

"Yeah, and I got nowhere." She spit the words out like they were acid burning her from the inside. "Forget it, they'll give up eventually."

"Except they haven't," Jamie said.

MJ's snap trap focus, eager for a misstep, shifted to Jamie and I took some deep breaths.

"What the fuck do you want me to do? Go on the site and comment, whining how they're not real customers. You ever read when other businesses do that? They look pathetic and desperate. Once people come and see for themselves, they know how good we are."

Jamie's body remained relaxed in spite of the rapid-fire words coming her way. "If people read these then they're not going to give us a chance to prove how awesome we are."

"Then we need to find another way to get people in here," MJ said.

She didn't seem to understand how influential review sites were. Action needed to be taken. Plans needed to be made. Preferably with bullet points.

"Maybe you could sue them to make them stop," I said.

MJ angled herself so she faced me directly and I automatically took a step back. Her shoulders weren't actually much wider than mine, but she seemed so much larger. Her attitude, her dark hair, dark eyes, and the black pants and steel-toed boots she favored all added to that impression. Pretty much everything about her made her seem big and scary.

"Yeah, I'll get right on that. Got my lawyer on speed dial. Think he'll take payment in ink?"

I squeezed my hand tighter around my notebook, the pages curling. "There's some lawyers that take on cases and only expect payment if they win."

"My cousin used one of those," Kayla, the artist two stations over, broke in. "He's still in jail."

MJ nodded as if to say point was made.

No. It wasn't made. They had to do something. "You…"

"Enough." She crumpled my design in her hand. "This is what you need to be worrying about." She held the ball of paper up to my face. "Don't give me something unless you know it's your best."

She walked past me, her shoulder barely clearing mine.

I stared at my drawing still clutched in her fist. I wanted to ask for it back so I could refer to it, which was probably why she'd kept it. There was nothing about that she liked. Behind me someone snickered. Stress sweat drying on my skin, I could feel the stares. After pretending I was invisible for days, these people were all too happy to witness me being put in my place. Kayla, the newest artist, enjoyed it the most I was sure. She'd taken one look at me and treated me like a threat. I couldn't figure out why she'd be threatened by anything about me. She was outgoing, gorgeous and accepted by the other artists.

MJ made it seem so easy. To be strong. To speak up. Well, I'd spoken up and now all I wished is that I hadn't. Instead of making headway, I'd taken a step back. I didn't know how many more of those I could take before I was out the door.

God, I missed Zan. I missed knowing what was expected of me. Most of all I missed being liked.

Don't miss
New Ink on Life *by Jennie Davids,*
book one of the Thorn & Thistle series.
Available now wherever
Carina Press ebooks are sold.

www.CarinaPress.com